Blue Billy's
Rogue Lexicon

DAVID LAWRENCE

For Mika,
Who has kept me sane (well, mostly)

"Pity the fall of young fellows all
0 well-a-day! 0 well-a-day!"

— FLASH LAD, *18TH-CENTURY*
HIGHWAYMAN BALLAD

The Mint, Southwark, 1771

CHAPTER ONE

Abram Cove

   – among thieves signifies a naked or poor man; also a lusty strong rogue

---

" And what have we here?"

     "Let us in, Moll. Beast of a storm tonight, ain't it?"

"Aye," returned Moll, cinching her silk wrap while maintaining a hand behind the front door she'd opened just an inch. "Stormy for some by the look of it."

The wind sent rain barrelling into this secluded yard in the Mint, taking the standing, shiftless dregs of chamber pots for an airy jaunt. Souls Yard, a misshapen cul-de-sac of three freestanding abodes consisted of a squat, squalid cottage, from which no light entered or emerged. A converted barn with modish ventilation in every wall and door, the slope of its gambrel roof rather like hands praying for intervention. And the jewel of the Yard, Marathon Moll's: a double-fronted, two-story block tethered at east and west with slender chimneys touched with scoliosis.

"Have you lost your way tonight, Billy?"

With a look of wounded indignation, William Dempsey said, "Ain't it enough to wish the company of an old, dear friend? 'Old' meaning previous-like," he added, "nothin' more."

The door remained unmoved; Billy was left to shiver on the tilted stonework of the front elevation. Wiping the endless stream of August rainwater from his face, he pressed himself against the opening until their faces nearly touched. Moll's – with its native jaundice, like dirty lemon juice upon features which arrived at too many points. Billy's – a canvas of creamy white, flushed with health and whose boyish pout Moll herself had often declared a criminal provocation.

"'Old' you have defined, Billy, but how do you define 'dear friend'?" said the bawd, pushing up her aquiline nose. "That term implies paying calls of friendship, or at least of courtesy (which are *not* calls to steal from my house, mind you), and I've not seen your pretty face these two years."

"That Blue Billy outside?" came a second voice from within. "Let him in out the rain, for God's sake."

Recognising the voice of one of the house's most devoted patrons, Dempsey said, "'Dear friend' I define as Dip-Candle Mary there behind you, who I hear's set to be married next week, so I come to bestow my congratulations."

All around Souls Yard, eyes were opening within cracks in the ramshackle barn and, one sensed without ever quite knowing, at the darkened front window of the cottage. For though a code of honour kept the inhabitants of each from inquiring into the business of their neighbours, scenes in the Yard were fair game for all.

After a moment, and a great sigh from Moll, the door withdrew just enough to allow into the vestibule Dempsey's small, slim form. Mary hurried forward to embrace him. He was a tallow chandler from Shoreditch, Dip-Candle Mary being his house name. Such names were customary in these houses, which referenced either one's profession or physical appearance. Indeed, Billy had never known him by any other, though the man had always been sweet on him. Sweet enough to forgive the trinkets Billy had lifted from his dressing table when staying the night. That silver-handled comb the man really didn't need seeing as how he kept his hair so short. That errant bit of coin taken from coat pockets…

From the dark vestibule, Billy looked toward the glow of the front parlour. The room was filled with claret wallpapering before which replicas of Roman forms thought or gloried or sported in alabaster relief. Chintz upholstered sofas and settees of various conditions reclined before the fireplace, currently cold, its salt shelf crammed with crucibles of scented oil waiting to ignite on crackling nights. The parlour was lit by two fat beeswax candles stuck into halves of an antiquated urn hung over the mantle. The widely cast light lifted a glow from the gold threading of the furniture and, for a moment, a glow in Billy himself as he recalled the handful of good times he'd enjoyed while living here.

No question, Moll had come up in the world. When his eyes returned to hers, pride shone in her face as though to say: *only observe all I have accomplished since I got rid of you.* When Billy took a tentative step forward she held up a thin finger, forbidding him to take another step, dripping like a rainforest. He began to undress.

"You keep those sodden clothes on 'til we fetch you a robe," said Moll, ordering the house fiddler, presently dozing on the chintz sofa, to grab an old, dirty robe from the back of the parlour cupboard – "the one Lord Chesterfield died in whilst having a frisk with Sook Stockings." Then she reached forward to slap at Dempsey's hand, which, despite the injunction, had continued to open his fine Holland shirt to his navel. "Sook Stockings, Billy. The boy I discovered after I kicked you from this house despite your prediction that I could never replace you. Well, let me tell you – he not only replaced but has indeed outshon'd you."

Billy returned to Dip-Candle Mary. The man smiled and kissed him, tugging at the stubborn tie in his long, drenched hair before venturing one large hand over his narrow belly. "Tremulous as a new calf from that chill rain," said the tallow chandler. "Upon my word it is lovely to see you. They tell me you are kept by the Marquess of Argyll these days – he is a lucky man."

After taking Mary's hand for a kiss, Billy slipped from his shirt and into the filthy robe presented to him which smelled of all shades of nastiness. Stepping wide to leave his shoes, knee breeches, waistcoat, and frockcoat in a steaming pool in the vestibule, he took Mary to the spot on the crimson sofa previously warmed by the fiddler. Then, hitching up his robe, he bid the man unfasten his garters so they might peel away his silk stockings. "But do it ever so carefully. They're my best vampers."

As Mary reached tentatively up his thigh to begin the operation, the lady of the house entered the room, cinching her wrap violently across jutting hip bones. "Moll is my dear friend too, despite her abuse," continued Billy. Then, addressing the man directly: "Not in a hundred years would I begrudge you another attraction; I wish you ten pairs of Sook Stockings if they fetch the cash. And now, while my Marquess tends to some important business in France for a few months, I've decided to make myself available to you again."

At which point Dempsey squirmed and, touching his attendant's shoulder, said, "Mary, a lad don't tie garters that far up his leg."

"Get your bloody hand outta there!" shouted Moll, and after an imposing look from his hostess, Dip-Candle Mary withdrew in a cloudy frown to the opposing end of the sofa.

At this point, footsteps descended the stairs to produce the slight, slightly bandy-legged youth known in the house as Sook Stockings – a very small, effeminate youth, airy in a long cotton smock which extended to his knees. This landed angel had only just appeared when the front door opened to allow in Miss Irons, a beefy blacksmith from further up the Borough Road and Mary's betrothed. After bringing Irons beside himself upon the sofa, Mary said, "We've an old friend in the house. From before you knew me, my love, but no doubt you've heard us speak of Blue Billy."

After glancing at the boy of about eighteen tugging off wet stockings, Irons turned to his companion and said, "Blue Billy, the thief?"

Mary hesitated. "Yes… that's the one. But you know Harry, those accusations have never been proved––"

"They was your own accusations."

Mary smiled at the tactlessness of his big fella, then said expansively, "That was, what, two and a half years ago now? A regular lifetime. I for one am delighted to welcome him back. He's a great success now, in high keeping for two whole years. A year and a half under the protection of no less than the Marquess of Argyll." Turning to Billy, "I don't wonder you've waited until he leaves the country to come see us again. Everyone says His Lordship is wildly possessive and never allows you out of doors."

"That's not quite true, is it Billy?" interjected Moll, bringing to her side the wisp of a youth in the long smock. Her new pet had an open face centred around a large nose, a head of chestnut hair cut into a Caesar and crowning a some-what bulbous head. Moll pinched a speck from his shoulder and said in her story-hour voice, "I have it on good authority, darling, that the Marquess very generously gave our Mr Dempsey an airing one day a week. Friday, to be precise. Which was the very day a certain *Mr Evans*––"

"You Sook Stockings, then?" interrupted Dempsey,

shocked to hear that the miserable old biddy, though always known to be a famous snoop, had even learned about Evans.

The boy turned to the visitor. "I am. But unless you are a client, I prefer Sukey Chandler." His small, brown eyes assessed Billy, as though bringing into focus the double image of this visitor and the dastardly scoundrel who had been thrown from the house for stealing before he'd arrived.

"Hired to replace me. I suppose Moll told you that."

"Moll has employed many in her house."

"And always has a house pet, a favourite: what used to be me and now it is you. How do you do on the trapeze?"

With a furrowing brow Chandler said, "The trapeze…?"

"*Friday*," continued Moll, stepping forward. "The very day a certain Mr Evans, a silly man with a taste for dirty, lying, thieving little punks also found himself at liberty…"

Turning to Moll, Chandler said, "The *trapeze*. Moll, he *is* joking?"

"Don't worry yourself over that, my darling. Billy has fallen from the dazzling heights he knew before: the heights of his days as a popular boy in this house. The heights of a wealthy and powerful Marquess. All the way down to a lowly Mr Evans. *Mr Evans*, Sukey, is the trapeze to which our visitor refers: a thing to catch him during his fall. But, alas, I hear even his tenuous grip upon Mr Evans has faltered…"

"It has *not* faltered," said Billy, for the first time with a slight tremor in his voice. "Anyhow, there is no Mr Evans. I continue with my Marquess as the toast of the town. I am treated with turtle soup and claret wherever I go."

"No," said Moll, "no, you are not. I have followed your career and you have at last done yourself in with your wretched deceitfulness. Now you must beg a return to old Marathon Moll's in the Mint. Well, the answer is no. You insisted on coming into my house to request it of me, so I have the pleasure of telling you, to your face, as you sit in a filthy robe and before my loyal and cherished guests: *no!* Now return to my vestibule, pull up the puddle of clothing you left there – for I do request the immediate return of my robe – and exit once more into the dark, dreary night from whence you came."

His eyes widening, William Dempsey said, "I know other bawds keep houses like yours—"

"And in each one the name Blue Billy is synonymous with infamy – hell hath no fury like a woman scorned, so you may be sure I have warned my sister brethren about you." Then Moll summoned the house fiddler, who served as well as a footman and who knew what else, to come forward. He seized Dempsey by the arm and hoisted him to his feet.

"Moll, I beg ye!" cried Billy, "I haven't a place to go. Really and truly I have not. There is much more to those stories of the Marquess and Mr Evans, and I have not one blessed farthing to my name."

"I believe that. And I can add you haven't much of a name either, leastways what anyone would call a good one."

"*Moll, I beseech your mercy…*"

"Try returning to the alley outside that tavern in Holborn. What was the name? The Hook and Crook – where you ended up the last time you were ejected from this house. No doubt you recall it, and your lures for snagging those dead-drunk punters stumbling out the door. Though I must say, eighteen is a bit old to pretend to be a linkboy anymore. 'Tis a tragedy to grow old, Billy, isn't that what you said to me once?"

"Moll, I shall faint…"

"Then a spot out in the rain shall revive you," said the lady of the house, then gestured to the fiddler: "*Out.*"

"Oh God!" said Dempsey, turning to Dip-Candle Mary, who was now fully engrossed in his blacksmith and studiously looking everywhere but at the scene before him. "Mary, I have no choice but to beg a place at that accursed tavern. A place I vowed never to go near again. Perhaps only to sleep in the alley outside, and for even that I must beg…"

"Then fall to your knees and beg," said Moll, following him to the door. "Where else can one ever expect to find you but on your knees, for one reason or other, in the alley outside the Hook and Crook? There we may always discover London's one and only Blue Billy."

THE DOOR CLOSED. The rain came down. William Dempsey stood amidst the muck of Souls Yard. The squalid cottage withdrew into its burrow of night. The hands of the lofty barn prayed to the blackening sky.

A flash of lightning lit his flight into Red Cross Street. He jumped over rising pools until, coming into Finch's Grotto Garden, he huddled under an evergreen to consider the wreckage of a ship broken upon too many hostile shores.

The Marquess.

Mr Evans.

Now even that old bitch Marathon Moll.

But for pursuing that milk-sop Mr Evans, he might be snug in his West End apartment tonight. Welcoming his Marquess. A mutual laugh as they embraced at the door. A touch of sherry; the Marquess reclined upon the sofa as he patted Billy's knee. Talk of his day and his abhorrence of all the Lords, Ladies, and Earls of his acquaintance.

Then three days ago, all that had ended. But *could* it have ended? Could a life change so quickly and so dramatically? A person was meant to climb ever higher. And so he had done. Graduating from back-alleys and bawdyhouses to Mr Sallow, who had kept him well, if not lavishly, for half a year. Then a year and a half with his Marquess – the apex of any boy's dreams. And Billy had done right by him. So many romantic nights spent just the two of them, lavishing the man with affection and praise. Then to dinners hosted by discreet intimates. Or riotous masquerades, the man occasionally withdrawing Billy's masque to the praise and scandal of the room. Then he would sweep Billy off his feet and order his chariot to return them home…

A few more days, then. Give it a few more days. Then he would approach the man with tears of remorse. Charm him, flatter him, and win back his place. Then he would never, ever go behind his back again…

But just now, he needed a place to shelter. And Billy was not so long risen as to forget he had started life as a vagabond boy from Wapping. Of a den of thieves, shifting from one hovel to the next for most of his childhood. This, if nothing else, had taught him to be resourceful.

So under the old, sagging bed of Hardware Nan did Billy crawl for the night. Nan had been a friend of Moll's from time out of mind. And from time out of mind, Nan had passed Monday evenings ragingly drunk and carelessly fastened his front door. As he was too repulsive to be invited into anyone's bed, and too cheap to lure anyone back to his own, Nan was by ten that evening snoring in solitary splendour, one arm dangling off his narrow bedframe.

Closing the front door, Billy tip-toed across the creaking floorboards of Nan's single-room hovel. He stripped off every stitch of clothing, hung them up to dry. Then, below the lifted toll gate of the protruding arm, Billy shimmied with one of Nan's blankets to a warm, dry place beneath the bed.

Naked as the day he was born.

CHAPTER TWO

Sundge

– one that lies under the bed to rob the house

D awn opened its cloudy eye to meet those of the boy beneath the bed. Billy had slept little, instead spending his time listening to water dribble into Nan's washbasin. The water originated from the garments he had pinned to holes in the ceiling beams using the man's hairpins. Dribbling at one edge of the washbasin – his silk breeches pinned to silk waistcoat pinned to the lapels of silk frockcoat. Dribbling at the other – his entire suit of linen small clothes.

As dawn progressed the rainclouds cleared, and the suits of clothing came into view under the glare from Nan's bare window. Rather like two visions of himself deflated of all their pretensions. Against the miserable morning shine he closed his eyes and declared, "I am treated with turtle soup and claret wherever I go." Then he said it again. And again.

Then he hadn't the heart to continue. Nobody was listening. Even the dust balls under Nan's bed looked unconvinced. He *had* blundered with the Marquess. Terribly. Going behind his back to earn a bit of pin money had been wrong. Yet little he'd done in life had been what you might call *right*. He'd climbed from that community of aimless street vagrants to a private, luxury apartment in the best part of town. He'd done it using the same tactics he'd just been punished for – telling fibs, sneaking about. The odd betrayal.

Letting his head sink onto his hands, Moll's face flashed before his eyes – that hatred at seeing him again last night, that glee in pushing him away. No question that, of all the bawds he'd known, he'd done best by her. But what had it got him? Nothing. So was the lesson from this to do people worse? To be more conniving? His only answer was Nan's endless snoring.

Into the strengthening light of day there came a cry from the street. A cry which arrived each morning in the Mint, be it muffled with rain or ringing the crisp, clear air to echo through the alleyways: "*Old clothes… ooooold clothes!*"

"Bloody hell," muttered Billy, horrified at the reverberation within the room, as the clothes collector sounded to be standing directly outside. Nan's snoring, however, continued unabated as the collector continued, loud and lusty and long, eventually moving down the alley to lure from other inhabitants their saleable rags.

With the calls subsiding, Billy was on the point of making his escape from beneath the bed when, in place of an incoherent exhale from the snore just withdrawn, he heard in its place: "The happy pair."

Billy froze as Nan, stumbling and elephantine, rose from the creaking bed to balance upon bluish feet. Bringing a chamber pot from a sideboard, he held the ceramic basin before him and, pissing lustily, addressed the two suits of clothing suspended from the ceiling:

"My tall, dapper fellows," he said. "Slim where I am fat. Side by side where I have nobody. Shoulder to shoulder to face the world. Well, Nan has had his fill of love. To you, my man in linen, I say this: your silk man will betray you for another in silk. I faith, for whatever he says to you now, whatever promises and talk of devotion, he cannot ultimately bear another so far beneath him."

Addressing the other: "And to your companion, the fellow in watered silk: you think yourself very fine. And perhaps you are. Perhaps you wish to do a good deed: to raise your linen fellow, to dress him in silks like yourself, and so buy lifelong devotion. But this cannot be – for your linen friend will merely take whatever he can get from you. Will repay generosity with ingratitude." Then Nan cried out, "Then take *your* silks to clothe *himself*!" as he sealed the chamber pot and returned it to the sideboard.

Then, rounding upon both men, he said, "And so for as long as you may proceed together in life. But one or other of you (I predict it will be both!) *shall* suffer in the end…" The man shook a finger while attempting to maintain his feet, concluding: "Only Hardware Nan *has* had his fill of love. And so withdraws from the game. So goodbye… to love… *forever*…"

Then Nan turned on his heel, tipped forward, and crashed onto the bed in a snoring heap. Upon which Dempsey tore from beneath the bed, snatched his clothes from the ceiling, and dressed himself, cursing Moll and her low associations.

He was on the point of departure when he hesitated at the rusted doorknob. Nan's performance, having sapped every ounce of his energy, meant he was again unconscious, and Billy experienced that hunger, known so often while a street boy, which was actually two pangs – that for food joined to an itch to enrich. As such, he remained for a time, breakfasting upon bread and cheese while perusing the paltry contents of the man's keepsake chest, sideboard, and wardrobe. Rubbish, the lot. Garments into which two of himself might easily fit. At last he took a walking cane of stout construction and coin amounting to two pounds five shillings.

Then, once more faced with the rusted knob, he hesitated. Was he... *reluctant* to go outside? Could it be he would rather remain in this dingy den than go into the world again? It was almost as if, after two years in those fine apartments, he had begun to grow soft.

Rounding on the slumbering wretch, Billy said, "Your friend's a right bitch, you know that? I been shunned by everyone I know, but what hurts most is Moll's look last night when she pushed me out in the rain. I was used to bring heaps of cash into that house but what a return! Utter contempt and disdain!"

Nan produced two wet snorts then smacked his lips.

"Alright then. She had her reasons for kicking me out back then. I *was* stealing, but I never took much from that house, not really, cus I was always scared to death of Moll. That's the God's honest. And that's why I reckoned she'd let me back if I really needed it..."

Tiring of his own voice, Billy fell silent then looked once more about the room. He crossed to observe himself in a small oval mirror above the washbasin. Combed his hair, straightened his collar. Then he approached the bed and, holding his nose, tugged a woollen blanket over the snoring mess that was Hardware Nan. At last, with another sigh, because he really was trying to be better, he returned five shillings to the pocket of Nan's dressing gown.

Then he turned the rusted knob and proceeded into the day.

THE MINT, that diminutive district south of St Saviours parish west of the Borough High Street, had for much of its life been

known as a haven for London's debtors. A special charter
exempted the area from City control, notably those officials
sent to incarcerate citizens for unpaid debts. As such, the Mint
became known as a "Liberty" – a refuge for London's delin-
quents both, as it were, rich and poor. Six days a week, the
area was guarded by bill collectors, waiting to seize anyone
who ventured outside the Liberty of the Mint – every day
except Sunday when debts could not be collected. Sundays,
then, became the day when residents ventured out of the
district – the men dressed in their best in the hope of being
taken for carefree came to be known as "Sunday gentlemen".

In 1722 a law was passed withdrawing that special exemp-
tion from City laws. However, despite the change, the Mint
had so entrenched itself in a colourful assortment of Sunday
men, Sunday women, and whatever Sunday children they had
produced, that the area seemed doomed never to recover a
respectable populace. For some, respectability was attained by
comparing east with west. For to the east of the High Street
stood Newgate and King's Bench prisons, the residents of
which, but for hefty bribes, were never allowed out of doors,
even on Sundays. Yet, in truth, there was little to distinguish
the population of either side of the High Street, as the
inmates of the east often began life as heroes of the Mint's
creating upon the west.

Running out of the Mint, William Dempsey fell into step
behind the old clothes collector, who would undoubtedly lead
him to a good second-hand dealer. There was nothing for it
but to turn pedestrian for a time; Billy's heeled slippers were
meant for little but stepping from carriages into drawing
rooms. The change must be immediate. And without fine
shoes, so too must go, though it vexed him to admit it, every
stitch of his silk garments.

The roving collector deposited his armful of wares with a
clothes seller in Three Tun Alley, and when he departed,
Dempsey proceeded into *The Sign of the Jolly Tailor – All Sorts of*

Men's and Boys' Clothes, Both Rich and Plain. After the traumas of the night, his suit sat somewhat angularly upon his frame. Still, undressing and handing the garments over, he narrowed his eyes, daring the merchant to inquire. When the man's brow furrowed, Billy announced: "I am treated with Turtle and Claret wherever I go," pulling from between bolts of blue damask a dark brown cotton suit which he paired with a waist-coat of shocking yellow.

"Are you now?" said the clothes dealer, examining the silk suit against the light of an east window.

"Those fine garments can leave no doubt of it."

From the floor Dempsey snatched a tarnished lace doily which appeared to have lain under a fingerbowl for much of its life. Upon pulling it into shape and setting it across the yellow of the waistcoat, whose saturation mellowed the tarnish of the doily, he deemed it the most he could do by way of jabot. Slipping on the ensemble, he pulled the doily gently around the top button of his undershirt and stepped to a sliver of dirty mirror to judge the effect.

"You treated as well with plunges into the Thames?" called the merchant. When Billy failed to respond, he continued, "...plunged deep, then drawn out again in a fisherman's net?"

To this impertinent man, Billy said, "No, my dazzling wit, not the Thames. The suit was merely kissed by a bit of errant mist at Carlisle House. Last night I was too long upon the famed Oriental Bridge which stands near a fountain. A very pristine fountain, I can assure you, only too lively."

"...and the coat," continued the merchant, appearing not to have heard, "pulled hither and yon, quite out of shape. Tell me, have they great tempests blowing at Carlisle House?"

After dallying another moment before the mirror, Billy sighed and approached the clothes merchant. "Only the winds of life, sir. What I reckon everyone must bear occasionally while seeking a path through it."

The merchant looked up expecting to see a smirk on an impudent face – only no impudence, no smirk. Billy's dark, expressive eyes had expanded to catch new morning light – a boy of no more than five foot four, pathetically garnished with an ugly old doily tucked into his shirt like a child's napkin. Maintaining the merchant's gaze, Billy continued, "You understand, sir, better than anyone, that London will knock a lad about; wise men such as yourself have the businesses to profit by it. But I have discovered that wind don't break a tree that bends. That's why I reckon cotton and wool will, with time, reclaim my silks for me."

The merchant remained silent, annoyed to have additional jousts with his humorous lance countered with a stab at sincerity. Extending a hand, he said, "Let us have the shoes," from which Dempsey was only too happy to step, having had his eyes on a pair of alternatives sturdy and flexible enough for an errand boy. "No inconsiderable wear here as well..." complained the merchant, licking his thumb and rubbing at a heel.

"Sedan chairs come only so far into the Borough," said Billy, "but I spent my last farthing on a chair solely out of consideration for those shoes. Then I caught lifts upon carriage boots where I could, and tiptoed with vast care where I could not, to my destination."

In the end, the clothes merchant offered decidedly less than Billy had hoped for. Owing to the boy's resigned nod, and his extending his hand for the coins with only a slight tremble of his lower lip, the man ordered Billy to take something additional. "Boys like yourself always wish a hat to go with their walking sticks and frilly jabots, do they not?"

"With an ostrich feather, thank you sir!" said Billy. And upon snatching a plain hat with a wide brim, he took from the counter an ostrich feather quill pen which may or may not have been part of the offer. Upon verifying the end was entirely dry, he tucked the nib under a ribbon which ran around the hat and, with a deep bow, exited the shop.

The High Street roared as he entered that strong north-ward current of Hackney carriages and cattle driving for Smithfield market. With an idea of crossing London Bridge for the City, Billy proceeded: a pedestrian, with all the free-doms and limitations thereof. The black feather in his hat danced. The glossy cane he extended like a physician taking the pulse of the Borough artery, for a pedestrian's London was a place no longer known to him. It was, as he knew quite well, entirely unlike the London crossed in a closed carriage.

Soon enough, his cane became a scythe cutting through organic obstacles – things inattentive, even downright feral. Among these: a dog frothing at the mouth for a choice bite of his silky calf. A pale young cripple with a harelip and a runny eye demanding alms into a rusted receptible. An ox driver taking but minimal care of his herd. After applying his cane to a few of the oxen, and to the brawny ox driver himself, Billy hurried up Counter Lane where it branched from the High Street at St Margaret's Hill. This would bring him to the crossing at Blackfriars's Bridge, which had not existed when last he'd resided with Moll, nor the subsequent arrow of new activity it had ushered in. An arrow which had pierced the wharves of the Southern bank – down through market gardens and rambling orchards, through timber yards and tenter grounds with their acres of drying dyed and bleached cloth. In the arrow's wake had sprung up a decidedly mixed collection of new housing, varying in completion and craftsmanship, but an undeniable sign of lives taking root north of St George's Fields.

What had not changed, however, was the certainty that what lay south of the river was but a reflection of something better upon the north. He experienced an increased urgency to cross. However the dressing down of William Dempsey was to continue, for as he proceeded toward the Triangle, the

Borough reached out and snatched his new hat. This was achieved by an urchin aiming a broom from a first-floor window, and another creeping up Stoney Lane behind him, arms extended to catch the prize.

Surprise lost him a moment while, prize in hand, the street urchin fled up New Rents in the direction of St Saviours. But rather than follow him, Billy sprinted in the opposite direction, for having once worked these streets himself, he knew the crowds of the market and those of the High Street would snag a thieving urchin like briars. Equally undesirable were the grounds at St Saviour's, which left you entirely exposed. A loop through Rochester Yard then up Dirty Lane would, however, deliver a boy with hot booty to a nearby den of thieves, the *flash ken* as he had been used to call it, known as Three Crown Court.

Arriving in good time, Billy waited just around the corner of Three Crown Court for the hat thief. At the sounds of approaching footfalls he leapt out, delivering the sprinting boy into a wall of roughhewn Greystone, retrieving his hat and returning it to his head. He gripped his walking stick into a cudgel, prepared to sacrifice it to the loftier goal of a sound drubbing when the stirring denizens of Three Crown Court came forward, delaying commencement. Then the sound of his name called by one of the onlookers prevented it altogether.

"William Dempsey – as I live and breathe!" With that, a young man a few years his senior stepped forward. Gripping him about the neck, he brought their foreheads together, and despite a separation of more than five years, Dempsey submitted immediately. As the man held him, touching with grubby fingers Billy's cheek and his hair, he asked where on earth he'd got himself to. Then, without waiting for a reply, he turned to the loiterers in the courtyard and announced: "This is William Dempsey, my brother!"

"Pull that child out the muck before he drowns, Tantivy,"

said one of the onlookers before returning to his group. After the ragamuffin was pulled to his feet, he cast Dempsey one long, petrified look, then ran to safety. He fled up a flight of stairs while his kinfolk eyed Billy exchanging judgments in the cant language, that cloaking dialect of London's street vagrants. A dialect which Billy understood perfectly well.

"That was the son of a lady friend of mine," said Tantivy by way of introducing the child. Seeing no interest, he continued, "But where you keeping yourself now? Back in the Mint, then?"

"How's Mama?"

As the man considered, he picked at the scars from smallpox which peppered his face. He was a stooped, stringy young man whom Billy had helped name while he was a youth still learning what their people called The Stealth. "*Tantivy, Tantivy!*" they had taunted during evening practice sessions, for initially his stumbling gait had put some in mind of the cacophony of horses' hooves.

Presently Tantivy pulled a hand through his hair and laughed. "Aw, you know Mama. It's like you to ask about her. Well, she's just like yourself, ain't she? Wild and free. We ain't seen her these ten months; being kept by a new man, something in the military. Those things never last, you know – men grow bored right quick, even with pretty damsels. Always moving on. She'll be back, never you worry, then you can come round to find her."

"Perhaps she'll stay on," snapped Billy. "Ain't ye never heard of love? Life-long love? Men adore a pretty companion to go about with. Pretty ones with dazzling conversation ain't common to get."

Once more consulting his scars like Tarot cards, Tantivy said, "Alright. I heared of love, sure enough. And I know what you mean. I got some of what you term *life-long long* for my Abigail, mother of that there boy you knocked about. A right *dimbermort*, let me tell ya…"

"Warmest regards."

Suddenly annoyed at this testy exchange, Tantivy took his companion by the scruff of the neck and held a fist up for emphasis. "Now you know we ain't forget you, William. I called for you once myself in the Mint, years ago that was now. And was informed you was kicked out and nobody knew where you had got to. So I ask again, where you keepin' yourself at?"

Billy pulled away: "The house in Souls Yard, like you said."

The look of disappointment which met Billy told him nothing had changed – low-down robbers, beggars, and pickpockets though they were, his people still looked down on anyone making shift for themselves in a bawdyhouse.

"Come back to Barbary, William. To your people. You know we never go hungry. We always find a way!" he said, as though glorying in the shifting sands of their past. A quicksand which had sucked at their feet with endless uncertainties, endless itinerance. Faces hidden behind a dirt of anonymity, full bellies only for the scrappiest and meanest.

Waxing mystical, Tantivy continued, "You appearin' before my eyes just now, reckon it's in the cards."

"Reckon so. Anyhow, I've an appointment to keep, so I shall be on my way—"

"Sunday then. We shall send someone round to fetch you from that place in Souls Yard round about ten. Come to think of it I know just the lad to do it. Have him bring the horses, Galahad and Lancelot – same as when you was a boy. Remember? We shall saddle them up special for you and see if we cannot find a means to help ya." Billy nodded. When his brother saw there was to be nothing more from him, he said, "Alright, then…"

"Ask for Blue Billy, that's what I go by now."

At this, the man clapped his hands together and patted Billy's cheek. "Bluuuue Billy!" he crooned. "Finally got a name for yourself, then! *Blue Billy* – bless my soul it suits! Never in my life saw a child more desperate to get a name than was William Dempsey. Well, and now he's got one!"

So ENDED the interview and so on with his day. Billy arrived in Holborn; but how he arrived, he could not have said. With any luck, he would never see Tantivy again, yet his thoughts were now brimming with the past. The cadences of the cant language had entered his head, stairs were *dancers*, cloaks *doashes*, pretty wenches *dimbermorts*. Field Lane was leading him to a tavern called the Hook and Crook, yet simultaneously he was upon Cannon Street Road, the artery of his youth, running on spinning child's legs through the streets of Little Barbary…

Past sooty men heaving coal, through the boat yards. Past the German shops where vats of sugar churned in slow boils. Where plumes of sticky sweet haze kissed the docks then froze into brackish sugar plumbs.

Suddenly, through the piscine fog: a silk handkerchief, gleaming white.

Caught in one hand, he held it aloft. It sailed through the gloom and the haze as a flag of triumph. This was his first trophy, lifted from a foreigner wandering about St George's. Just a beginning, but surely enough to bring him to attention. And with an apple-bright, juvenile conviction, he had been certain of receiving his name that evening.

For a sparkling sobriquet was a prize above all others. *Tantivy* – a name given in gentle mockery prior to the youth's rousting his inelegant stumble into a rolling, almost frighten-ingly silent gait. The gait which had thereafter lent him excep-tional stealth.

Tantivy.

Nimble-Fingered Meg.

Freddy: The Flagrant Vagrant.

All shadows dancing upon the bare walls of imagination. Shadows following him into the ever-shifting confines of childhood abodes: the ramshackle barns, the boarded-in boathouses, the crumbling rooms stacked pell-mell, like bricks strewn about the new work sites at Marylebone…

Ten years ago, that handkerchief had fluttered through the byways of Wapping, and he had thought: why not *suggest* a name for himself? Why not *invent* something dazzling and declare to his mother, to his siblings, to the sea of men he called *father* that henceforward he would be known as *Brazen Billy* – a fiery, fascinating name! Perhaps something simple and dignified: *Billy of Little Barbary.* Or, if you like, *Little Billy of Little Barbary…*

Yet none of these, or indeed any other, had been bestowed. He had arrived home that evening to life as it actually was. Nothing was to be so easily decided. Not even a name. One did not bestow a name upon oneself.

You performed in the world. The world judged you. Then the world named you.

CHAPTER THREE

Whip off

 – *to run away, to drink off greedily, to snatch*

W ith his hat tipped over his nose, Billy settled into a corner of one of Holborn's seedier establishments, crouched in an alley just off Field Land, the Hook and Crook.

The publican, Old Sam, with a dash of white about the chin and temples though he was no older than fifty, stood behind the bar. He noticed Billy as he was wiping his mouth with a bar rag, holding his eye a long moment before turning to draw a pint for another patron. Billy looked away as well, experiencing a stab at this less-than-cordial reception. Old Sam had no call to snub him. They'd parted on entirely good terms – Billy had merely failed to return one day after that rich American put him in an apartment. Still, something had changed – both in Sam's manner and in his establishment. Today nobody lingered in the alleyway. Not one boy smoking in the lean-to or tossing about a taper he might, at sundown, offer to light the way of an intoxicated man.

Having rapidly burned through his hopes for the place, what remained of Sam's tavern descended over Billy like a layer of ash. He didn't mind change or a dingy environment. But he did mind a look which said a man knew him and wished not to. Christ, but Sam used to joke and laugh with the boys. Supply them with food and hot ale. And on winter nights, blankets for the night in a room behind the bar. Perhaps there had been a run-in with the law. Such run-ins were not unknown, but even so, Billy was not propositioning any of the men here. He was merely a patron enjoying a beverage. Who was Old Sam to take on such airs?

So he decided, to spite Sam, to bring out an old gem which had served him well on other occasions. Because at that moment, he felt a figure standing just behind him. A male figure. An interested gaze. And an urgent wish to speak to him. Billy said:

"A bob gets me down to vampers and duds
I'll cavort as you take care to handle your affairs.
A solitary crown for a kneel and buff,
Half for my hand, and double for a fuck (two and six to be
added if you fancy getting rough)
For the same a second may join for a tease
Add a bob and I'll thrash with a whip as you please
But a sovereign is king; I'll be yours for the night
And receptive to however many you might…"

Then he lifted the drink to his lips and waited for the man to approach. When he did, Billy found himself facing none other than Sukey Chandler.

"It's only me," breathed the boy, settling down with a wooden mug of sweet wine crowned with a head of yellow froth. Chandler was perhaps two years Billy's junior, rather too thin and no beauty. Yet he savoured of nothing low, was well-spoken and curiously self-assured, and so in a way was rather appealing. Billy eyed him a long moment, certain he was after something.

"So you are the big punk at Moll's these days."

Chandler nodded.

"You've a silky way about you and speak better'n most."

"A trained thespian must speak better. That is my true calling."

"That's which?"

"The stage, of course! Not just acting but every aspect of the Bard's forum – set decoration, costumes." After coughing delicately into his hand, having ingested a portion of the foam which topped his wine, Chandler continued, "I have painted scenery and cleaned set pieces at Drury Lane. Most people never consider that, but one must understand a play intimately before projecting an appropriate vision onto the set. I performed once, too, though in an entirely silent role. It was in *Elvira* – happen to see it?"

Dempsey looked at him like he was out of his mind. "What I happened to see was you assessing me at Moll's like you wished to know all about me. You nigh on devoured me! Lookin' for a fuck?"

It was some satisfaction to see the stars fade from the boy's eyes, as what remained was a look Billy understood far better. With a sigh which told him they were not so very different, Chandler said, "Why would anyone in my trade be looking for that?"

Dempsey held his mug suspended. "Aye," he said, then added with a wolfish grin, "but despite your stage passion, you wish to keep your top rank at Moll's, so I reckon you come to ask me about the trapeze, at least."

The call for forthrightness appeared to stick in Chandler's craw, but he said, "Very well. I *would* like to know something. I should like to know what happened with your Mr Evans."

Then setting his drink aside, he looked his companion in the eye. "And what is more: I believe fellows of our trim should stay together. Regardless of what happened with Moll before, we should try to look out for one another."

Billy frowned. Once Chandler assured him he would help get him a bed for the night, though suspecting his motivations more than ever, he agreed to talk.

"Well to start, I ain't betrayed nobody. My Marquess was all day in his own house. Then on the town two, three nights a week, doing whatever he liked and keeping me like a mushroom in that dark apartment. Cunning bastard; bought all and sundry for me 'til I thought I was a prince. Yet never a farthing of pin money, nor the freedom by which to earn any. We fought like brawlers about that. I threatened to leave unless he allowed me one bloody day a week by myself out of doors. I won that fight, leastways I thought I did. He had me followed, but I quickly learned my spy had a prodigious thirst for liquor, so I bribed him to remain in my apartment with a couple of bottles of Old Hock while I went out.

"That was when I found speaking to a crowd on a street corner Mr Evans, who is what's termed a 'Member of the Commons'. Well that's an important title, ain't it? Politicians got power and such like. What's more, just the week before I'd seen this self-same man staring at me in a coffeehouse in that way, so I knew he was ripe for a plucking."

At this, Chandler produced a look of grave disappointment. "High keeping. Do you know how many boys would kill to be placed in—"

"Shut up with talk of high keeping! What happens when a man tires of ye? Where would I be with nothing put by?" Appearing slightly abashed, Chandler nodded and remained silent. "Right. So after his speech and the crowd broke up, I approached Mr Evans and asked what I could do to serve my country. On Fridays."

More regret must have been betrayed than he had

intended to show – seeing Billy had emptied his mug, Chandler reached for his hand and insisted on buying something else to cherish his nerves. "A measure of claret if you please," he said after summoning the pot boy. "Served in a clean mug and without a head. *Clean*," he stressed, "and without a head."

"Alright," said the serving boy, "ye needn't shout it at me."

Billy's pride could scarcely endure pity, but Chandler seemed to possess that rarest of all commodities: a genuine wish to help. And so steeling himself for what remained of his story, Billy said, "One Friday, the Marquess went to my apartment and discovered the spy incoherent upon the floor. Friday after that, he followed me himself. I had that coming, I suppose, but what I can never forgive …"

Chandler nodded.

"What I cannot forgive is his searching out *Mrs* Evans. It was with that red-faced wench on his arm that he arrived at our next rendezvous. That was a riot, I can tell you. Screaming, weeping, vases thrown… The Marquess said he would not tell the world what Evans was if his wife would promise to keep her husband away from his *nephew* henceforward. 'I shall keep him away from *everything* henceforward, you may depend upon it!' she shrieked. When we were out in the street, the Marquess told me I was not to return to my apartment. The locks had been changed, and all my belongings, clothes, trinkets, everything was already out for sale. I was left with only the clothes on my back and what Evans had given me, which I used to take lodgings for a coupla days. Then I proceeded to Moll's."

Soon arrived the claret, a substance sufficiently clean in appearance and with it, a grey rag with which to wipe away anything which might form along the surface.

"Let us consider now," said Chandler. "Is there anyone in the metropolis who might still retain an affection for you?"

After a long draught, Dempsey shrugged. "Moll Dowager. Keeps a boys' house and brandy shop in Soho. We parted worse than I did with Marathon Moll. I don't dare go near him now, not without a peace offering."

Chandler rephrased his question. "Is there anyone, from whom you have not stolen, or by some other means done wrong, from whom we might ask assistance?"

"Tub Nan. She gets her bread that way, making and selling wood washtubs. Weren't never nothing in her workshop to sell."

"There you are. Let us proceed to Tub's and see if she won't take you in."

"You work in a hatter's? I already been and she wasn't there; languishing in a sponging house somewhere for debt. Unless the Bailiff can find more to sell in her workshop than I could, she'll be in The Fleet this time next week."

During this exchange, a woman had emerged from a back room. She was talking to Old Sam and nodding in their direction. "And perhaps," said Chandler, "after you have finished your claret, we might continue on a merry little pub-crawl. I expect we shall be approached."

The sight of the dour-looking tavern wench delivered a memory to Billy. A memory with the smarting force of an open palm, as she seemed to encapsulate just how far he had fallen. The woman offering to bring a patron into the back room. If rejected, the offer of cheap liquor then another approach. And for those who rejected her a second time, a word from Old Sam to the boys in the alley to approach the man when he departed.

Billy put his face in his hands. Noticing the publican approaching their table, Chandler began to drink off what passed for claret in this place.

Said Old Sam, "Don't suppose either of you two might wish to meet Miss Olive in the private room?"

As Dempsey wiped his eyes, Sukey lisped, "No sir, we intend to be on our way once we have finished our beverages."

"Up with ya," said Sam, "I run a respectable establishment here."

"Sir, we may be allowed to finish the wine—"

"No time for that now. You two been loitering about long
enough and are starting to draw attention. So now—"

Dempsey took his mug of claret and tossed the contents
into the face of the publican. Then he jumped into the man's
initial blind swing at him – Sam's arm came around in more
of an embrace, Billy succeeding in bringing them both to the
floor and himself promptly up again. Then he scrambled for
the back room and the alleyway door beyond it.

"*That son-of-a-bitch picked my pocket!*" shouted Old Sam,
hauling himself to his feet and starting after him.

WILLIAM DEMPSEY WAS ONCE MORE RUNNING through the
streets of London. The streets he had known all his life. Yet
not as before. Upon outrunning Old Sam, he continued
forward in the belief he was once more the active agent in
pursuit. Yet something within him was calling to be heard –
over the horseshoes skidding across cobblestones, over the
knife grinders at their rhythmic work in Covent Garden, over
the maids hallooing to sell buckets of milk gone sour. Crying
that he no longer wished to pursue. That he could *not* pursue.
For pursuit was the thing which brought rejection – what now
seemed continual rejection.

Yet flight, for the young and desperate – for the disillusioned and disheartened – one may believe to be pursuit. For
the motion is the same.

Billy was but chasing his hat again. The discreet corners,
the blind turns, the byways – these were his domains, his
means through life. Yet when Tantivy had pulled that boy
from the muck, Billy had observed a look he had never before
encountered. A look not merely of terror. But terror of

himself. Yet how could one frighten who was so frightened himself? Who was, in fact, beginning to doubt himself?

And so run though he might, Billy feared he would be the one taken by surprise. And with a shove from around a corner, delivered into a wall of Greystone. Stunned from his wild advance. Breath knocked from him.

Then down into the muck.

CHAPTER FOUR

Bob Ken, or Brownmanken
– a well-furnished house

"Well, well. And what have we here?"
"Let us in, Moll. I've a beast of a bloodied nose, and nowhere to go…"

Billy swooned, his eye swelling, the bridge of his nose a busted dam through which a red torrent was flowing. Drowning under his tearing vision stood Marathon Moll, folded arms in a silk banyan, appearing as just another wall into which his face must be driven.

Yet, somehow, something was different. It seemed he had an arm stretched across someone's back, stretched taut so he wouldn't fall, stretched until the tendons might snap. Looking down, a tanned arm protruding from a workman's smock was gripping him tightly about the waist. A thumb previously broken and reset was cradling him across the belly. The man was speaking, and as he did, the strength left Billy's body and he sank toward the opened collar of the workman's smock. Into the smell of sweat and clinging sawdust. Into the smell of deep, clean strength until it was all he could do to keep his fractured, bleeding beak from taking refuge under that wing.

A casement window creaked. Chatter from over their heads.

"But do you *know* him, Moll?" the workman was saying. His large, coarse hand came forward to draw aside Billy's matted hair. "William, is it?" he asked, holding him up as though it was merely an uncertain identity preventing his admission.

At which point Billy turned to the house and, praying that Chandler was within, bellowed for the youth at the top of his lungs. He bellowed lusty as a new-born, bellowed so that Moll held her ears, bellowed until at last the boy appeared. With a shriek of horror, Chandler squeezed around his unmoveable mistress to assist the blood-soaked wretch. Next to appear: a large black man who set Moll to one side. Lifting Billy from the arms of the stranger, the man swept him onto a flying carpet, to an island far from all noise, harm, and distress: the first floor. Here were the boys' bedchambers, and in one, under a canopy of pink clouds, within a forest of fat mahoganies, Billy was stripped of his soiled garments and deposited into a feather bed.

Chandler's face drew close, came into focus. Biting his lip, he dabbed at the bleeding nose with a scrap of cotton, the fringe at his forehead, short as it was, still managing to appear utterly dishevelled. Then at a shouted order to come downstairs Chandler withdrew, handing the cloth to the other attendant, asking him to tend Billy while he tended to Moll. Then he hurried downstairs, his footfalls in the stairwell like bubbles rising from the seafloor where the monster lay.

"Out!" shouted the monster.

"Moll, I have asked Caligula to guard him, to assure you that—"

"*Out!*"

"—and shall vouch for anything that goes missing from the house—"

"*OUT!*"

"—of which there shall be nothing, as theft simply will not be possible. As a favour to me. Your best, most loyal employee, as you have said yourself many times…"

A broken, attenuating response. A long pause. Another word from Chandler. Then a wail of surrender – music to Dempsey's ears. From the soft, dry bed, Billy observed the bedchamber door close, sealing out the subsequent noisy exchange from downstairs.

Caligula approached the bed. He loomed over him under a sky of pink parasols suspended upside-down from the ceiling. Blinking his vision clear, Billy saw the forest of mahogany had been felled, shaped, and polished into functional furnishings – a wardrobe, an escritoire, a nightstand. Mezzotint portraits of David Garrick, the stage actor, crowded the walls around a ceramic sock and buskin. And upon every surface: perfumes, breath-sweetening tinctures, and cosmetic washes.

"William Dempsey," said his guard in a reproving tone. Billy opened his eyes, unaware that they had closed, to observe Caligula, house heavy in Moll's for many years. Bald, six-foot, a cotton waistcoat left undone over a rippling, ebony torso. "What you doin' in this house again and looking like this?"

"I got nowhere to go, Cali—"

"Don't call me that."

"Why not?"

"*Cali* – like you was used to do. Makin' me consider the passage of time, and how you was one bird flew out this cuckoo's nest wasn't never supposed to return. But now here you come landing in the Yard like some gentleman's been out snipe shootin'."

Billy grabbed for his hand and put it to his heart. "I've missed you, Cali."

"Don't do that." But the man's warm hand closed over Billy's. After a long moment, he sighed. "Well, who was it?"

"Who was what?"

"The one smashed your nose and busted your eye; the one I gotta kill now. Loiterin' about outside?"

"Long gone," said Billy. Then he paused, understanding for the first time he had achieved his goal: he was back in Moll's. With its leaky windows, its scent of lavender stirring about the heart-chambers of the house, breaking from some deep part of himself memories from earlier and, somehow, what felt like more innocent times. "Anyhow, I reckon he's done me a favour if Moll's to let me stay on a while."

"A *favour?*" Caligula drew closer. "You tell me what happened now and why you seem ta' have lost what little sense ya'ever did have."

Billy shrugged. "The cash; I needed some. Round about dusk, I snagged a bit of trade at Savoy Gate."

"Mighta guessed as much. But went bad for you?"

Billy exhaled. Then closed his eyes.

AFTER A MELANCHOLY HOUR roaming the city, without even a Chandler to speak to, his spirits had risen upon discovering a candidate – a man reading a book outside Savoy Gate. Blotting his brow with a white handkerchief, Billy came forward. As soon as he could, for there was a terrible throng, he passed by, twirling the kerchief behind his back in the manner of a horse's tail. He turned once to observe the man, who was now scrambling to his feet, and, grinning, continued on. That voracious look meant a sovereign for himself, a meal, and a bed for the night at the Talbot Inn.

And so full circle into Southwark into the picaresque arms

of the Talbot, a rambling, two-storied building ranged in dormer windows. Mr Leonard was a man of decent, though not decadent, means. He confessed to being somewhat inexperienced, upon which Billy raised his fee to one guinea. As they supped, Leonard laughed overmuch, nodding incessantly as though fearing a rebuff for what he was already assured of attaining. By his frequent glances about the Inn, he appeared not to understand that the Talbot was long established as a place of assignation for their lot. Dempsey made much of his inside knowledge, flirting openly with him before the waiter, then summoning the chamberlain to garnish one cosy bed with two nightcaps and two romantic red-tinted candles.

"And a tankard of claret," he added, as he often encouraged a companion to drink. This Leonard did prodigiously. Once upstairs and half the tankard had been consumed, Dempsey donned his nightcap and, relieving himself of every other stitch of clothing, slipped under the bedclothes. The man followed, stripping off and jumping in, growing so excited at the touch of the young, warm body against his own that Billy contrived to discharge his obligation with what should have earned him just half a crown.

"Bloody hell…" sputtered Mr Leonard, "I didn't intend—"

"Oh, but the night is young, Leo!" said Dempsey. "We shall remain together for many hours more. 'Tis a usual manner of commencing a night of frolic. Now take a tipple, then rest in my arms as we consider how next my lion shall ravish me."

The man took his tipple and was soon snoring like a docile lamb. An ideal moment to slip away, but tonight, having no place to slip away to, Billy remained where he was. During his wine-scorched daze, the man placed wet kisses on his cheek, forehead, nose – anywhere his claret-slumber led him. Something in the man recalled to Billy his first long-term benefactor, Benjamin Sallow. Gullible to the point of foolishness. But kind. Loved reading to him. And hardly ever bothered him about the other.

"You're a reader too, Mr Leo," Billy crooned at eyelids too heavy to open entirely. "Though reading that book was just a pretence while hoping a boy would pass by waving his tail at you. Still, I know a book lover when I see one. You'd like to read to me, wouldn't you, my lion?" And believing this a stroke of insight, Billy was cradling the book to his chest as Leonard emerged from his peat bog of inertia.

Leonard immediately grew ardent in his addresses but pushing him gently back, Billy propped the book between them. "I knew you was my sort of fella when I saw you reading this book. My favourite of all time."

"Spare no thought for books now," groaned Leonard, now fully awake, "not now…" sucking at Billy's neck and crushing the book between them.

"But I adore this novel. Do read to me…"

"*Read?*" said Leonard, as though *The Vicar of Wakefield* were an actual rival to himself. Casting it to the floor, he threw his companion onto his back, then commenced upon a better compensation for the loss of his guinea. Billy tugged the lip of his nightcap down over his eyes while his lion nipped and nuzzled them into a twisted and trembling embrace, at last grunting to a roaring conclusion as he held their slick limbs together, the air punctuated with one perfect, round belch from the fermenting claret below.

Hopping gingerly off, Leonard retrieved his book from the floor. After lighting a fresh candle and placing it on the bedside table, he returned to bed, tugging Dempsey's nightcap up to reveal his eyes.

"Not sleepy yet? It's not gone nine."

"Christ crucified, I can't again as yet!"

Mr Leonard shook his head. "The book, Billy. You said you admire *The Vicar of Wakefield*."

Suddenly showing more life than at any point during his ravishing, Billy sat up and said, "Yes. *Sure*."

Leonard handed him the book and, settling back into his pillow, said with a dreamy smile, "How about you read me a bit in that sweet voice."

After rather a long moment, Billy laughed, "Nay, you don't want that Mr Leo. You want to read *to* me."

"I think I know my own mind, lad. Read us a bit now, go on…"

"Sir, I don't enjoy that sort of thing. And you've such a sweet voice, much sweeter than mine."

Leonard held the book between them in the candlelight: "Nothing to be embarrassed about. I shall begin. *'I was ever of opinion, that the honest man, who married and brought up a large family, did more service, than he who continued single, and only talked of population.'*"

Dempsey snorted. "That is the famous *Vicar of Wakefield*? Doesn't promise much of interest, 'pon honour." He was chuckling for some time, then said, "But go on, it must improve, and I adore the way you read."

Leonard frowned. "You lying to me?"

"Lyin'?"

"You told me this was your favourite novel. Haven't you read it?"

Shaking his head, he replied, "I thought it was *Sir Charles Grandison* I observed you reading. I'd have laid half a dozen of burgundy it was *Sir Charles Grandison*, but my eyes ain't worth spit, and there's the God's honest. *Grandison*'s my favourite, not this."

Leonard propped the book open on Billy's chest. "High time you read Goldsmith then. Read me the first page."

"Sir, I just said my eyes ain't no good. Anyhow," he added, extending a hand into the nether regions of the bedclothes, "you shan't have a willing lad in bed forever. I'm feelin' right neglected…"

But Leonard failed to succumb, appearing to see him in an entirely new light. "It ain't a crime you can't read, Billy. Many cannot. But a man don't like being lied to…"

"Shut *up* with talk of I can't read! I read, and write, beautifully. My Marquess often had me write out special notes and billets for him simply for the high craft of my penmanship. That's the Marquess of Argyll, what maintained me in luxury in a West End apartment."

With disgust, Leonard said, "Christ Almighty. You're a pretty piece, but you need to leave off lying. I ain't a fool and won't be treated as one. There is no Marquess, and you are illiterate. I don't condemn you for it. Just admit what you are and let us have no more words…"

Billy pulled away, dropping the book to the floor as he sat on the edge of the bed. "You know nothin' of me, or my Marquess, who told me daily I was the prettiest in all London as he strutted with me on his arm, the regalest hanger girded to his thigh with the most elegant handle of pure gold. And, nightly, he presented me with another hanger of comparable size and strength I can tell ye, unlike that melted bit of butter knife ye've got down there…" Billy kicked the book across the floor. "Aye, and—" but received such a crack on the head, nothing more was heard until his face connected with the edge of the bedside table.

"Shut that mouth, you dirty little whore!"

A moment of stunned silence elapsed. When Billy remained on the floor, sputtering, and choking, Mr Leonard experienced a twinge of remorse. Seeing his companion would remain bracing himself on the bedside table, he rose and came around the bed to observe at a safe distance. Then, retrieving a posset bowl from the tallboy, he placed it under the red stream issuing from Billy's fingers where they cradled his nose…

Billy opened his eyes.

Caligula had departed; Chandler reappeared. The boy was sitting at his bedside, turned toward the nightstand where he appeared to be preparing something. He listened as Billy told him of his flight from the Talbot down the High Street, then his hazy recollection of encountering the Good Samaritan who had helped him to Moll's door. While he listened, Chandler brought into his lap two slabs of raw beefsteak as though set to commence upon some barbaric feast. Observing Billy's confused expression, he assured him these were not for consumption, but rather for external use as an aid in healing his injuries.

"Excellent for the skin," he said, angling the first across Billy's cheek to butt up against his clotting nostril. "What I use myself twice a week to maintain a fresh, rosy appearance."

"Thank you, my angel," crooned Dempsey, nearly gagging at the stinking leach clinging to his face. Then he did gag. "I – swear on my life I shall take nothing from this house as long as I remain."

"Betray my trust and I shall flay you alive," sighed Chandler, rather like he was required to say this. Then he moulded a second slab with his agile, tapering fingertips.

"Who was it helped me to the door? Seemed to me he's known here."

"Tom Baker," said Chandler, joining him in bed with a dog-eared play.

Billy repeated the name to himself, then glancing at the play, said, "You on the stage tonight, my lovely?"

Musing: "Oh no. Not until the season begins, which is November, and even then only after a fashion."

"A fashion?"

"It shall be my dexterity which pulls my fair actress into her corset. My taste which ties my gentleman's cravat. My flourishes which grace the set pieces. So in that sense, yes, I shall be present."

"Your play must be enchanting like no other."

"The rollicking 'Miss in her Teens.' Everyone's favourite."

"Who is Tom Baker?"

Twisting his head around, Chandler raised his brows. "Well, you're recovering nicely. That lovely man is Moll's carpenter. He's done various jobs for her here and there and is currently working up shutters for the windows."

"Oh," said Billy. After a time he said, "Do me a favour."

"Certainly."

"Read out the choicest bits of your play. Once I have regained my place in the city, it shall be the first I seek out. Only I reckon nobody in the metropolis could perform the parts as well, even those intended for the mannish sex."

"Oh may I?" said the boy. He was a moment looking over the cast of characters listed at the front of his play. Then, imbuing himself with the essence of each one, he cast forth his hand, and with a dazzling reading of the stage notes, parted the ruby-red curtains. He set out the props, then papered, carpeted, and lit, floor to ceiling, the first scene.

Billy closed his eyes. The power of Chandler's performance, along with the extraordinary loss of blood he'd sustained, soon overcame his restlessness. He fell into a doze to the sounds of lively dialogue under the constant watch of two raw and greying beefsteaks.

HE DRIFTED IN A HAZE.

When the beefsteaks were removed, it seemed his mother was beside him, with her head on his chest as she was used to do when they were alone together. That pervasive sting of lavender was bringing her to him, that smell which pierces the skin to stir memories. It should have been his last memory of her, as the scent had been strongest the day they'd parted.

Rather they were lying in bed somewhere in Little Barbary conversing in the cant language.

Speaking the complex dialect of Wapping had been the only part of life among his people to come naturally to him. Theirs, they believed, was a centuries-long bloodline. Free-thinkers of the London streets, persecuted by a Society which could not accept the transitory nature of the material world. Yet the bloodline brought expectations. Expectations of skill and stealth. A something no one else could do as well, which brought benefit to the community and informed the giving of a street name. Only Billy had never found that skill to set him apart. And as the years passed, it had come to trouble him greatly. Mama had understood this, and so had spoken in the cloaking dialect even when it was just the two of them. She understood speaking it came easily to him and would give him pleasure.

These thoughts of Mama arrived when he was unprepared to keep them at bay. That companionable closeness. A haven from the world. A home for two like minds. But these memories were wine upon a dusty shelf; consumption might deplete the store. And he banished her.

It was now Mr Leonard lying beside him. Only they were not in the Talbot. Instead, they were in the apartment in the West End and had taken down from the shelf a copy of *Gulliver's Travels*. Billy was holding the book open before them. And though he was not reading the book, he *was* reading – from a list of questions he'd been compiling about that strange and elusive art.

During the final months of his incarceration in the Marquess's apartment, he had begun perusing some of the books in the sitting parlour. A cover which showed a man surrounded by little people announced one book was *Gulliver's Travels*. He could read neither the title, nor any but the most commonly used words on the first page, but the picture on the cover had communicated with clarity that this was the famous tale by Swift.

It was a moment of pure comprehension. As though he had tricked the book into betraying itself. His heart surging, he was determined to chisel out more from it. And so he had begun a list of questions, legible to himself if to nobody else, which he might ask some unknown person at some unknown point in the future about the art of reading. The list was now lost, along with everything else he had been forced to leave behind. Yet it was here in his dream. Complete. Every line recalled; every question concise.

Leonard answered none of the questions; Billy had no expectation that he would. The point was to recall the list to its end. After which, he folded the paper and sealed it once more into the pages of *Gulliver's Travels*.

Then he returned the book to its shelf.

Waking with a start, he observed Caligula once more towering over him, holding a dancing orange flame amidst the darkness. "Downstairs," he said. "Moll ain't lettin' you lollygag up here like a princess 'til you've faced the house."

It felt to be about midnight. Billy groaned and clutched his head. A quarrel involving Chandler sounded to have resumed downstairs. Rising to his feet, into the flickerings and swayings of candlelight, he caught a glimpse of his reflection in the looking glass. He recoiled, nearly sick. For a moment, he couldn't even speak.

"What in *Christ* will I do, Cali? No man will look at me now! I'll be driven to the basest bulk-mongery!"

He turned toward the bed. But no, he *would* look again. Look at what Leonard had done, not just to his face but to his fucking livelihood. He found a crumpled newspaper, dipped it in a ewer of water. Then at the glass, he blotted his engorging, crusting nose the care of two beefsteaks had done little to assuage. Caligula set the candle down, then brought Billy's nose nearer the flame.

After an inspection he said, "Ain't nothin' to write home about. It ain't broke. The swelling at the eye will go down in a day or two. You're young, alright? So stop that blubbering."

The man maintained his chin until Billy nodded and wiped his eyes. And though suspecting Caligula wouldn't like it, he came in and kissed him on the cheek, taking care to keep clear his offending orifice. Nothing at all remained of the ensemble purchased from The Jolly Tailor, and it seemed unlikely anything would fit him from Chandler's diminutive wardrobe. So he reached for the roomy smock the boy had worn the night before, no doubt left by a patron. When he was dressed, he presented himself to Caligula, attempting a smile. The man could only sigh and shake his head.

He led Billy onto the first-floor landing, all ancient green wallpapering and walnut wainscoting. Punctuating the forest were four bedchamber doors and another containing a box staircase to the attic. The light flickered and then failed. When Caligula relit the candle, Billy's former door, directly opposite Chandler's, flashed like an unbidden memory. As the flame passed, imperfections in the oak deepened and lengthened.

As they descended the stairs, landscapes new to his eyes appeared in a jagged sequence, placed where he recalled various tears and scuffs in the papering. At the base of the stairs stood the dark vestibule. To the left: the dining parlour, and the slack legs of a plate warmer dozing after a lately concluded meal. To the right: the front parlour, filled with candlelight and every member of the house.

Moll was standing somewhat dramatically between the split fire of the urn which flanked the mantle. Towering over Chandler, with an accusing hand extended, she appeared slightly manic with her mass of thin, longish hair pinned into a disintegrating bun. Grouped with her were the fiddler and the three other working boys of the house, no doubt more inclined to support their mistress over the favourite in a conflict.

"...I said nothing about Saturday, Sukey," Moll was saying. Turning to the newcomer: "Here is the little monster. No, do not tell me what it was, Billy, I should like to fancy it was a hardbacked dining chair applied with gusto."

Moll's new favourite was clearly Sukey Chandler. However she always had another in the wings, and this appeared to be the one in the attitude of a cat on a floor pillow near her feet. Rising up, the reedy young man commenced shrieking at the sight of the bloodied newcomer. He slipped an arm through that of his mistress, then clutched at an imaginary string of pearls. "*This* is Blue Billy? My dear Moll – I knew you had made a success of yourself, but I had no idea the depths from which you had risen!"

Moll was too smart to let rise beyond secondary favourite anyone inclined to such clumsy flattery. Still, she patted his hand as she inspected the appalling state of her visitor's nose.

"You share a long history with William, that must count for something," said Chandler, "As you can see, he is suffering now for his wrongdoing."

"That boy stole from me," snapped Moll. "Not only me, from my guests. From my *employees*," with a significant look at the young man on her arm, whose hand again sought pearls which were not there.

"Mary desires him at his wedding," continued Chandler. "He wished to tell you, but you get in a rage at the mere mention of his name. We must always strive to make long-time patrons happy. The ceremony is just a few days away and Billy can assist me with the costumes..." Then he looked once more toward the boy in question. "And for my part, I wish to do what I can to assist him. We should all wish to help one another. There are not many who will."

A sudden rapping at the front door broke the thought. The house fiddler rose to answer the door, but the interruption seemed to lend itself in Chandler's defence.

Moll hesitated. "I wish to help those who help me, Sukey.

Not betray me. Billy has betrayed everyone he's ever known. Argyll, Moll Dowager. That American put him in an apartment. The list is endless. All used ill. And they are fools who will not learn from history."

"None will improve without some faith shown. William knows it is a risk to trust him. But should someone take that risk, just once more, he will understand this same faith is what he must have in himself."

"Oh save it for the stage, Sukey…"

"Beggin' your pardon, mum," said the fiddler, returning to the room. "A visitor is requesting to see the new one – Mr O'Donnell, I take him to mean. You desired to be present at his introductions." At this a particularly well-built, stoic young man who had been lounging on the sofa stirred and met Moll's eyes.

With a sigh as though the entire world were against her, Moll informed the fiddler they would arrive presently. Then, "Very well. Billy may stay until the wedding."

"Oh my *dear!*" said house pet number two.

"Be quiet, Humphrey."

"I am only thinking of *you* Moll, whose generosity—"

"I know, dear. I am thinking of me too. I shall take as compensation seeing the wreck of those pretty features whenever I wish." Moll turned to Chandler. "And to secure myself against the risk, I shall have two guineas. Paid in advance." Though somewhat taken aback, the youth retrieved from his pocket two pounds two shillings. "You will keep Billy away from our guests, of course – he cannot represent me looking like this." Then she turned to the one called O'Donnell, whose silence Billy interpreted as a newcomer's fear not just of meeting a customer but of Moll herself, which, for many, never went away.

Once the pair had departed, Chandler turned to the group. "Stellar. Now, you should meet the boys." At this the one called Humphrey strode to the sofa and pulled up the last of the boys, who, for good or ill, was not unlike him in appearance – another slender sylph of about twenty-two with snub features. They came forward in united opposition to the newcomer, and in a manner which declared them something more than just fellow employees.

"I'm Harper. This is Applegate. We share the first-floor room at the northeast corner. And you should know, Moll runs a differing sort of establishment to the days when she accepted such as yourself into her house. You are at the bottom of the heap here, understand?"

"I ain't in the heap, just a guest."

"Aye, you fancy yourself in the heap if I know anything of William Dempsey. I can tell you we are all fiercely protective of our mistress," continued Humphrey Harper, pushing forward his concave chest. Then, glancing at Chandler, "Leastways most are. Any questions?"

"Harper and Applegate," said Billy, "no house names then?"

"Oh, the *gall!*"

Chandler put forth an appeasing hand. "Pray, let us not search for conflicts which are not there. He merely asked a question."

"Yes…" said Harper, "*just* a question." Returning to Billy, "We do indeed have house names, you little bug. We are The Princes in the Tower. Known far and wide by sparkling reputation. Been with Moll these eight months. That other is O'Donnell just come to us from County Meath with no experience whatever. I suggested we call him Cat-o'-nine-tails, and Moll agreed as it has an Irish flavour and himself is a bit strapping. Reckon we might get him into flogging after he's got some experience."

"There we are," said Chandler, tugging Billy toward the stairs. "Halfway friends, now we have humanised each other. One need only speak civilly and learn respective names."

"Oh, Billy's name is well known in this house."

"He did not know yours, Humphrey, is what I mean."

"The Princes in the Tower, at your service," said Harper, and still joined to his companion, stooped in a deep bow.

"When two are required," sniffed Dempsey. "I always get the job done myself."

CHAPTER FIVE

Smelling Cheat

– a bouquet of flowers, a garden

Asolitary day in Chandler's bedchamber passed in relative incoherence. Billy's waking hours were filled with anxieties over money, his dreams heaped with guineas dancing in a golden light, the glittering profile of George III eying him accusingly.

Chandler had a small, black feline named Eva Marie, named for the wife of his hero David Garrick. The cat was a testy bundle of nerves continually in and out of the room in search of her master. When Billy lifted his head from the pillow to inform her Chandler would be out all day with a beau, she hissed wildly and, with back arched, backed out of the room. Later when he rose from bed to use the chamber pot, Eva Marie actually vanished – or seemed to. She was, in fact, hanging halfway up the lace curtains where she was to remain for nearly half an hour.

Billy was some time attempting to open the room's grimy casement window, which seemed hopelessly stuck. A glimpse of Tom Baker in the back yard was a reasonable, if ultimately futile, hope, given he was working up shutters for the house. He wished for a glimpse of him. Just one, to cool an unaccountable and growing fixation. Chandler, strange as he was, Billy at least knew now and had thanked for his kindness.

Tom Baker was an unknown. He'd never even seen his face. A face which could then be categorised and understood, and in some way got the better of. This Baker was nothing but a baritone voice with an exceptionally lean and muscular body. And a scent. Or rather an odour – anything so pronounced and unhidden must be called an odour – yet that was not right, not at all. It was the musk of a man who worked in the sun, yet without the oiliness to turn him sour. Only something earthy, like the wet of a mud-bound spring heated from some deep and unknown source…

Frowning, Billy checked these thoughts. They were too much like the babble of people *in love*, a condition with which he had never been afflicted. It required, as he saw it, that mixture of lust and ignorance found only in the celibate who had not yet learned how rotten people actually were. And it was what made the loss of the Marquess so much more painful. Theirs had been a business arrangement without the ups and downs of emotions to get in the way. After so long together, they had fallen into a comfortable routine. There was comfort, stability. Everything he'd dismissed as boredom only a week ago he would sell his soul just now to have again.

As time passed, Billy dozed. The sun grew long, and the room filled with the scent of oranges as the pyramid Chandler had left by the bed went down. That evening Tom Baker was at last driven from his mind when his boy guardian attacked him with another round of unprovoked kindness. This was not merely a place to stay and two guineas for Moll, but a frontal assault upon everything Billy thought he knew about his brother punks.

Upon entering the room Chandler dived into a drawer of his vanity. Then, like a great thespian at the end of a long and storied career, he drew out a slender volume, worn and weary, and insisted Billy take it as a token of his affection. This little guide had been key to his development in the art of beautiful pronunciation, and anyone, anyone at all, might benefit by a perusal of it.

"I got no use for the theatre."

Settling beside him, Chandler opened the first page. "A common misconception, I hear it constantly. Everyone *must* have use for the theatre. It is life distilled. A model for all our behaviours good and bad. So too a model for our speech. Every fine girl must attend finishing school. That is what this is." Then urging the book into Billy's lap he prompted him to observe: "'*I – love – you – O-li-vi-a!*' You see? Every vowel synthesised into one charming sentence. Now: rrre-*PEAT!*"

Sighing, he repeated. Then, placing a hand on Billy's throat, Chandler directed him to the second line, offering once more to speak each word slowly and deliberately as he traced the words with his finger. Or did Billy, perhaps, wish to attempt pronunciation first? Why not have a go? Nobody here to judge. Chandler would sound the words out with him if he liked, but they must always, always remember to *project*.

Gorging himself on oranges all day allowed for the only appropriate response to this horror – Billy's face went blood-red from shame. In his half-conscious telling of the incident with Mr Leonard, it seemed he had let slip the origin of his anger at the man.

After a time, his eyes returned to the pronunciation guide. He told himself he *could* read out *I love you Olivia*, not from the memory of what he had heard but because he could now read. He had once believed that after staring at the writing of others, say for an hour or so, things would become clear. After which, one could start copying words over to make one's own writing. Many hours of failure had disproved the theory, so it seemed unlikely he might suddenly… Yet it *could* still be true, couldn't it?

In the end, however, he muttered something about wishing to learn proper "pronunciation" but only if Chandler first reminded him of the "basics". His new friend needed nothing more to commence his instruction, much of which Billy needed to have repeated for the blood pulsing in his ears. He went to bed long before his instructor, exhausted and increasingly convinced that Chandler's do-gooding must be in compensation for some obscure guilt. Nobody could be so kind without a hidden agenda. It might be that he was a crusty old cynic at the tender age of eighteen, but there it was.

All these concerns faded away as he fell to sleep, where there were many, many gold guineas waiting to taunt him. Ever gleaming. Ever golden. All just out of reach…

DAWN BROUGHT from the shades of night the strong, square tower of St Saviours, the watchman of Southwark. Brought to life the skinners and the tanners, the brewers and the malt makers, the confectioners and the biscuit makers, the ship makers, the sail makers.

Under a white, woollen nightcap, Chandler snored from a cleft in the counterpane while Billy, from his perch at the window, stared at the skyline. He had often observed the dawn from his window across the landing, though back then it was with a pipe before bed rather than as a waking image. But on either side of sleep, he found some obscure contentment in first knowing that the darkness contained the tower, then, gradually, in having that knowing confirmed.

Flowers.

The image and the word came together like two open palms. *Flowers.* Turning toward the bed, he knew it was what he must do. The slumbering saint might not accept coin or even a word of thanks for his kindnesses, but flowers he would accept. He would clap or cry or, by some other means, be made abominably silly. And as he slept late, Billy might return with the gift well before he awoke.

Rising from bed and feeling considerably more himself than he had done the day before, he stretched and drank a glass of water. After rubbing at his nose with a bit of old newspaper, he combed his hair, then slipped into the one suit of clothes he'd found to fit him from Chandler's wardrobe. He was on the landing when he recalled a dour directive from Moll not to set foot outside the room without an escort. He rapped smartly on Caligula's door.

"Somebody need tossed?"

"I require an escort outside."

After an interminable pause, footsteps thudded across the floor and the bedchamber door swung inward. "*Damn* you, Billy," he hissed. "You woke me for that?"

"*Damn* you, Caligula," hissed Billy. "Moll ain't trust me to proceed anywhere by myself, not even out the front door. I promised I'd do nothing wasn't by the book."

"You damned mis-trustworthy thief," said Caligula. "So I gotta dress and hold your hand a few steps to the door?"

"You damned shiftless porter!" said Billy. "It's yer job to see folks in and out. Rowdy, brawling folks what's misbehaving, and I'm gentle as a lamb on a lead. I ain't ask you to dress; escort me down in purest natural livers for all I care."

"But they *ain't* no brawl, *damn* you. You wasn't infamous, you'd be fit to see yourself outin' the door."

Billy clutched his head in his hands. "I'm beggin'! I must fetch a nosegay for that boy in there! He wouldn't hear my thanks last night so I reckon he ain't quite human, yet if I can make him blush or squeal or something with a bunch of flowers I'll at least know I ain't living with Jesus Christ hisself, and also I gotta repay something towards what he gave Moll for my stay, and a pound's likely all the money I'll have after I buy the nosegay, seein' as how I can't give the money without no preamble, as the sayin is, or nothin' additional what says something from the heart and——"

Caligula seized Billy by the shoulder, turned him toward the stairs, and marched him down. They crossed the vestibule. Then he reached around his charge, opened the door for him, and prodded him out.

"Bless you, Cali. And when I return if I might trouble for an escort back upstairs——" The door slammed. "*I shall toss a handful of pebbles across your windowpane, like the lightest rainfall, to inform you of my return.*"

JUST UP FROM SOULS YARD, along St George's Street, stood Finch's Grotto Garden, an expanse of evergreens and various sheltering trees surrounding walks, intimate enclaves, and a ballroom, the so-called Octagon Room. Some ten years before, the Gardens had been constructed to be a smaller, more exclusive Vauxhall and an all-out campaign waged to convince the *ton* to descend into the Mint for their outdoor diversions.

Yet fierce competition from London's more established gardens had seen interest decline, a consequent lack of maintenance, and the Garden left in an accelerated mode of disrepair. Situated, as were most things in the Mint, below the level of the river, the Garden's mineral spring stared resignedly at the creeping sludge. Shrubbery: overgrown. Buildings: peeling and wearing. The Octagon Room greeted all with the bleary eyes of smudged windows, then turned to pull a blanket over its head against the day.

Upon the Garden's northern green, huddled about a

dying bonfire, a party of about twelve vagrants were partaking of Sack as they prepared for a day's begging. Billy's eye was immediately drawn to a slim, pale young man of middling height posed in a buff girdle. He sported a cap of matted grey hair which descended partly over his own, which was somewhat shaggy and of silvery white. He held a cage in which a fat rat chewed a morsel of cheese and was speaking in a dramatic character while moving in a series of almost balletic movements.

Reclining on the ground as two pieces of leather, well slathered with soap and lime, were laid over his leg, an elderly beggar asked, "…but my dogs, my beloved canines, Mr Ratcatcher. Your schemes must affect not one hair of my dogs."

"Nay sir!" declared the young man. "For rest assured, I am ratcatcher to Lord North, Prime Minister of Great Britain, and a famous lover of animals of all varieties. My schemes are laid within the most impenetrable of contrivances. The low: canny enough to avert the most curious canine paw. The high: oblique and slippery enough to repel the most daring of your airborne parrots! And felines, sir, are particularly immune…" The old man winced as the leather was bound to his leg, splitting to lend the effects of gangrene over which a child splattered concealed pigs' blood.

"William Dempsey!" called the man who had been guiding the child in this delicate art. "Reckoned Tantivy was out of his nut speaking of William Dempsey traipsing about the Borough again." This was a man known on the streets as Freddy: The Flagrant Vagrant, known for his "*You don't mind if I take a bit o' this for meself, eh?*" accompanied by a hypnotic gaze. As Tantivy had done, he stepped forward and took Billy around the neck: "My brother. God be gracious, William, your face! What's happened to you?"

Without waiting for an answer, Freddy beckoned to the ratcatcher, his gesture declaring *this is the one I told you about.*

The young man set his cage down. As he approached, he gave Billy a long, assessing look, appearing particularly keen to examine his busted face.

Bringing them into a decidedly motley morning circle, Freddy said, "This is the one they call Blue Billy. Of my own people in Little Barbary."

The young man withdrew his cap, and with it the mop of grey hair fastened inside, then stooped in a deep bow. He rose again with a luxuriant shake of his silvery locks, grinning grandly while allowing his fingers to linger amidst the glory. At last he announced, "Roger Calcroft, of the Common Fame: Cripple of the Clink Liberty, Beggar Extraordinaire of Grace Church Street, and various appointments down the Borough Road. At your service." He then produced an oddly shaped morsel of polished glass, stuck it to his lip to invoke a harelip, and touched something into his eye until it began to stream. Then, going to the ground, he drew a foot into his belt so expertly it was nigh on impossible, from any angle, to believe the limb did not end at the knee. The effect was startling, yet strangely familiar. Once he had withdrawn the glass and returned to full height, Calcroft said, "I see you recall our first meeting – when you struck me with your shiny stout cane while walking up the High Street."

Before Billy could bring the encounter entirely from memory, Calcroft reached forward to acquaint himself with the technique he had employed to make a mess of his nose. In instant agony Dempsey sent out a fist; Roger, doubling over from the blow to his stomach. He managed one of his own off Billy's face, opening a fresh flow from his nose, and so forth. They were at last separated by Freddy, Calcroft holding his head up haughtily while attempting to regain his breath.

"Of the Common Fame?" laughed Billy, wiping the blood running fresh over his lip, "Your reactions appear rather less than common."

"And I," choked Calcroft, "was told that Blue Billy came

from good thieving stock! —Was a pretty piece besides, and one I should like to make! Only now—"

"Keep a civil tongue," warned Freddy.

"Only I forgot!" shrieked Roger, "that William Dempsey was dumped in a whorehouse by his own mother upon proving himself without a scrap of ability in the thieving arts!"

His eyes going wide, Billy took another wild swing at him. Freddy was quickly between them and Calcroft already leapt ten feet to safety, hands in the air.

"*Don't ye dare speak of my mother!*"

"Get back to your rat now, Roger; I shall speak to William myself."

Billy made one last effort to pull away, kicking up a great deal of earth which missed its mark quite spectacularly. "*I'll kill him…*"

Freddy struggled to contain him: "*Forget* him now! Let us speak a moment, you and I. Ain't ye happy to see Brother Freddy again?"

"I got more brothers and sisters than I know what to do with. What good are any of 'em to me?" He then served up a look of loathing the man appeared unprepared to digest. After a moment fumbling about for a kerchief, Freddy took Billy's chin and began to blot his rupturing nose.

"Criminee, it ain't me yas angry with! I never done ya a lick a harm."

Billy attempted to pull his head away, but Freddy maintained him expertly in one hand as he continued to dab the nose.

In a more sober tone, Freddy continued, "Mama put you out too early, alright? She hadn't patience with you. Neither had she any with herself. And so you hate the whole community and don't wish to look back. But we're kin. What does a man have if he hasn't his kin? Sometimes it takes kin to say what needs saying, and it's this: you been doing what you're doing long enough…" At Billy's affronted look, Freddy continued: "Now I ain't mean it that way. Having a taste for men ain't nothing to us, never has been. You wish a nice fella to care for ya and kiss ya and all that; lads like yourself deserve to be happy too and you'll never hear that in the world at large, I promise you that. Only working in that brothel ain't right; I'd say the same to a female whore."

Billy remained silent.

"Right. The community's been considering the matter now you are known to be back in the Mint. You and Roger got off on the wrong footin', as the saying is, but…" and here he attempted to judge his words: "But he ain't no street boy like we was. If you can believe it, he's actually the son of some well-known grocer in the City. But a natural at The Stealth as one rarely sees. Puts me in mind of Grandfather Carew—"

"You compare that clown to Carew, King of the Beggars?"

"Listen to me now: the lad's a talent. And as he happens to be… *that* way, of your own persuasion, you take my meaning. And your being put out unfairly so long ago and desirous of guidance – the thought is Calcroft might take you under his wing a bit…"

After a moment of stunned silence Billy cried, "*Fuck ye!*"

"Watch your mouth, William. Your people want something better for you than what you're doing at present. It ain't who ya are, as I said before and what I hoped to prove by introducing Calcroft to you. Only what you're doing with your life – it ain't right."

LATER THAT MORNING, Chandler burst from his counterpane cocoon with a cry of "Flowers!". He threw on a favourite sprigged muslin day dress and with proboscis extended descended upon his gifts – a nosegay of primroses and sweet violets set beside a penny custard into which he touched a finger. Once he was sufficiently intoxicated on his gifts Billy held forth fifteen shillings.

"What's this?"

"What I owe. Well, it ain't half what I owe but it's the most I can do at present. Don't look like that."

Once more dipping his nose into the flowers, Chandler said with prissy disdain, "You may set the coins on my dressing table if you wish," then from the same table he retrieved a French *medicament* reeking of sub-par essence of lilac. Coming forward to apply some to Billy's nose, he frowned at the fresh damage and at the look he discovered there. "You've had an upset."

An upset, thought Billy – that was the understatement of the year. *The understatement of my life*, he stirred tentatively into the private thought, like wormwood into ale in the hope of producing a bracing morning purl. Instead what it produced was a self-pitying gruel, repulsive in the extreme to him. It was that weakness he'd smelled on that lover of Harper's the night before. Applegate. Hiding behind his outspoken companion during the entire exchange like he'd pissed himself. Without a word, without even a house name, of his own.

Then the piss and the purl and the fight in the Grotto Garden came into Billy's gullet and he said to Chandler, "You *do* fuck men for money, right? You *are* the one they call Sook Stockings?"

"Yes, of course," said the boy, furling his medicating fingertips and withdrawing half a step.

"Then by God and all the Saints behave like a punk, or I shall see Moll changes your name to Mother Mary or the Babe Jesus."

"The Babe…?"

"You belong in a church singing hymns, upon my honour. Never in all my years have I seen the like—"

"But the flowers—"

"Yes! The flowers! Because you—"

But at that moment cries sounded in a resonant bass from the room across the corridor: "...*Battersea'd! Battersea'd! Moll, come quick!*"

The boys stared at each other. Then as one, they said, "O'Donnell."

As they exited the room, Patrick O'Donnell was emerging onto the landing, naked as a new-born. Making a snatch for him was a man of about fifty who, upon seeing the rough condition of Billy, appeared to think better of it and retreated again into the room. O'Donnell was indeed a fine piece – about twenty-one, broad-shouldered, well-muscled and well-endowed – but with a look on his face as if he had seen a ghost. After catching his eye, Billy took him by the shoulder then directed him back into his room.

"I shall proceed downstairs, this moment, and demand my money returned," said the patron, a Mr Frost, to the horror of the Hibernian. "'*Cat-o'-nine-tails', fresh from Ireland.*' I've heard of frigid wives, but a frigid farmer's son from County Meath?"

Young O'Donnell cast his eyes heavenward, appearing about to weep.

Coming into the room like a Fury in a sprigged muslin day dress Chandler said, "Sir, you arrived in this house asking for the freshest on offer, did you not?

"What of it?"

"You did not proceed to the fleshpots of Covent Garden, to Weatherby's or to Haddocks, where a maidenhead twenty times refreshed is sold as intact."

Frost stepped forward and, assessing this effeminate youth, smirked, "That where you are employed?"

"No sir, I am not. I am employed in this house because I have a penis and testes. And because I have those things, I know very particularly how to pleasure a man, and to such heights of frenzy he must be peeled from the ceiling once I am done with him. However, I did not understand those things from birth and was quite as shy as this one when I began."

This was said with such brazen confidence Mr Frost, upon reassessing him, leant in and said, "You… available? We might come to an agreement, and Moll need never receive my complaint…"

"I am available to those who pay me. Thus far you have paid Moll for Cat-o'-nine-tails and nothing more."

"But received no satisfaction."

"*Bugger* you, you corny-faced bastard!" cried O'Donnell. "I lay with you the entire night, as desired. I lent my hand. And later, you…" he fixed upon Billy two widening eyes, "took your pleasure of me."

"*Pleasure?*" said Frost.

At this the horrified young man did begin to weep.

Billy pushed by O'Donnell and, yanking at the patron's wrap, went to his knees.

"What in God's name?"

"He declared you Battersea'd," said Billy. Turning to O'Donnell, he said, "Ninny, you're tell Moll immediately, not after an entire night."

"He refused to light the candle…"

Billy tugged Frost around to face morning light. "OH!" cried the man, but before he could decide what he thought of what was happening, Billy had risen and stepped away. "Scars from some ancient distemper. He ain't got nothin'."

After a prolonged silence Mr Frost, rounding on O'Donnell, said, "You thought I was clapped? Sir, now I *insist* my money be returned. With an apology!"

"My goodness, my good man," said Chandler, easing off the patron's robe and helping him on with his shirt, "next time you wish for a night of enchantment you ask for Sook Stockings. Your adventure tonight merely proves O'Donnell was what he says he was – what you requested and desired. Close your eyes in your bed tonight, sir, and recall the experience. The uncertain touch. The shuddering from a foreign sensation. The 'yes, I promise that feels good' and you will understand one of the best nights you've ever enjoyed with a man. Marathon Moll sells no cheap thrills, as you should have understood coming in. We sell complex experiences which mellow upon reflection."

Sukey continued to sell as he helped the man to dress. Then he escorted him out of the bedchamber and out of the house. Billy refrained from laughing out of regard for O'Donnell's tears. The young man was now so confused he knew neither what to do nor where to begin. He settled on, "I cannot do this!"

"You fared well enough," said Billy. "There's scarcely a misfortune happens what cannot be sold as success if you know how. But Moll told you to call 'Battersea'd' within the first five minutes. For God's sake, light the candle yourself next time if he refuses."

After some twitching at the very thought of a next time, O'Donnell nodded. When Chandler re-entered the room, Patrick wiped snot from his nose with the back of his hand and shrugged. "Mighta been worse." As he crawled resignedly back into bed, his visitors made to depart. "Remain with me until I go to sleep." The boys regarded each other. Then Chandler drew up a chair and Billy leant against the window frame. "What's that mean: *Battersea'd*? No end to the things a life in County Meath fails to teach you."

"Ain't you never heard of Battersea Park?" said Billy.

O'Donnell nodded.

"*You must go to Battersea, to be cut for the simples*, was the saying," said Chandler. "It's where they used to cut herbs for that particular medicine. An old expression, but if there's better to delineate 'blistered over with the clap' then I don't know it."

"…I cannot do this; I *cannot* do this…"

"Listen to me," said Chandler, "I did my best, but Moll may come to hear of this episode. She will be most displeased.

She told you everything to do within the first five minutes. You have the advice. Now you must *take* the advice that is given."

Wiping his eyes, then regarding his advisor with an expression approaching desperation, O'Donnell said, "After which I shall be peelin' them from the ceiling like Sook Stockings?" Chandler took him by the shoulder, then nodded with such grave assurance Billy could hold it in no longer and let out a snorting laugh.

"Something funny?"

"Only that you've convinced me you ain't the Blessed Mother. I suppose you might retain the name of Sook Stockings." When Chandler sniffed, Billy added, "Unless you fancy the sound of Mother Mary or the Babe Jesus?"

"Not particularly. A Christian must reject all such out of hand, fitting though they may appear to some." After a moment, he added: "Still, I might consider 'Jesu, Joy of Man's Desiring'."

CHAPTER SIX

Spanish Money

— *fair words and compliments*

The morning Tom appeared Billy slept in late. As Chandler was out all night, he had slept roomy, the dream that was the feather bed making it almost criminal to interrupt that dream. Still, sleeping in these days simply meant rising after dawn and after looking for the workman in the backyard through the windowpane, he was performing his morning ablutions at quarter to eight, waiting for his friend's return.

As he dressed, his thoughts turned to his small saviour, with whom, after the upsets of the previous morning, he'd spent a leisurely day eating and chatting. A newspaper entertained with every bobble and pearl of a gown Lady Northumberland had worn to a Haymarket assembly. For Chandler, who came from the country and had scarcely any exposure to the *ton*, enough could not be said when the topic turned the fashionable set. After so many months dining and masquerading among them, Billy was able to tell him much that the papers failed to tell, and the boy had examined him with endless, starry-eyed questions.

However Chandler had a pronounced reticence to speak of other things, namely Moll and her carpenter. His dismissal of Tom was somewhat surprising, for though he reaffirmed the man was quite handsome, he had been aloof when approached by the boys. He was abrupt, unfriendly, with time only for the project at hand. As such he deemed him not worth Billy's trouble.

The reticence to speak about Moll, however, who quite worshipped her little pet, Billy found entirely confounding. Much as he questioned him, he could make neither head nor tail of it, Chandler all the while insisting he had nothing at all against his mistress. *He liked her very well. She had been very kind to him. She was always very mindful of his health and safety which he very much appreciated.* From which Billy learned nothing but that *very* was to be the word when Chandler was lying.

At last, growing desperate to change the subject, Chandler returned to Mr Baker, believing it his duty to say that handsome faces were not everything and all efforts must be given to winning back the Marquess. Billy bit his tongue, assuring young Sukey that he was, every minute of every day, reminded of the urgency of winning back his rich benefactor. The state of his face, however, would make a hasty approach into nothing but a burlesque. He must have time to heal, so Mr Baker, who he admitted *had* asked Moll about his recovery, had piqued his curiosity.

After completing his morning toilette, Billy was looking over the perfumes scattered about the vanity when he saw Tom through the filthy windowpane. He was a *tableau vivant*, entirely without movement, considering a plank of wood he had placed across his sawhorse. He was so completely motionless Billy could not have said just how long he had been standing there.

Jumping into the window seat, he cursed the panes grimed over with dirt and prehistoric calcium deposits. The damned thing *must* open. A window was *made* for this sort of exchange, which required nothing more than a wave and a word of thanks. No putting oneself forward, no making an unwanted approach, yet quite enough to form a judgment about him. Should his net bring up nothing but a cold fish, he would simply throw him back. But such was the condition of the window he could not even rightly see the man's face.

Billy pulled the latch and threw his shoulder against the pane. The pane resisted. Then, to his horror, it failed to resist, sliding to one side like a rotten tooth primed to fall from its socket. He jumped back with hands splayed, praying that the pane would fall inwards if it must fall, cursing his rashness, cursing everything…

This was quite enough to bring attention to the first floor. The figure at the sawhorse looked up. Then, bending and bulging, it moved down the pane to stand nearer the house. Billy rubbed at the relatively clean inner panes more to show his interest than to clear the sightline, as most of the grime lay without. The figure below brought a hand to its face to tap its nose. To which Billy, driven to a style of overacting he was happy his thespian friend was not present to witness, gestured that *all was good, absolutely, safe as houses.* The figure nodded. Then, after a prolonged look down at the ground, he returned to his sawhorse.

With nothing at all accomplished by this ridiculous display, Billy determined to go down and speak to the man properly. As this would require disturbing Caligula for an escort, he steeled himself for the man's abuse and was on the point of exiting the room when the door swung inward, and Chandler stepped inside.

Billy grabbed his hand and led him back down the staircase. "Please and thank you."

Now in the vestibule he was stuck on just how to approach Baker. But for pans in the kitchen and the sounds of stirring in one of the bedrooms this was one of those rare times of quiet in the house. For a moment it was all quite disorientating. Then a thought came. He squeezed Chandler's hand before releasing it, then took a large glass from the dining table and tipped in water from a ewer.

"What's the *sturm und drang*?" Then peering into his eyes, Chandler continued, "Tom Baker? Oh Billy…" Then he sighed as he could see his friend was not to be dissuaded. "He did ask how you were recovering. Maybe he needs drawing out. Perhaps he is just extremely shy." His tone having slipped into disbelief, he added quickly, "Well he must have some reason for returning here. It never has made sense his continuing to come round to do these piddling tasks for Moll. Surely he has bigger and more important jobs in the shipyards."

"The shipyards?"

To Billy's great wonder, Chandler then informed him the man had served two years as master carpenter aboard the *HMS Dolphin*, an exploratory vessel sent into the South Seas in the summer of '64. In the five years since his return, he had become one of Southwark's premier consultants on large-scale seafaring projects.

Quite startled by the information, Billy stepped outside with his glass of water feeling decidedly less certain of the man he was to approach. As he proceeded, he observed the evidence of his exsanguination still winding ingloriously across the Yard. Though much had been absolved by the more forgiving earth, the pebbles and stones wore their crimson coats with the pride of British soldiers traipsing through the forests of America.

Along the side of the house, hitched to an aged grey steed, stood a large, square cart. It was rusted at the bolts and hinges, filled with lumber of all conceivable sizes, with a workman's chest set on the lowered tailgate. Round the back, Tom stood in the tangle of dust and sturdy weeds assessing a woodwork pastiche – slender planks, some approaching the size of window shutters, one or two the size of a door.

With some odd monkey grace he took up a medium-sized board, measuring once, then again, using the length of his forearm in a series of supple pivots. Withdrawing a blade from his belt, he made a mouth of his hand, then with the blade edge bit into the board at each end. From his belt he produced a long iron file for a guide, and with the blade drew four surgical lines at right angles into the skin of the board. After this a stout saw driven across these lines produced the pattern by which to cut multiple shutters.

Tom had the kind of agile body which clothes seemed not quite able to understand. His loose cotton smock and trousers seemed superfluous, yet one sensed they suited him better than anything else. A suit cut by a good tailor might contain the stationary man well enough, but it would not account for what seemed an exceptional understanding of his own body. Never had Billy seen such harmony of movement, apparently entirely at ease while in motion, though with a kind of austere self-sufficiency which seemed to say people were almost as superfluous as garments.

"Mr Baker?"

When Tom turned, his lean, tanned face was rather a continuation of his movements. Harmonious. Introspective. Lovely. After a moment to take in the newcomer, he leant his modelling board against the sawhorse, set the saw beside it, and stepped forward.

From under the shallow brim of the workman's cap each iris shone as though light had been brought to points under glass. It was a fixing gaze, something in it attempted to fasten an object. When he took up the water he looked away, and

Billy experienced a singular feeling of having been himself set down.

"Much obliged."

His eyes returned to Billy's. Then to his bloodied nose and the discolouration around his eye, the continued sight of which upsetting what had seemed a contented layer of formality. It was a serious countenance, a man of about thirty-two, who had seen much and internalised all of it. The only relief was a certain impishness around an unusually full upper lip, which appeared perched with a tart reply for a schoolmaster. In it one could see the boy that had been before he had been shed like so much inefficient fat.

The words subsequently exchanged were like pebbles into a riptide. Words bought the time to study the other, neither entirely hearing what the other was saying. Billy was certain it was the same for Tom, and that it was his injury which somehow enthralled him. His injury which excused his continuing to look, which compelled his attention just as he'd been compelled to help him stumble to Moll's door.

Then Tom replied, "…so you know carpentry."

Billy tried to recall just what he was replying to. "Well. One or two things. *Measure twice, cut once.* That is one thing I know. Words to live by, I reckon."

"Did you come outside just to speak to me?"

"Give you my thanks for services rendered. You needn't have helped me."

Tom's expression sought to assure him he would not ask what had happened, but Billy also understood he was not to inquire too much into himself. That Tom prized nothing so much as privacy, that he might be pleasant and engaging but only if one maintained a respectful distance. After giving Billy a moment to understand this, he said, "A man isn't much of a man who cannot assist a brother in need."

The thought was somewhat grander than what Billy was used to engage, and he said, "Maybe I deserved that smack on the nose. Maybe my opponent was left in worse shape than myself, and he was the one needed assistance."

"I've a good sense for people."

"So do I, occasionally." Billy waited, hoping Tom understood the compliment. "I been through a bit lately, as you can see. Mostly self-inflicted wounds. But still you helped me so there we are."

"Where are we?"

"Arrived at my invitation. There's a wedding tomorrow, in this house, four o'clock. I'm in the damn thing to please one of Moll's patrons but I'm a bloody horror to regard so I'll likely be relegated to a corner. If you come, I'll have someone to speak to like decent folks and I promise I'll show you a good time."

There was a long, to Billy inexplicably long, pause before Tom said, "Another time."

"Won't be another time, unless you are free tonight."

"I am working."

"There's your chance, then, gone. Moll's letting me stay only 'til the wedding. Then I'm out."

A brief twitching of the lip betrayed amusement. Nevertheless amusements did not control Tom Baker and as though reciting his *curriculum vitae* he declared: "I don't attend parties. Soirees, routs, whatever you call them I don't go to them. Nothing but a mess of babbling fools and the drunks are only marginally better. I have nothing in the way of small talk, a failing often condemned but which should be to a man's credit."

"Ask me about my nose."

"Your nose?"

"'*Hey fella, how's the nose mending?*' It's an instant conversation piece. I reckon more people should get such-like embellishments, makes everyone else in the room feel better about themselves."

Tom pushed his mouth to one side, but a short, clipped

laugh broke through anyhow. Billy laughed as well and, grinning, took his hand.

It was a coarse hand. And though just moments before so intimately engaged in work, Tom seemed, momentarily, to have no connection to it whatever. As though it was no more than the sleeve of his smock. Once he understood he withdrew the hand. He looked at it, then with an odd gesture seemed to set it aside. Continuing to look away he remained silent.

Billy was a long moment waiting for him to look up again. When he did his eyes remained slightly averted as he said, "Are you recovering then?"

"I'm alright."

"I—" but Tom left the thought unfinished.

"You… will see me tomorrow at four," said Billy, happy to complete his thought for him. While attempting to catch his eye he thought, *Good Lord, he* is *a bit shy. What kind of ninnies are working here anyhow who can't get past a bit of shyness in this lovely man?*

Tom nodded somewhat uncertainly. At last, somewhere under his breath, he said, "I shall be the most miserable wretch in the room."

"Come after the ceremony. Four-thirty, when everyone is too drunk to care about small talk."

When Billy stepped away and proceeded to the side of the house, he expected to feel a glow of conquest at what he'd achieved. Moll's establishment had always been one of competition between the boys; Tom had been hard to get, he was exceptionally attractive. Yet *why* Billy had convinced him was unclear, and so left him uncertain what to make of the encounter. He'd learned early that much in life could be achieved by boldness. Showing confidence you didn't feel was often enough to convince others. This is what he had done – done particularly well given how he looked. He had approached. And the approach had worked. But should it have?

As he came around the front of the house, Humphrey Harper was waiting for him with a look of great irritation. "Damned impossible to locate. Moll wishes to speak with you. Who let you outside?"

Harper led him to the dining table, kicked the leg of a chair and told him to sit down. When Billy opted for a seat on the floor his escort let out a trilling little laugh, rolled his eyes, then tossed a bread roll in his direction. As he ate Billy was obliged to listen to a drawling, simpering conversation between him and Applegate about some generous new patron they had secured. This was broken at last by O'Donnell's pounding down the staircase and into the dining parlour, red-faced.

"Where is Moll?" he asked. "I've something to tell her."

"Just rising," said Harper, nibbling a roll.

"There's a suspicious man loitering outside – peering in at windows and working the fastenings. I shall bid her fetch her pistol. We mustn't tarry."

"Expect it's the carpenter come to fit the window shutters."

O'Donnell's wide, well-proportioned face, when it did anything, turned from tomato to beet-red. "There is a fair bit of crime in the Mint. Are you willing to risk the life of your mistress?"

"Never," smirked Humphrey. "Be sure to tell her of the intruder the moment she steps from her room."

"That I *shall* do," said O'Donnell, before moving to the dining parlour window to search out the prowler. He stood there quite a long time, silent as the Princes simpered behind his back. Then, rounding once more upon Harper, he said, "I was to have fetched William from upstairs this morning," a vein throbbing in his forehead. "I wish to pull my own weight here, as I have said to Moll, and she vowed that I could fetch him!"

The Princes were now openly laughing at him, apparently unaware of his experience with Mr Frost and the damage it had done to his self-image. Growing up, O'Donnell had been handsomest and ablest in his village. Young and strapping, with scarcely a notion of failure. And now, so ambitious for instant fortune, he would even sleep with men to attain it. But there was a saying in London which, if he had not heard it before arriving, he certainly had now – that the Irish were *rarely paid and frequently beaten, light in purse and strong in appetite,* said both as commentary and prescriptive. Billy was no Good Samaritan, but he should have liked to say something in O'Donnell's defence just then. He had felt desperation too keenly of late not to recognise it in a fellow human.

At this point a stooped young man ran into the room, snatching Applegate's recently emptied mug of whey before returning to the kitchen. A moment later he appeared with fresh place settings. His limbs moved as though continually stung from the memory of being told he was too slow. And though no more than twenty-five, his hairline had already slipped to his ears, which seemed somehow owing to the great speeds he maintained. Nevertheless he avoided crashing into anything or slamming anything too firmly upon the table. Only after all had been set out (plate, utensils, fingerbowls, mugs, orange slices, and a tankard of small beer) did he note the person seated on the floor. In a tone of breathy surprise he descended to his haunches and said, "Sittin' on the floor then?"

"Aye."

"Got a busted and bloodied nose, have ya?"

Dempsey simply nodded. And though met with no warm reception to his questions, the young man liked what he heard so much he hitched up his breeches and took a seat beside him, persuaded that the floor was indeed the place for those who knew.

"Name's *Hen*-ry," he breathed. "That's what they call me. Reckon you're the one they call Blue Billy."

"Some do."

"But that's pretty, ain't it? I'm Henry *Spar*-row, of Spital-fields. Been cook here these eight weeks. You've come into an odd house, I faith. What I told my friend Joe, who lives at 13 Craven Street, Strand, one might term a *Frisky* House. There's two as visit playing at getting married, name of Miss Irons and Dip-Candle! How's that for a frisk, eh? I'm to make a great feast for their *wedding* tomorrow. And you know what I figure?"

"What's that?"

"*I* figure one of 'em must be the wife! But I cannot, the entire time I have known 'em, make out which it should be."

A stirring in the bedchamber just off the dining parlour announced the house mistress – Billy felt his stomach contract. Moll appeared. She directed Sparrow back into the kitchen to prepare a plate of eggs and summoned Billy from the floor. Then, mercifully, she directed him out of the room and away from the ears of the other boys. Through the front parlour she led him, then down the intervening corridor into the back parlour.

Billy seated himself gingerly on a sofa as Moll commenced shuffling across the carpet, methodically covering every inch in a move to announce territory. At last arriving at her reflection in a looking glass, she said, "You know, I used to subscribe to an Eastern philosophy. Was I wearing the banyans when you lived with me?"

"The what?"

Turning grandly, Moll gestured to her shining, silvery garment. "My Oriental robes. As I have on now."

"Reckon you was," said Billy, recalling her in little but

flowing things, usually thrown over a smock and flannel breeches.

"From the moment I saw David Hume painted in that *killing* turban, Eastern dress has become *quite* my thing. For a time, Eastern thought was my thing as well. Then one day I learned the turban the great Mr Hume wore in that portrait was nothing but a common velvet house cap. Well, I was never so disillusioned in all my life. Then, upon closer inspection, I discovered that Eastern thought, too, disappoints, offering one only the blandest of life philosophies. Passive non-resistance, everything in its place, all that…"

Billy hadn't an idea what she was talking about and neither, he suspected, did Moll. When he began shifting in his seat she came forward and said, "Nevertheless, I retain my Eastern garb because they are the finest garments I own and because they suit me. Nothing at all suited me in Oriental teachings except this idea of patterns. Patterns in all things. Lovely idea. I have always understood patterns of behaviour, of course; one must managing a bawdyhouse. But it seems to me there are also patterns within the very fabric of life. Repetitions. Things that are *cyc-lic* (the word sounded somehow obscene on her lips). One must mind the patterns and learn to heed them. To not resist those things, even odious things, which for whatever reason are continually pushed in one's face."

"And I am one such odious thing?"

"You are. I refused to look at you when you first arrived. Yet here you are again and with a bright red stain on your face one can scarcely look away from. You never were subtle, Billy. So here I am. *Me voilà.* What have you to tell me? What have you, as the mystics might say, to *teach* me?"

Rank bitch, thought Billy. Leave it to Moll to invent such nonsense. She did it to intimidate and make you uncomfortable. Yet somehow, as he searched to find the words to tell her so, he hesitated.

"You see?" she said.

"I ain't see nothin'.."

"You've matured, William."

"What's that mean? That I'm old now too, I suppose?"

"It means you stand a bit taller than you were used to do. You speak a bit better – when you allow yourself to."

"What's that—"

"You've benefited from keeping company with the Quality, darling. You've seen more of good things. I reckon if William Dempsey becomes angry and fights today, they are for very different reasons than those of a couple years ago." Then, so he might not forget his disfigurement, she tapped a finger to her hooked nose.

"Can I go now?"

"Not before you have told me of *my* admirable qualities."

"Your ever obligingness to let outta your company folks what ain't enjoying themselves."

"That is *not* one of my admirable qualities. Now: you returned to my house when you were dumped by every last gentleman of your acquaintance – why?"

"Cus I reckoned you would take me in, and I reckoned wrongly."

"And why did you reckon this?"

"You know why."

"Because you like me? More than, say, Dowager?"

"No, I liked him more'n you."

"Much more, from what I hear. But dared not return to the house in Soho because you did worse by him than you ever did by me. Why was that?"

"Because I was always scared of you. Alright? Does that make you feel like a big man?"

"*Respected*," said Moll, tasting the word. "'Because I always *respected* you' is what you mean to say. We return to those who are strong. That is why I abandoned Swamis and returned to the West. But what is it that makes me stronger than others? More respectable? *Scarier?*"

Billy shrugged. "You wasn't three sheets to the wind all the time like other bawds. Damned if I ever seen you drink anything but small beer."

"And?"

"Can't nobody run a business always in drink…"

"And?"

"…not even selling boys' bums."

"And?"

Billy hesitated. "You wasn't keen on diddlin' the employees." Moll raised an eyebrow. "And you had Caligula and others around to keep us safe from rowdy-types. Made it… more business-like."

"More business-like. Even while selling boys' bums?"

"That's right."

Moll gave one of her more unbecoming smiles. "I hear in your words, dear, an enticing presentation to an errant young stud loitering at the Registry Office. Is that what you hear?"

Billy's eyes went wide. Then, sitting forward, he said, "And should you ever wish to Eastern falafasise about why nobody likes Marathon Moll it's comments like that!"

"Whatever did I say?"

"You *know* what you said! I was never so low or unpopular as to be sent fishing at the Registry Office. My dancing card is always filled!"

"But sweetheart, the heels of your dancing shoes are broken at present. Two guineas from Sukey or no, I shall have nobody in this house isn't doing for me. You must avoid the patrons looking as you do, as I said before. But you will not lay around all day being shiftless. Now. How else might you make yourself useful?"

"I already *been* useful."

Moll waited for him to continue. Wasn't this the place to insert Tom into the conversation? Wasn't this the time to throw the handsome carpenter into her face, then tell her what a fool she had been to reject someone of his abilities? It was likely she would not believe him at first. When she did, she would slink out into the Yard. Find Tom with that smirking, flirtatious manner she had and say she *knew* he could not resist the charms of her house forever. *Knew* something more had been *rising* when he'd fixed a stair riser last month. Then Billy recalled Tom's expression as he'd withdrawn his hand. Withdrawn, then fallen silent.

"I been useful to Patrick O'Donnell. He's about to run; I shall talk to him."

Moll frowned. "What do you intend to say?"

"More of what I said yesterday after that upset with the client."

Narrowing her eyes, she said, "Sukey assured me Patrick did well with the patron." Billy remained silent, fearing he had stepped in it, then Moll groaned, "But he is my new, lovely lad! Mouth-watering. He's to have a premier role in the wedding ceremony tomorrow. And he is the requested love toy of our happily re-marrieds! Don't *tell* me that delicious, strapping lad is a dud!" Billy assured her all was not lost. He could help, he only needed to know a bit of his history. "There's not much to tell, beyond Sukey's discovering him at the Registry Office. Even my top performer is not too good for that, when it is required."

"But he used the old chestnut didn't he?" Moll pushed up her nose. "He did, didn't he? '*Potentially offering services for neglected wives and older women*'?"

"It worked, didn't it?"

"Did it?" said Billy rising from the sofa.

"O'Donnell," he said returning to the dining parlour. "Moll wishes you to show me the Registry Office. She likes the cut of your jib and reckons between the two of us we might bring in another like you for the attic room."

"Moll is pleased with me then," said O'Donnell as they departed on foot twenty minutes later. "I fill a niche, fancying girls – I knew that." This put a spring into his step and for a time he favoured every woman they encountered, young, old, or middling, with the puffed chest of what might be hired for absolute pleasure. Waxing more serious he said, "Listen. I don't mind fishing, but I can't imagine it will be difficult discovering another of the normal persuasion. My seniority in the house must be made clear. As yet we are not absolutely overrun by members the fair sex; I daresay word has not travelled. Still, I must have first choice of—"

"Moll's customers are men."

"Yes, though offering services for—"

Stopping them before a busy brewery, Billy said, "Men, O'Donnell." After letting this sink in, he continued, "And as I see it you got two niches. Do you wish to hear them?" Frowning as though he was being tricked into agreeing, O'Donnell nodded. "Coves wishing to break farm lads what fancy girls—"

"*Break?*"

"And coves wishing domination. You must enjoy dominating them, and show that you enjoy it, or this excursion to the Registry Office should be for you. Queue up for a brick-layer or coal-heaver and remain to see who wants you."

After this the flow of conversation dried. They proceeded on their way, Billy shrugging off the odd, irritable comment, even an absurd accusation that he wished his former room again.

He was thinking of Moll. Never before had she spoken to him as… well, as an adult. Despite his complaints, her request that he go fishing was not so unreasonable. During their previous collaboration he had always assumed she was merely fixated upon tormenting him. How startling, how freeing, to realise she was, simply, the owner of a business. Years ago, after the theft of a patron's timepiece, of which there had been no witness and which Billy steadfastly denied, she had shouted this at him as he lay on the crimson sofa puffing his clay pipe.

"A business-owner?" he laughed. "This ain't no business. Real businesses keep regular hours and don't change into a boarding school soon as the law comes sniffing about."

"It is a *business*, you little horror!" she had shrieked. "How on earth can I remain operational if my place of business comes to be known as a den of thieves? I shall be queuing for employment like a common country wench at the Registry Office!"

"What's that?"

At which point Billy had been obliged to jump from the sofa to avoid Moll's fury, losing most of the contents of his pipe.

Presently the queue snaking from the Registry Office came into view. Still displeased with him, O'Donnell was happy to stride ahead and begin assessing the men. Billy, however, continued in his private reverie, wondering that, during his life, he had managed to keep company with those who were either too high, or indeed too low, for the Registry Office. Despite what Moll had been led to believe years ago, he did know the place and had done since a child. His people had referred to it as *Smithfield*, usually accompanied by a laugh. He was ten before he knew to distinguish Smithfield market, with its cattle for sale, from the office which connected laborers and domestic help with potential employers. London's Registry Office was often the first stop for fresh faces from the country – once he'd begun at Moll's, he'd learned it was also a prime place to recruit for brothels and bawdyhouses.

Yet the employment-seekers he observed today were not at all the restless herds cowering under a master's whip he had thought to discover. Modestly dressed to be sure, but well-behaved, many reading newspapers, no doubt the adverts for help. A peek inside showed a young woman with a quill pen scratching a document in four places. This rather incensed him – what on earth had labourers and domestic help to do with reading and writing? Why must he be so continually reminded of all that?

Sometime later he re-joined O'Donnell, who had spent the entire time leaning against a wall, caught in an inner turmoil which ended in his declining to join the queue himself. His previous bad temper was now exchanged with anxieties for his future. Billy assured him, if he truly understood what working at Moll's required, he would have his own advice about patrons once they were home. O'Donnell took one last look at the men hoping to be put to work. To a future in which he might never need to call out *Battersea'd* and God knew what else. To a future which might well leave him destitute, and even worse off than when he'd left his home. With a nod he agreed to stay at Moll's.

They were returning to the Mint when he crossed a street in the Strand to purchase a newspaper. Billy followed, peering around his companion as he approached the table of offerings. So very many. Too many. Even O'Donnell was undecided which to purchase. That thick one – stacked upon others like itself? Or that bit of curling scroll, pinned with a rock against the wind? Or perhaps one of those pamphlets just a few pages long?

"Something with a detailed account of Captain Cook's voyage," said O'Donnell to the newspaper vendor.

The vendor selected a newspaper and set it before him. "At the moment the *Herald* has the only account worth your money; this issue contains nothing but the account. All official journals from the voyage were taken at arrival and will not be published for some time. But this being the *Herald,* you can trust the details have been authenticated as being from an actual member of the crew."

If one event could be said to define the summer of '71, if one event unified the rich and poor, the young and old of Great Britain, it was without doubt the triumphant return of Captain James Cook from his three-year voyage round the globe. Though Cook and his ship, the *HMS Endeavour*, would be remembered for the discovery of Otaheite, the charting of Venus's path through the heavens, and landfall upon the hitherto mythical land of *Terra Australis Incognita*, Cook's voyage the summer of his return was the subject of as much misinformation as information, and so captured the popular imagination as would never occur again.

Was *Terra Australis Incognita* actually one quarter the size of the globe? And what of the island in the South Seas said to be inhabited by giants, who painted multicoloured rings about their eyes and who would trade all they had for a handful of little beads? And what of the young women of Otaheite, or *Tahiti*, who danced naked upon a series of mats? Mats which were placed ever closer to their male audience, who were waiting to devour them in scenes of debauchery once they reached their destination?

That evening, Billy found the newspaper in the back parlour and brought it up to Chandler's room. Settling down he stared at the symbols at the top of the page.

Then to those at the bottom.

Then to the curvy writing beneath the illustrations.

He was entirely at sea. A sea of shapes grouped into block after block of endless, meaningless variety. Some words he knew, small and often used, floating like buoys, connected to nothing. He came ashore every few seconds to the only things which held meaning for him: An etching of the *HMS Endeavor* at launch. A map with a dotted line showing a winding course around land masses. A scene which appeared to portray a human sacrifice.

He realised that Tom Baker, given his history in seafaring, must love to speak about Captain Cook – the voyage would be the perfect topic of conversation. If Chandler would help him through the article, Billy could speak to him as an educated, inquisitive companion – and he very much wished Tom, or somebody like him, to see him in this way.

Ever since Mama had begun despairing to him about her age, as she had often done towards the end, Billy had been of two minds where physical attraction was concerned. Beauty attracted. Yet, with time, a companion might become accustomed and grow tired, as he'd feared would be the case with the Marquess. Or you might receive a crack in the face, one which would not heal in a few weeks. Then what? What else had he to offer? Tom appeared taken with him in some way – he'd stared past what was wrong, into his eyes, and seemed to see a person worthy of compassion. However reserved in manner, he had liked something enough to suffer a party so they might know one another better. If Billy didn't improve himself, a second inspection might show him there was, in fact, little of value to discover.

When O'Donnell rapped at his door, he realised something else. He was a position in life considerably worse than that of the newest employee of the house. Moll was still starry-eyed about the young man's potential, and with advice and the fear of becoming just another hungry Irishman at the Registry Office, he had at least a fighting chance of becoming a success. Billy, however, would be out. Moll had no stars in her eyes for him anymore. She had taken him in to please Chandler, that was all. After the wedding, he would be on his own again.

And Tom Baker, however unlikely the prospect, would be his only hope of a place to stay.

CHAPTER SEVEN

Autumed
– married

W ith the wedding just an hour away, O'Donnell's nerves were tuned to a high pitch. His head now brimming with Billy's advice on seduction, flirtation, and whip-wielding, he had almost forgotten he had been given pride of place in the ceremony. As guests were heard arriving downstairs the knowledge returned, and he appeared ready to sink under the weight of expectations.

His anxieties were not unfounded; Moll's signature offering was, without doubt, the weddings. Even in a niche market, she wished to set herself apart – while turning a tidy profit. A patron had but to show interest in a house boy or visit with his lover to receive her proposal of marriage and with it her own seductive charms. Hers were a combination of arch innuendo tinged with the overbearing, no doubt the same she had employed as a performer before turning bawd some twenty-five years earlier. Such affected manners were common enough in the profession – Humphrey Harper had them in spades – yet Billy believed his own successes had been attained by foregoing all that and simply giving a man undivided attention.

"Which is *not* what Harper does?" said O'Donnell, some-what panicked as Moll's shrill laughter drifted up from the vestibule. "I do assure you I am *committed* to fulfilling the role I have been designated: I am Cat-o'-nine-tails. I shall *dominate*. I shall *enjoy* dominating. And I shall *show* that I enjoy it. But I shall not always be employing the riding crop; one must behave in an amusing and captivating manner. And Humphrey has given me precisely the opposite advice to what you have just done!"

"Ask a patron who he is, listen to what he says, and don't look at anyone else while he speaks. Tell yourself he is the most interesting man in the room, and act like it."

"And this is *not* what Harper does?"

"Humphrey Harper behaves as though *Humphrey Harper* is the most interesting man in the room. Understand?" After a long moment considering, O'Donnell appeared to. His brow cleared: the laboured innuendo, the batting of lashes, and sly looks over a shoulder when departing the room – one need do none of it!

"Oh, William Dempsey – you gamahuchin' Skye Farmer – I could kiss you. With my tongue and clear down your throat. It is enough, then, that I am a robust, well-looking lad bestowing my attention upon a patron?"

Billy nodded, though was obliged to add, "Open your shirt to your navel and it is enough."

UNTIL RECENTLY, weddings had been performed in an empty bedchamber on the first floor called the chapel. Now with a full staff, and with the increasing popularity of the weddings, the front and back parlours, along with the intervening corridor making to extend the aisle, had been transformed to contain the ceremony. Lending itself best in the endeavour was the back parlour, with its tall, dramatic windows unobscured by curtains and a back bay suggesting a holy enclave. The intervening passage was rather dark with scarcely enough room for chairs. The front parlour, with its Roman urns and statuary, too much an altar to the men who had persecuted the Saviour to be a very fitting monument to him. Moll placed a portrait of Jesus on the wall and beneath this a large bowl of punch tasked with the remainder of the convincing.

Wedding themes varied according to the tastes of the couple and remained a closely guarded secret until the ceremony. As this was not the first wedding of Miss Irons to Dip-Candle Mary, it was widely believed there would be less of romance and more of spice than on previous occasions. As such a flood of guests, of all sizes, descriptions, and combinations, milled about the rows of hard-backed chairs in high good humour. Some were single, some couples, all with house names but for the newcomers who would receive theirs at some point during the evening.

Libation flowed. Manners: somewhat worse than Sunday-best. Billy appeared with Chandler, each habited in white robes, which were tugged at and tossed up as they passed by. Next to emerge was Hardware Nan, always dependable for duty as master of ceremonies. He was followed by the Tower Princes, each swinging what appeared to be thuribles at the end of chains, but which were in fact decanters of brandy – for a small contribution the Princes would sit on the lap of a donor and tip a bit down a thirsty gullet.

Once Billy and Chandler had taken their places on either side of the pulpit, Nan directed the revellers to take their seats.

He was a few minutes into a sermon of John Wesley's, performed with pomp in a carrying baritone, when a shriek from upstairs signalled the commencement of festivities. The Princes, having already made conquests of hearts and other parts, threw arms around their new beaux and waited with bated breath for what was to come.

First down the stairs, with hands bound behind his back, was Miss Irons. In an apron and wielding a rolling pin, Moll was hustling him forward. "Scoundrel! Villain!" she was shouting, red-faced, hair askew even more than usual, and in particularly fine form: "Stop the service Reverend! You must perform a marriage ceremony this instant. We cannot delay!"

From the back parlour Nan set Wesley aside, then boomed: "A marriage, my child? Do you wish to marry this wretch?"

"ME, marry the footman?" shrieked Moll, then struck Irons across his beefy shoulder with her pin. "My daughter – the little hussy – must marry him! BRING HER DOWN, OSTLER!"

Upon which a terrible cacophony tumbled down the staircase, across the vestibule then arrived at the back of the chapel. The parishioners, all of whom had turned round in their chairs, were rewarded with a strange and heavenly sight: the doubled-over form of Dip-Candle Mary and, towering above him, the house's newest treasure – farm fresh from County Meath, Óengus, the God of Love, Summer, and Youth, though known in his London incarnation as Cat-o'-nine-tails!

O'Donnell stood apprehensively but radiantly in taut riding breeches, smock opened to his waist and brandishing a horsewhip. When audible gasps, even a bit of applause, were heard his eyes leapt across the chapel to find his instructor. *Oh William Dempsey*, he seemed to say, *you never said there would be applause.* And with this every ounce of his former trepidation fell away. He tugged to a standing position the slumped over

Mary, who was holding a weight at his middle which threatened to tear through his loose-fitting shift.

Cried O'Donnell: "Your footman, Moll!: The blackguard has bragged to every member of the staff of his villainy! And hark," tugging Mary up by the sleeve, "your daughter approaches her time!"

Weeping, Mary embraced Patrick tightly about the waist, nuzzling his face against the musculature of the young man's chest. "Oh save me! *Save me*, Cat-o'-nine-tails…"

"You scoundrel!" wailed Moll at Irons. "I trusted you to be my footman and now look what you have done! You must make an honest woman of my girl before it is too late!"

"Bring the sinners forward," commanded Hardware Nan from the pulpit. "I shall marry them as man and wife, the girl cannot be long for her lying in."

"Marry her?" laughed Irons, pulling violently free from Moll's grip, in the process overturning an empty chair at the back of the chapel. "I shall never marry the wench, though she was a fine piece to tumble in the hayloft – aye, and once, there was even a delicious romp in her own virgin bed…"

At this Moll collapsed in a heap in a hardbacked chair, fanning herself and declaring her entire family had been undone.

But stepping forward, O'Donnell declared, "Fear not, madam. All is not lost. Not if I can help it." Then, addressing Irons: "*Strip to the waist, villain!*"

The attendants stirred in anticipation at this dramatic turn of events. Some moments were required to strip and move aside a few chairs, so Billy took the opportunity to parcel out mugs of alcoholic punch while Chandler passed around a tray of biscuits, grapes, and orange wedges.

Miss Irons, shorter and stockier than O'Donnell, when stripped to the waist displayed a blacksmith's powerful upper body. Unlike his smooth adversary, he was covered in dazzling runs of black hair, front, back, and down his arms to the tops of his hands. He waited in a crouched position as O'Donnell strutted up and down the aisle flexing his muscles, pausing to be admired, which for the young man was so intoxicating he nearly lost the thread of the narrative. Once he returned to the back of the chapel, Irons reached forward and slapped him lightly across the cheek.

At which point O'Donnell lost the thread entirely, and Moll almost all control of her wedding ceremony, as during the ensuing scuffle a genuinely enraged Hibernian overturned a good number of the chairs, some containing guests, in an effort to seize hold of Irons. O'Donnell slapped Irons. Irons slapped O'Donnell. Then jumping forward, Irons took the younger man into his powerful embrace. After rubbing their bodies together a good long while, much to the satisfaction of the onlookers, Irons brought them crashing to the floor in one heaving bundle of testosterone.

Guests began shrieking as the rolling men hazarded their seats, Moll hustling Dip-Candle Mary up the aisle to the pulpit. At last Irons cried, "I surrender!" after O'Donnell had pinned him to the floor with one arm twisted behind his back. "I shall do anything! I shall marry the wench! Only leave off brutalising me, for love of God and Country!"

O'Donnell jumped off, tugging Irons to his feet and, turning to his audience, bowed deeply to receive a wild round of applause. Upon retrieving his horsewhip, he marched Irons down the aisle to join Mary at the pulpit. Guests were by now shrieking with mirth, one elderly gentleman nearly fainting from excitement while Applegate, supine upon the floor, struggled with a guest who had grown intent upon discovering what lie beneath his white robe.

Hardware Nan performed the ceremony. Billy brought forth the rings and kissed the bride. At which point Moll glanced with some trepidation toward O'Donnell, for at Irons' hesitation at saying "I will" her new protégé was to apply the horsewhip, just once, across his back. But all came off without a hitch – at the crack Irons shuddered quite pleasantly and burst forth his compliance.

Overjoyed, Dip-Candle Mary fell backwards into the arms of guests in the front pew. And in all his emotion and with the help of Moll, he was safely delivered of a fine Cheshire cheese, which until then he had been struggling to maintain beneath his shift. Chandler promptly brought the cheese to the sideboard where he began slicing it for his tray of appetisers.

Miss Irons kissed his lovely, slimmer bride, who appeared very much to stoke his fire again now he had lost his cumbersome burden. Moll pushed a flushed and sweating Patrick O'Donnell toward the loving couple. "See he does right by my girl, now."

Mary reached forward to grip O'Donnell's wrist – his pulse now visibly quickened, eyes dilated, dizzy with anticipation. At which point O'Donnell betrayed a moment's hesitation. But after partaking of a nearby thurible, and with an approving look from Moll, he directed the glowing couple down to the cellar bedchamber which had been prepared for them.

Slipping upstairs after the ceremony, Billy fell onto Chandler's bed, pleased to have the wedding done and even more pleased not to have been waylaid by a patron before Tom arrived. There was yet to be a sign of him. But Tom *would* arrive. He was certain of it. Well, mostly certain. And… and if he did *not* arrive. Well…

When Hardware Nan stumbled into the room and ordered him down to meet a guest, Billy's heart leapt and he followed it into the air. He slipped into a new smock and knee breeches lately purchased from The Jolly Tailor, entirely plain and what must appeal to a no-frills type like Baker. After tugging on a pair of shoes he rattled downstairs after Nan, who led them forth holding a mug of punch suspended like a guiding light. He continued into the dining parlour and almost into a man of about fifty-five, who appeared a bit dazed and clutching a thurible to his breast. He smelled terribly of fish and Nan, in the same booming voice he used to wed couples in sacred union, took his shoulder and introduced him to Billy. This, he announced, was a member of Captain James Cook's illustrious crew.

"Midshipman Jonathan Monkhouse," said the red-faced, red-nosed man swaying as though the sea he had ridden for three years still churned beneath him. At the announcement eyes turned, some came forward for a look, among them a deeply sceptical Moll. After a quick inspection she took Nan to one side, chastising him for making the introduction, which, if he really were a member of Cook's crew, must cause a major upset in the house. All guests, let alone such an illustrious one, were the rightful property of *her* boys.

From across the room Harper met Moll's gaze with a flash of anger, pushing from a wall to make his approach. Upon which Billy produced his most winning smile for this Monkhouse. Should Tom fail to appear, he'd be damned if he'd let slip the opportunity to earn a bit of desperately needed coin. The midshipman was three, perhaps four, sheets to the wind, but his eyes shone good-naturedly, and he appeared harmless enough.

As Harper sauntered over, Moll took Monkhouse's hand and sniffed in Billy's direction. "Nothing I should ever recommend. William is *not* an employee of the house Your… Midshipmanship. I *have* to believe Nan mistook your request; for I am in a position to offer you a truly stellar boy, one of the feted Tower Princes."

"Blood, Moll!" cried Monkhouse. "There's been no mistake! Your Prince looks a nice enough fella, but I wish the lad with the flowing dark hair. This is the one."

"But such a battered..." said Moll. "Humphrey, would you believe we've a member of Captain Cook's voyage with us tonight? A voyage which, as I heard it put so charmingly in some little newspaper report, has put a girdle 'round the globe!"

"Stars and planets, *how* delicious! Such talk is just to my *taste*," and, leering at Monkhouse, Harper circumnavigated his upper and lower lips with a lascivious tongue.

Returning to her guest Moll said, "John, you must reconsider."

Looking steadfastly away from Harper, Monkhouse said, "You been to sea, Moll? With hard-workin' lads, roughed-up like this one? All lonely for love and seldom able to reach for it. Such have been the knock-abouts I've known, and some very much to taste. Yet in such confined quarters, I was little able with any of 'em. Got so bad I nearly attacked the cabin boy napping in his hammock."

"The cabin boy? Oh John, Billy is *far* older. Eighteen, perhaps even *nineteen*..."

Monkhouse's eyes went round. "I ain't *want* no runt like the cabin boy! This Billy's a small lad but I'll warrant a man in the places what matter. A man that can take what I got to give him. How many ways I gotta say it?"

This was clear enough even for Moll, and as she stepped aside Harper came forward with a sneer for Billy. "Yes... youth without beauty still has its charms."

"And nothin' without nothin's got no charms," said Billy, "that's why he stepped past a down-market guttersnipe and asked for me."

Moll clapped a hand over Harper's mouth and, after a brief struggle, tugged the young man away.

Monkhouse advanced. "How much to pound ya, Billy?"

"A sovereign."

"A *sovereign?* Good God——"

"Moll'll demand half my earnings." While the man was

trawling his breeches pocket for the money, Billy cast about the room desperate for a sign of Tom. He could not have stood him up. He said he would be here and with men like that his word meant something. Still, with no sight of him he had no choice but to accept the sovereign from Monkhouse. He pocketed the money. Then not bothering to disguise his increasing gloom he said, "I haven't a room so you must take me to the Tal—"

"Midshipman Monkhouse – of the *HMS Endeavor*. An honour." Tom was suddenly standing with them and had taken Monkhouse's hand. "I was present at her launch." Aiming his eyes at the man a long moment: "Present, too, at her return. Just one of thousands, but close enough to discern the face of every member of her crew. I'd recognise you anywhere."

Baker gripped the man's hand until his oddly set thumb seemed about to pop off. With an oath Monkhouse withdrew, wincing. Billy nearly did as well, for though the features of Tom's face remained impassive, his eyes were flashing with black anger. It required a moment to reconcile his joy at seeing Tom with the man's extraordinary agitation. Billy was not novice enough to believe it was jealousy on his own behalf. Tom was more likely angry at a man he took to be an imposter, which perhaps Monkhouse was. Such things were not unknown in the sort of wishes-fulfilled establishment Moll sought to cultivate. But why on earth should he care so much?

Once his hand was free and he had assured himself nothing was broken, Monkhouse said, "Happens all the time, lad," then to Tom, "my decanter's just run dry, my boy – I could do with a nip. And a bit of fiddle music."

Tom looked as though he had more than a bit of fiddle music to organise for him, but he said only, "Let us have *Sweet William*."

Shooing him aside, Monkhouse said, "As you like. Fetch that drink now and leave us in peace."

When Tom withdrew, Monkhouse led them to the settee in the back parlour. Exhaling a great and gratified sigh, he drew Billy down beside him, then, after looking him over, grabbed him between the thighs. "Theeeeere ya are, lad. Respectable, but I'm bigger!" At this excellent joke he laughed raffishly and ruffled his companion's hair. "Weeeell, I'm a decent enough fella once you get to know me," he said, withdrawing a stained handkerchief from his waistcoat pocket to blow his nose. With a shake of the head, "Christ, the savages I've encountered in my time." Then turning to his companion: "And a stump for a foot won't put ya off? That's all I got on my left leg and scars up and down me what's right repulsive to some."

"You're a man," said Billy, somewhat reflexively.

Monkhouse's eyes lit before taking them into a closer attitude. "That I am, lad. And ye shall feel the man I am once I get another drink in me."

"Aye aye cap'n."

When Tom returned he was holding three goblets. After distributing them he drew up a chair before the pair and made a toast to the *HMS Endeavor*. He directed each to empty his goblet in a single go. All agreed, first holding his goblet suspended. Then bottoms up. Billy tasted nothing but sweet punch, but Midshipman Jonathan Monkhouse experienced something beyond the effects of that syrup-water Moll doled out to her guests. He started awake. Then, laughing uproariously as his sails filled with the prevailing trade winds, he declared he could take on the world! Then, just as quickly, his sails came down, his eyes rolled back, and he tipped toward oblivion as Billy retrieved the empty from his hand.

Holding the goblet to his nose: "A lethal elixir; my very eyebrows are scorching!" Tom shrugged, though by a faint blush it appeared he was not exactly a ruthless assassin. He gave a look which asked forgiveness. And Billy, flattered beyond anything and seeing nothing to forgive, could think of nothing to say. At last, lifting his own goblet, he asked with a small smile, "And only sweet punch for me, lover?"

The word lifted a hand to Billy's cheek. Tom said, "Lover," running the backs of his fingers across the skin, the tips seeming to continue in lines of quicksilver the length of his spine. Tom *had* been thinking of him since their meeting. His easier manner said everything. Said he wished to be more engaging. This first sign of affection from him quickened Billy's breathing, a reaction Tom observed and smiled to have produced. Yet it was as much fear as pleasure, as Billy had rarely had to contend with attraction for the men he entertained.

Tom set a finger gently to his nose and told him he was mending nicely. Swallowing, Billy smiled, unaccountably fluttered and again unsure what to say. Then Tom slipped a hand under the fall of his hair, and if words had been forming, they fell away. Tom was so altered from what he had been. Determined now to show his interest, determined to push beyond his reserve, and it heightened his attractions exponentially. Now he seemed wishing to say something himself, and when the words failed to come, Billy put a finger to his lips to tell him it was alright – they needn't speak.

For a moment, each had his ear to a conch, and it was the sound of the surf – deep and hollow and constant.

They were set to continue in this manner when a snort from the slumbering seaman roused their attention. The man was stirring and, after a handful of coins slid from his pocket, seemed liable to awaken. Billy slid a throw pillow under his head and said, "And if your sleeping potion wears off?"

Tom lifted his hands to grip an imaginary collar then mimed with a dip of his head a quick, elegant head-butt. Billy let out a laugh which contained the fruity notes of a giggle, then clapped a hand over his mouth, lest he rouse the sleeper. "You rogue!" he whispered. "What'd this poor man ever do to you?"

It was the wrong thing to ask. He was dismayed to see Tom lose his growing easiness. Reverting to his previous formality he said, "He offended me. Jonathan Monkhouse, along with many others, died of dysentery after leaving Batavia. It was the last leg of Cook's voyage, only months before returning after so very long at sea. Such a grotesque display was to me intolerable, certainly nothing to be amused by."

Though sobering, Billy saw his opening to speak about Cook's voyage, facts from which he had memorised for just such an occasion. As this was also an opening to tell what he knew about Tom's seafaring history, he began with, "Reckon your time on the *HMS Dolphin* makes such things—"

But now it was Tom holding a finger to Billy's lips. "Please. Nothing of the past just yet. Let us leave our baggage behind."

Just yet. Those were the words; Billy had not imagined them. *Just yet* meant there would be a later. Something *was* happening between them, Tom felt it too and wished to be with him. Once you got beyond that no-nonsense exterior, he was as hungry for affection as any. Perhaps he didn't wish to talk much, but what could that matter? Billy was actually *attracted* to this man. Tom had already helped him once when he was in a bad way. And just look at him: without the workman's cap, that head of auburn waves lit by the light of a wall sconce – he was beautiful. When you came to think of it, having no bedchamber in this house, far from being a hinderance, might be just the thing. He would wait until Tom was good and heated, then ask to see his home. Come morning, if all went well, there might just be an offer to stay…

Though never much of a drinker, tonight Billy did wish a drink. He needed it. Too much depended on this night. They must have a marvellous time and a dose of brandy would relieve all worries.

The brandy soon arrived and oh – that bright relief. That freedom from tomorrow…

Billy filled the fiddler's head with songs of sailors, songs of adventure, though summoned him first to:

"Adieu, adieu, I must meet my fate,
I was brought up in a tender state,
Until bad counsel did me entice,
To leave off work and to follow vice
Which makes me now lament and say,
As in the dismal cell I lay,

Pity the fall of young fellows all.
0 well-a-day! 0 well-a-day!

At cups and cans I took great delight,
Singing in alehouses day and night;
A pretty girl was never a joy,
I took greatest delight in a lusty boy,
Which makes me now lament and say,
As in the dismal cell I lay,

Pity the fall of young fellows all.
0 well-a-day! 0 well-a-day!"

From there to a livelier, then still a livelier tune. And as Billy skipped about what was left of the wedding chapel, bellowing in a fine tenor, and falling to one knee before his companion with his arms cast forth, Tom began clapping his hands in time. His face began to glow. Lifting Billy from the floor, he took him about the waist and spun them in a country dance. They retrieved more drinks, milling about the rooms sipping and spilling as others joined for the next song.

"Tears of the tankard!" called Billy, dropping to his knees to catch in his mouth the ale which Baker's stepping about prompted over the rim. And soon enough, he knew again the joy of casting himself into a lively tune. The utter silliness that could be life in a bawdyhouse, far from the sombreness of his experiences in keeping. Even Moll, upon entering the room, was compelled to perform her version of a dance, her goblet of sweet wine suspended as she marched back and forth to the music…

Soon Tom had one arm wrapped about him, nipping at his ear, and declaring in a heated voice, "I want you, Will. Right now. Let's get upstairs."

But Billy resisted, wishing to stay among the revellers, drunk on the knowledge that he might enter into this micro-cosmos of lives, these Toms and Molls, these Chandlers and O'Donnells, and not blunder too terribly. That like a comet he might dislodge their orbits, dislodge but not disturb. But rather cause them to spin more beautifully, and for one night at least become the solar body at the centre of things! And…

And then.

All went black.

CHAPTER EIGHT

Stow your Whids

– be wary

---

hat evening Chandler made his move. Slipping away
just after the marriage ceremony, he had hurried up the
High Street and hired a chair out of Southwark. In his hand
he held his copy of the *Harris's List of Covent Garden Ladies*,
1770 edition. His destination: Fleet Market. He was now
wandering the streets and byways between the Market and
Temple Bar thinking of, and expecting every minute to see, a
voyager of rather a different cast to that of Midshipman
Jonathan Monkhouse.

His aim was to meet Sally F., starlet of page 74 of the
List, which for years had been London's premiere resource
for men wishing to meet ladies of the evening. No more
ambling about London Bridge for whatever presented itself.
No more brothels where one must contend with Madams

and upsells of all variety. Inside the *Harris's List* were the name, location, and typical working hours of every lady worth knowing in the city. After more than a decade, the *List* now reached far beyond Covent Garden, and was updated annually to contain the freshest, most desirable offerings. Conversely was it updated to disparage those previously recommended who were known to cheat, steal or in some other way displease. The publisher of the list, who remained anonymous, had the power to raise or lower the desirability of a lady at will, and it was precisely because Sally F. had apparently displeased someone that Chandler wished to meet her:

> "*Sally F. At a Chandler's Shop, Fleet Market. This delicate lady is to be met with between Temple Bar and the place of her abode. She sets sail between the hours of seven and eight. If she meets with any captures, she generally sets fire to them and bears away with what plunder she can conveniently carry off. She is Dutch-built, broad-bottomed, and carries a great deal of sail. Goods put on board her reasonably freighted.*"

But after half an hour Sally F. was yet to show, and Chandler was beginning to fear this excursion would end just as his previous outing to meet Fanny B. had ended. Fanny B. had been chosen for an unflattering review which implied she was hard pressed for money, which he had hoped would make her receptive to his inquiries. He had been lucky to get away that evening, Moll scheduling nearly every hour of every day. But he had got away and so travelled north to meet Fanny B., who had:

> "*Married a brass-founder in Houndsditch. She launched out into all the fashionable follies, and soon melted all her husband's brass into caps, handkerchiefs, and aprons. He became a bank-rupt, and she has sent him into the country, to his relations, to*

graze, that she might take her swing at pleasure more uncon-trolled."

But he could find no one by that name at the direction, and no neighbour willing to say they had ever known her. He was beginning to believe the fault lay in an outdated edition, a copy of the newest, updated for 1771, being notoriously diffi-cult to locate.

And so the appearance around a corner of Sally F., for it could be no other, was a pleasant surprise. Her size was considerable, her speed perhaps measurable in knots, yet by all appearances having lowered her sail for the evening taking on board nothing but a bottle of gin. As she approached the candle-maker's shop, she observed the figure leaning against a brick wall. They made eye contact. Sally smiled. Then, narrowing her eyes at the slim, effeminate youth, a youth inca-pable of appearing as anything but what he was, she stashed her bottle in a pocket and produced a cudgel from somewhere beneath her voluminous sails. With time only to drop to the cobblestones, Chandler kept clear of her instrument as it connected with the wall.

"*Bloody he-whore!*" shouted Sally, looking about in the hope of retrieving him from the shadows his slightness had allowed him to slip into. "*Every day more of yer lot offering it up, I faith, taking trade from us more honest whores!*"

Though fearing for his safety, and careful to stay deep within the shadows, Chandler hissed: "More *honest? Damn* you, you wench, I get my bread same as you!"

"*Honest, I say*! Using honestly what God gave, whilst you manipulate what you got to steal my trade. Aye!" she added, "and selling it as safe harbour for ships wishing to avoid the clap!" She gave the brick wall a second whack from indigna-tion. "*Come out and face me like a man!*"

Sukey at last appeared from shadows perhaps twenty feet from where Sally had last seen him. He approached, and at her look of growing outrage, during which she improved her grip upon the cudgel, Chandler extended an offering of his own. A peace offering – one shining, golden guinea.

"For you, Sally. If you will help me."

"*Help* ye?" she said with a sneer, though blended with the sneer for Chandler was a smile for the guinea, there being little to distinguish one expression from the other.

"You may interpret what I have to say as taking trade from you. I cannot help that, madam. But I can tell you this guinea might go to any in the *Harris's List*. It needn't be you. And it shall *not* be if you continue to aim that cudgel at me."

"How do I know that's a real piece?"

"It's real."

She hesitated. "What is it ye wish to know?"

"Two things; a name and a location. Who is the author of the list, and where can he be found?"

"What's this about?"

Chandler took in the moment. A moment he had so long wished for. The moment to tell someone just how unhappy he had become at Marathon Moll's.

"I cannot remain with my employer," he said. "She makes requirements of me, of my purse, of my time. Perhaps you have a passion too, Sally; my own is the theatre. Those glorious lines, written by our best. The Season begins in November, and I have met someone with connections to Covent Garden. Just a bit player and without much money. But he promises he can get me in as an assistant of some sort. And from there perhaps to understudy. You may laugh, but much of achievement is simply being present when opportunity arrives. To do that I must be master of myself, of my time, of my commitments. I need only a room in a good location and the ability to set my own schedule. Which is what you have, Sally, with your place in the *Harris's List*."

"You daft? Them ads is for the *ladies* of Covent Garden and surrounding vicinities."

"Yes, I know," he said, his voice faltering. "That will be my cross to bear."

Sally considered. The night not having been overly bountiful, she said finally, "Jack Harris is a bastard, as is his *List*. Called me a big-bottomed boat or some such, with a taste for piracy…"

"Said in jest and witty prose…"

"…settin' fires…"

"…while at the same time publishing your preferred working hours and location. My goodness, what I wouldn't give for such an advertisement! And were I so inclined, I declare: the thought of the buxom wench as you are described to be. With a hint of danger and selling at a reasonable rate. I believe I must adore to meet you in a dark alley."

"Takin' my trade…" muttered Sally.

Chandler shrieked, "*Confound you to hell, you harlot!* I have never taken trade from any seeking female companionship! They are tastes as differing as flogging and hair-combing!"

"Naw…" muttered the woman, narrowing her dark, beady eyes, considering whether a well-timed swing with her stick might not free the treasure.

Attempting a more pacifying tone, Chandler said, "They say it's three people who write the list. Or possibly only two. Or perhaps it's one using three names. Jack Harris I understand is a pseudonym."

"A what?"

"An alias. A fake name."

After some consideration Sally F. sighed. She was some moments listing forward and aft setting down the cudgel to bring out the gin. "It was three individuals – one has been dead these two years. Second is Jack Harris hisself, who is an actual man. It were only his name the dead one used for the list as Harris was for many years what was termed the Pimp-Master General of England. The third…" She trailed off, extending a hand for payment.

"On your honour, Sally: you will tell me?"

"I told ye already – I am more *honest* than ye. Now give me that piece." Coming forward, Chandler handed it over. Upon verifying it was genuine, Sally tucked it from view. "Third's a bawd. Charlotte Hayes. Far as I know she controls the list now. Sends the physician to see me. And holds my health bond verifying I've told the truth about meself and am well in wind and limb. She operates that famous brothel in King's Place, what calls itself a *nunnery*."

Chandler could not have been more shocked had Sally told him the list was maintained by the Queen Mother. The nunnery in King's Place was London's most exclusive brothel. How would he ever summon the courage to walk in and ask to be placed on the list?

"Thank you," he said, rather faintly.

"Go on with ya…" said Sally, turning towards the chandler's shop to meet a man just then descending from an apartment.

"Blood Sally, thought I heared ye down here. Back so soon?"

The man patted her bottom as he brought her into an embrace. He relieved her of the cudgel. Then he produced a grin at the guinea and stood aside as she advanced up the stairs.

BILLY STARTED UP IN BED.

"Alright, calm yourself. We're in the garret room, lying peaceably."

This was Tom: Tom speaking, Tom's arms around him, holding him.

Once he had assured himself of this, Billy closed his eyes and attempted to recall the previous evening. He took inventory of himself. "Two pounds. I got two pounds somewhere…" He dug in his pockets until he found them. Found too that he was still wearing his breeches. Oh, but his head was spinning. "I rarely drink to excess, Mr Baker, upon my honour. Thank you for not ravishing me while I was unconscious. I am a more amusing companion when I am awake. Only…" then he was on the floor retching into a chamber pot. Baker was soon at his side to hold his long, tangled hair from the line of fire.

After wiping his mouth, Billy continued an internal train of thought aloud: "…and I haven't a place to go, and how is it that even a Natural like Henry Sparrow can get a roof over his head when William Dempsey cannot?"

"Will—"

"Moll only agreed to have me here a few days, as a favour to someone she likes as she does not like me. Now the wedding is over—"

"I have spoken to Moll."

Billy was by this point leaning back on the bed, hanky to mouth with the heel of his palm over one eye. "You what?"

"Spoke to Moll. She was in a famous good mood after your midshipman was carried from the house. In his trail out the door he donated a total of five pounds seven shillings to her establishment. About that time I mentioned our circumstances, and she has agreed to let you remain in this room for now."

Moll agreed? Moll's *agreeing* meant Tom had paid her for the arrangement. Once Billy confirmed the watery contents of his stomach were at low tide, he crawled from the floor to the bed, under the worn counterpane which, though grown musty from languishing in a disused room, was quite warm. Tom came into bed. He resumed him in his arms, bringing them into a specific attitude. An attitude which said they had been this way previously. Billy shuddered, revolted that he must contend with this. Humiliated to know the man had waited so many hours while his bedfellow had languished in his arms, drooling on a pillow and on himself.

Swiping at his eyes and his mouth, Billy lay back on the pillow. Their eyes met. He set a hand on Tom's thigh, hoping both to distract him from his atrocious face and to show his readiness to comply. Tom set a hand on Billy's damp chest in a way that was both intimate and restraining.

"You talk in your sleep," he said, smiling. When Billy remained silent, he added, "Have you never heard that?"

As it happened he had not. It was the great irony of his profession that he awoke nearly every morning alone. Benjamin had had a wife and child, and the Marquess declared he could sleep only in his own bed. However the truth, in this instance, sounded like a lie, so Billy shook his head and waited to see if he would be believed.

"You do," said Tom. "And I must say can hold your side of a conversation quite well."

"What did I say?"

"Nothing much. Only every secret desire of your heart. I thought it would amuse you to know."

"I'm greatly amused," said Billy, actually rather sickened. After a moment Tom stooped his head and chuckled. "Please tell me."

"Something about finding His Lordship and asking for a place to stay. Made little sense to me."

"To me either," said Billy, greatly relieved, then before anything could be asked about the Marquess, he moved his hand up Tom's thigh.

Tom held the hand before it reached its destination, though was a moment considering. He said, "Let us postpone until the afternoon. We both stink to high heaven, and you need some rest. I'm due in the shipyard in about an hour and must change my clothes."

Because I am ugly. It isn't the shipyard. I am a monster, just as Moll said. But rather than cry, Billy said, "What are you working on? Or…" recalling his request from the previous night, "you ain't gotta say."

"Nothing special. A sloop with damage to her rudder languishing at St Mary Overies. I'm to meet with a smith and see what can be done. Work on the window shutters must wait a few days. However Moll has invited me to *tea*," he said, grimacing over the word. "I said I would stop by at four this afternoon if you will be here. Will you be here?"

Propping up on his elbows, Billy said, "I shall be nowhere else. Entirely rested and fresh for you. I shall count the minutes 'til you return and – and we shall have a lark."

"I hope so."

Tom dressed, but before he departed he said, "By the by, Moll says you are to come down for breakfast. She wishes to speak with you." Billy sighed. "And one other thing, she said you would know what this means. She will continue to hold the security deposit. But you may proceed up and down the stairs without the escort."

Billy groaned and pulled the blanket over his head.

Tom said, "Apparently things are looking up for you here," and closed the door.

CHAPTER NINE

Betty

– something to break a door

Though not particularly superstitious, Billy knew too much of the world not to believe he would soon pay a price for Tom's latest kindness. Noticing his scent upon him after he left, he delayed his morning ablutions, closing his eyes and summoning him from memory. A stern talk with himself at last brought him to the washbasin, though when he was done he felt as though he had lost a talisman. The universe must exact some revenge, and as Moll wished a word he could only assume she would begin introducing patrons to him. What else would she do?

And why would it be revenge? He had been overjoyed when Tom said he could remain in the house, yet less than an hour on felt disinclined to meet patrons? Why had he wished so much to come back to this house if he did not wish what came with it? Could one chaste night in the arms of a kind man change him so completely? Tom was not offering him an apartment, or even a stay in his house. Nothing for maintenance. Yet his presence was making the thought of maintaining himself in the old way rather repugnant to him.

Billy crept downstairs. He tiptoed into the dining parlour and took a seat on the floor, quite out of reach of errant lightning bolts. Henry Sparrow had just set out a plate of eggs and bacon for Caligula and was returning to the kitchen. Pausing before taking his first forkful of eggs, Caligula frowned at Billy. "Moll's letting you stay on. So why ain't you sittin' at the table like decent folks?"

"Superstition. What's Moll wish to speak with me for anyhow? I gotta get out for a while, I got heaps to do today."

"Moll wishes to know about Sukey," said Moll, slinking into the room. She sat down besides Caligula as though slipping under the covers with him. She appeared exceptionally pleased with herself, the wedding having been a great success – three guests ejected from the house before they commenced retching, and Patrick O'Donnell's dance card booked for two weeks solid. "My little darling, my Sukey, stole away in the middle of the festivities. He did come home, of course, but says he is unwell and doesn't wish to talk."

Moll was apt to grow enraged by such behaviour, however owing to her successful night this all came out as one long pout. Billy said he recalled something about Chandler's meeting members of the cast of 'Miss in her Teens'. And though never a fan of her employees doing anything without her consent, Moll admitted she had heard something about that play. No doubt that was all it was. Yes, she expected that was it.

The fluttering Henry Sparrow then re-entered the room, setting a huge spread before Moll, laying a napkin on her lap, then assessing the room. Noticing Billy on the floor, he brought him a roll and joined the grounded breakfaster with breathless excitement. "Still battered and bruised then? Say, Billy, with the money I'm earnin' I'm savin' for a ring for my girl. I never told you about her! She's Miss *Susan*, of *Spital*fields."

"She pretty?"

Yes she was. There were not breaths enough in the world to convey just how pretty was Miss Susan of Spitalfields. Her people were in the silk business; Miss Susan's hand was smooth as silk! The family fed a fluffy stray kitten which arrived each morning for his vittles; Miss Susan's hair was fluffier than that of the kitten. The family also kept a dog; Miss Susan was more loyal even than the dog...

He had been used to see Miss Susan once a week in church. But these days, his commitments in the Mint made this troublesome. Still, every two weeks he and his friend Joe, who lived at 13 Craven Street, Strand, went up to Cheapside to look at rings and place a bit of money into his account in the Bank of England. Joe had a spare room at 13 Craven Street, Strand, and was forever trying to get him to move in with him. But that would never happen because he loved it here in the Mint and could never think of leaving. This, then, was the life of Henry Sparrow. Billy knew it all now, and a very good life it was. Did Billy have a girl like Miss Susan of Spitalfields? Did he have a good friend like Joe, who lived at 13 Craven Street, Strand?

Billy had by this time come to his feet, quite ready to depart, but could not resist a grin at Moll. "Somethin' like that. His name is Tom Baker. He's the carpenter who makes all the fixes to this house. He's a dear friend."

Moll fluttered her lashes at him, but as she seemed to have nothing else to say, Billy commenced filling his pockets with rolls and a hunk of cheese, as he intended to be out most of the day. At the dining parlour door he turned once more to Moll, who was now resting her head on Caligula's shoulder, and said, "Tom'll be round a lot more to see me. Anyhow...

much obliged for letting me stay on…" then he ducked out before she could say anything to ruin the moment. It had all gone remarkably well, better than he could have wished.

And in a perfect world he would have escaped the house and proceeded into the day without issue. Moll's hazy happiness had set his nerves at ease. Perhaps he had even helped Chandler with his white lie. He was stuffing down a second roll as he stepped into the vestibule, when a rap on the front door announced a visitor and perhaps the last person he should ever wish to see here.

For in a suit of emerald velvet, waistcoat of cloth of gold, and powdered wig topped with a hat resplendent with ostrich plumes, stood Roger Calcroft.

Billy attempted to scramble around him and out the door. But as quickly Moll was with them, welcoming her guest, blocking Billy's hasty flight for despite her oversight the night before, she was a great clipper of wings. What was more, the scent of money worn by her visitor rivalled his scent of intoxicants, and she never failed to have her nose in the air. Calcroft was holding a large flagon of something at his side, and had a slight sneer on his lip, to which Moll immediately began patting her hair and straightening her banyan.

"Marathon Moll, I presume," said Roger, extending a hand which his hostess promptly snatched. Billy could only gape at the transformation of that beggar-turned-ratcatcher into this monied libertine, as there was nothing in his manner or ensemble to betray him as anything less than riotous nobility. Here he was: after a night raking at Almac's, he had left his gaming compatriots to the brothels of King's Place and slipped down to the Borough to fulfil desires of a rather different cast.

Dipping a hand into his pocket, Roger withdrew four guineas and dropped them into Moll's tremulous hand. With a long, seductive look into her eyes he closed her fingers around the coins. Then he commenced an examination of her home.

"As described. I was assured you are in possession of everything a man of uncommon tastes requires. Well," his lip rose as he motioned toward Billy, "I require this one." He continued into the front parlour, then peered into the back. At last rounding upon his hostess, with teeth bared, he said, "Will you not invite me to sit down?"

Dempsey's eyes dilated as Moll seized his wrist, hauling him forward then, after directing them to her chintz finery, dropped a curtsey. She then proceeded in her very worst attitude: "Deepest apologies *Monsieur. Mais quelle grande surprise* to be visited at such an hour and by such splendour. It was the shock, you see – *j'etais tellement choquée!* – that I tarried even a moment!"

"About two weeks ago," said Calcroft, drawing Billy to his side on the sofa, "I attended a most stellar orchestral diversion in the Grotto Garden. Afterwards, I asked myself why in Christ I have been so addicted to the King's Theatre. One must attend sometimes, of course, to hear Mr J.C. Bach. Yet I have *longed* to return to the Mint."

"I thank you, sir, very kindly. The Mint has been my home my entire life, and the Gardens are her jewel…"

"Her *jewel*. Yes – that is just the word, isn't it? A lovely jewel. Really, we are quite overrun with German influences at present. And what of the King's Theatre anyhow? I hope I have the good taste to be almost tired of the place. I am a *great* connoisseur of music, you understand. Nobody can equal my own love for the arts Moll, I truly believe that."

"Indeed…"

"I am quarrelling constantly with my friends to come south for new diversions. Why can nobody see it but me? One doesn't need a crystal ball to see the future lies right here in the Borough." With a smirk at Billy, "Mine does – the next hour or two most certainly. Is that naughty of me?"

"Oh goodness no!" his hostess nearly shouted.

Then Calcroft leant forward in an attitude of the starkest,

most open frankness, and whispered: "May I confess something to you, Moll, and make myself quite vulnerable?"

Sobering instantly, she bid him bare his heart.

"It is this: I've a most aching, a most *delicious* taste for the male sex. There, I have said it. Never have I dared utter it aloud: never to one soul. Yet I have been, though so stellarly connected from birth, too terrified to approach, or rightly know where our sort is to go. You cannot imagine how it has vexed me. Then, like the revelation of St John, I heard a fleeting reference to a place of diversion for those with my own cherished and secret desires. And so I thought: that is where Roger must be! Where he must invest his time, and his money. And just as I had expected, I had only to approach your door to observe this loveliest of young men."

"Blue Billy, my finest boy. The garret room with view of the skyline is his," gesturing grandly above her head. "Take him up and you will not be disappointed." Her eyes narrowed seductively to convey to Calcroft that her house was entirely at his service, then to Billy that he had better not disappoint. Calcroft rose, bringing Moll to her feet as he crooned many adoring words. He embraced her sensually, seized and kissed her hand, then extended his own languidly to be led away.

"Take his hand, Billy," said Moll. "You two proceed upstairs now like obedient schoolboys."

As Billy stood to take the hand, Roger said, "May I be Head Boy? Your Billy appears to have been in a few scrapes. Perhaps I might be a good influence on him."

"You certainly may, Mr…"

"Call me Rogge. Afterwards, I shall bring you a report on his behaviour and temper."

Moll clapped her hands so violently a bit of errant hair fell into her face, which she pushed back in careless dishevelment. "Oh Rogge! If you fancy a bit of role play, we shall get on famously!"

Readjusting his grip on Billy's hand Roger slipped into it

the ring he had taken from Moll's end finger. And Billy, who had never, not from his earliest years, been any good at maintaining an unreadable face, allowed his eyes to go large as saucers while attempting to jerk his hand away.

Observing something was amiss Moll said, "Shall I fetch one of our disciplinary rods, *Monsieur?*"

"No mum," croaked Roger, with a wink and a tug at his breeches. "I've brought me own."

At which point Billy hauled him out of the room and up the stairs. Once they were sealed inside the garret room, he opened his sweating hand to examine the ring which held a small sapphire. Seating himself at a table set before the room's small dormer window, Roger relieved himself of his feathered hat and sailed it into a far corner. Then he took Moll's hairpin from behind an ear and, withdrawing the silk hanky he'd lifted from a pocket of her banyan, began to pick out her initials with the hairpin.

Looking up he said, "Aren't you going to cavort for me?"

"No."

"Praise me as a handsome stallion?"

"No."

"Fetch me a glass of water at least?"

Maintaining the ring in his palm, Billy filled a mug from a ewer on the sideboard and slammed it on the table. Roger rose and seized Billy's hand into the sunlight, where the sapphire sparkled. "As a token of my affection..." He then stooped to snatch it with his teeth, hoping to produce a smile. When he did not, he rammed their torsos together so that his host fell back onto the bed.

"*Bastard!*" hissed Dempsey, scrambling to his feet, as he most certainly had squashed that hunk of cheese inside his coat pocket. Only the garment had been spared, for at a few paces Calcroft was studiously nibbling the cheese with his end finger extended.

"What next?" cried Billy. "Pull a dog from your waistcoat

and have it jump through a fiery ring? Pop a bearded lady out my wardrobe?"

At this Roger ceased talking, ceased moving entirely. He appeared quite taken aback, his pupils pulsing within the pale blue of his eyes. He set the cheese on the table, then the ring beside the cheese. He said, "I would do any of those things if I believed I might make you smile. I fancy you, Billy. After some reflection very much indeed. I was, well… *hasty* in my statements and assertions the other day. I have a passionate nature. But now I wish to make amends by making you smile and bringing you pleasure."

"I'm all a-tingle!"

Calcroft placed a hand to his chest. "I am a devious soul in all matters but those of the heart, Mr Dempsey. And you are, I must say, taking great pleasure stamping upon mine."

"You're here to humiliate me and tell me my lifestyle ain't no good."

"Am I?"

"You been talking to my people."

Roger came forward. "I've never attempted to conceal that. And I agree with them – your lifestyle *ain't* no good."

"*You* are a beggar and a thief! And I been five years with people says thieving ain't no good. Folks get attached to their things and maybe they got the right to. I weren't no good for my community, never was all the years I was with them, and I don't need no sticky fingers come to show me how much better he is than me."

"I will help you improve."

"What's in it for you?"

"I'm just doing a good deed."

"What's *in it* for ye?"

"Well, if you will listen to my plans with an open heart… and if it comes about that I can help you I… suppose I might like a kiss or something like that."

"A *kiss*? For four bloody guineas you can—"

"You think Roger Calcroft pays for his pleasure? Four guineas, along with this splendid coat and waistcoat, and that lovely hat, are merely my display – my peacock's tail – to catch your attention and to show you what someone of skill can produce. At will. The money, the costume, all this has been accomplished in just a few days, in anticipation of this performance. Had I succeeded in impressing you, which I have not, you can be sure I'd have taken whatever... favours you might have allowed me. But I am not in the business of buying affections."

Billy's look of relief Roger did not take unkindly. Indeed releasing him from this assumed obligation was the first thing his visitor had done which appeared to inspire anything like liking for himself. Roger leant in and said, "I spent my very last farthing specifically so I could *not* fuck you."

This, at last, prompted a smile.

"What you need, Billy, is a sweetheart."

"I ain't interested..."

"How do you know? Doing what you're doing you *can't* know."

The gall of this boy nearly took his breath. "Shut up about what I'm *doing!*"

"Aren't you tired of worrying over money?"

Despite his outrage, Billy tripped over a response. It was such an obvious, such a stupid thing to ask. And yet... he *was* tired of it. And the appearance of Tom in his life, his care and manoeuvring to get him into the attic – had it lessened these worries? Until this moment, he must have said that it had. Yet what had Tom done but shift him into a room in someone else's house? He was grateful. Yet whatever was happening between them, whatever the feelings being stirred, Tom *was* distant when it came to allowing a person beyond a certain point. Much as he seemed enamoured, he was showing himself to be nothing if not extremely cautious.

This left Billy with Moll, and he knew what she would

expect of him. Just when some wild, inexplicable horse was rearing up inside saying he no longer wished the lifestyle. What if all came crashing down? With Moll. Even with Tom. He would be driven back to the Marquess. To grovelling, to begging. Billy was not above that, yet knowing the Marquess as he did, his rages, his dignity, there were times when it seemed the chances of him taking him back were…

"Right," continued Roger, liking what he was seeing. "Those coins I gave your mistress were all I had in this world. But am I worried? Not at all! I just snap my fingers and make more."

He was speaking like any braggadocio from Little Barbary. Billy was about the last to find novelty in it, even if spoken by a wayward merchant's son disposed to slumming.

Roger continued, "You have one big plan upon which all depends. Perhaps it is a good one – your kin disagree, but I digress – but it is your *only* one. You crawl back to your Marquess, beg a return. He rejects you again, and then what?"

"How do you know about that?"

"Your people, of course. They've made it their business to find out about you. They are remarkable, Billy. We approach The Stealth in rather differing fashions. I am what you might call at the modern edge of things, the absolute forefront, while you were raised with the pickpocketing, the panhandling, the breaking of houses, in the real *classic* style. There's nobility in that, don't let anyone tell you differently. Little Barbary rogues are *legends* – their exploits, their language. This last week they've rather adopted me into their community, and the acceptance, the admiration, dare I say the *love* they have shown me…"

As he scarcely ever stood still, it was difficult to look away from Roger Calcroft. He danced across every inch of flooring, or in a chosen spot punctuated his lines with a series of poses. Something in him savoured of the court jester – threatening to split his tight breeches, his wig long since tumbled to the floor. A vehicle for disdain. Disdain for the tradesman's class in which he had been raised. Disdain for the gentry class from which Billy had been cast aside.

Yet despite the flash, Billy began wondering if this entire presentation were not a pose. If Roger were not inflating his knowledge in the hope of ingratiating himself with those vagrants he appeared to admire. As a kind of test he said, "I reckon you began by pulling trade from, what: Friday Street?"

After quite a long pause, Roger said, "How did you know?"

"A merchant's son must work down to begging. But you were raised with the coaching inns of Friday Street and so know the goings-on – shipments of fruit into the Home Counties and servants transporting bundles of plate to country boxes."

Unsure the aim of such an observation, Roger said somewhat guardedly, "It's well observed. Though from you it sounds like an accusation. Is Friday Street such a deplorable place to begin?"

"You tell me. I'm terrible at everything."

"It's a place," he began, then concluded grandly, "a place from which to *grow*. Confused domestics running about and losing the precious bundles of their masters requires little knowledge of the mind." He tapped his temple. "Insinuating yourself into someone's home, however, their sanctum of sanctums… or playing upon their sympathies, their guilts, now that…"

"Were you a failure at the coaching inns?"

"Certainly not! I succeed at anything I put my mind to. Calcroft & Son has rented warehouse space on Friday Street for twenty years, so I know the comings and goings like the back of my hand. I merely graduated from the inns."

"Why not return to your roots? I should like to learn from a plate master." Billy was rather enjoying himself – and something within him, something bright and quite exquisitely male, declared he should like to skewer this boy.

Roger advanced on him. "You think I recall very little don't you? Or perhaps never did know much? What would you say to the names of the best inns and their timetables of departure? How's that for a start?"

"It's a start."

"We have the intimate Bell, departures for the Home Counties at ten on Mondays, Wednesdays, and Fridays. There is The White Horse: Tuesdays and Saturdays at noon – a large and lively courtyard. Though nothing to the grand double courtyard of The Sarasin's Head, departures for Taunton and Yeovil Monday mornings at ten and Saturday nights at nine. Tomorrow is Monday, so we might select ten o'clock at either The Sarasin's Head or The Bell. Which do you prefer?"

Billy shrugged. "Either would do."

"No, either would not do. Timetables are not a starting point. You must begin with an aim. What is it you hope to achieve? A bundle of linen might do if you're to flee on foot and are assured of a good price. Plate or tea service perhaps, but only if you've a companion and a means of transport. You must have a companion to distract attention, as you cannot make off very quickly with your burden, nor would it be wise to. You must ask not only *what* do I know of the place but *why* do I intend to attack. You'll find nothing but fruit departing The Sarasin's Head at ten on Mondays, so best avoided unless you are a street vendor with a depleted orange cart."

Billy fell silent, and over the next hour listened to example upon example. In the process Roger seemed to gain more knowledge of his audience – stringing together thoughts long in Billy's unconscious, jumbles of old facts which had never been placed in much order. Roger joined all into a length of handkerchiefs, each tied to the next, then drew them out in a near endless, multi-coloured rope. There were times the effect was scarcely less than enchanting.

When they descended the stairs, every button of Roger's shirt and breeches was done up askew and he was leaning upon his Innamorato for support. Finding Moll in the front parlour rubbing her naked end finger, he strode into a dimly lit area of the room and, stooping to retrieve something, held it before the light of a window.

"Lovely piece," he said, then brought his discovery to the lady of the house: "I declare your home is absolutely constructed of treasures. Yours I presume…" No doubt beginning to suspect her visitor, Moll nearly shrieked at the restoration not only of her ring, but of her conviction of having attracted great finery into her house. Once she had returned the ring to her finger, Calcroft took the hand, kissed it, then placed into it his bottle of cognac.

"Take it. I've no use for it anymore." Turning to Billy: "I am drunk on a superior sort of intoxicant."

CHAPTER TEN

Bone Box

– the mouth

P rimarily to get Roger to leave, Billy agreed to meet him next day. They would go out, *keep company* as Roger called it, then in the evening speak on the specifics of working together. This was a scheme he had been teasing all week in Little Barbary, which everyone was now wild to hear. He had agreed to tell it to them tomorrow, presenting it as not just his own, but as his and Billy's scheme. Something modern, something quite fresh, something never before considered.

After he departed, Billy glanced at Moll before returning upstairs. He could take only modest pleasure in her somewhat dazed nod of approval. Never in his life had he felt so utterly confused. He must rest before Tom returned. His thoughts *must* be for him and showing him a marvellous time. Yet his mind was now spinning with coloured scarves and golden rings and the thought that Roger just might have something to teach him.

Long gone were the days when he'd longed for great skill, great Stealth. He could never think far enough ahead, never keep a straight face, always blundering in some way. Once he'd received his house name and become top boy here at Moll's, any thought of those former ambitions had dissolved. Yet might not a new kind of scheme, as Roger hinted of, be different? The proposal tugged at him with a power he'd never have imagined. He felt the call of those old expectations stir in his bones. Felt his blood rise to recall his bloodline.

Surely there could be no harm in meeting Roger. He'd gone to some trouble to make amends today. How easily he might have forced a sexual encounter. And just now, Billy must feel particular gratitude at his willingness to forgo all that. What was more, whatever these nascent feelings for Tom, he must be able to set them aside and handle his life like a business. Until Tom sought to secure him exclusively, he must risk losing him to someone else. He had a home in Lambeth Marsh and was much in-demand as a consultant in the shipyards – did any of that allow him to make an offer? There was no way to tell until an offer was made. But a man would never make an offer should he suspect, even for a moment, that his love interest had nothing to do but spend all day pining for him.

By quarter to four, Billy had had a full wash, changed the bedding, and set out every candle and candle-stub he could locate around the attic bedchamber. Suspecting Tom would find it vulgar to jump immediately into bed, he had also set out the copy of the *Herald*. Why not begin by speaking about that? Tom would agree to cuddle up and read about first sightings of the coast of *Terra Australis Incognita*. And that would be that.

Billy descended the stairs. The front door opened to allow in Hardware Nan, a regular at that hour for tea and sympathy.

As ever, he walked in with a favourite teacup, which, whatever it contained, was certainly not tea. And, as ever, he had nothing to say to Billy. Even after an absence of two and a half years, a couple of words only had been exchanged. Nan glanced at him, then continued into the front parlour, past Moll, to Roger's bottle of cognac.

In addition to his decades-long friendship with Moll, drinking and resisting advances from the boys seemed Nan's greatest pleasures. Billy had once known a patron whose greatest pleasure had been gossiping about his dalliances – the dalliances themselves being worked through somewhat grudgingly. Nan, however, took this a step further, glorying in the dalliances he resisted. Every couple of weeks, Moll would prod one of her employees to approach her friend simply to be rejected. After which, Nan would search out Moll, collapse onto the sofa with a drink, and for hours talk cuttingly about the boy who had approached him. Seeking out the clock in the dining parlour, Billy judged he had just enough time to be rejected by Nan, and so gain a bit more favour with his mistress, when he glimpsed Tom through the window and every other thought left his head.

Forgetting to maintain a cool demeanour, he ran back into the vestibule and flung open the front door. In a somewhat thoughtful attitude and with hands behind his back, Tom stepped inside, freshly scrubbed in a neat cotton shirt and waistcoat. From her seat in the parlour, Moll looked behind Tom's back, expecting some present for Billy or for the house, as was customary when a guest arrived to visit a favoured boy. When he produced nothing but the hands with which to encircle a waist, Billy almost had a tart comment for him. A *"what, no silk sash or bobble, not even a flower? There's a nasty trick,"* said with a trilling laugh which did not, however, remove the sting. Such had been his habits before, entirely approved by Moll, but Billy felt to have lost all his former spark where Tom was concerned. If he brought no gift, it was as though he was saying he alone was enough. That one need bring nothing to the other but oneself.

Tom was obviously quite fatigued, having slept little overnight then off to work at dawn. Still, here he was, pulling him close, leaning in as though to place a kiss on his forehead – he simply inhaled at the hairline. Billy had feared those moments this morning must be transitory, those touches he'd wished to pull away from then ached to know again. Yet they were, standing in the vestibule before the jaded eyes of Moll and Hardware Nan, just as they had been.

Moll was inspecting Baker's tall form with a mixture of interest and irritation, deciding how to chide him for so long resisting the charms of her house. Of denying that he even could be charmed when she had known incontrovertibly who and what he was about from the beginning. Nan, pleased to sit beside anyone in an irritated attitude, narrowed his eyes. Billy took Tom's ear and assured him there was no need to stop for tea, they might simply proceed upstairs. However Tom demurred, agreeing to go as one with no fear of a forth-coming attack.

"Never play Speculation with this one, Billy," said Moll once the pair had seated themselves on the sofa. "Some time ago Tom, you informed me you had been to sea. I know *that* about you most certainly. Is that where you learned to play cards? And to hold them so close to your chest?" When Baker's only answer was an inclination of the head, she continued somewhat curtly, "But *have* been to sea?"

Tom nodded. "As I said before. From the age of fourteen in one capacity or other. My father was a carpenter, and I've sailing men on both sides."

Moll nodded, uninterested. However Nan, after taking a sip from his teacup, swelled with a sort of restless, slurring indignation as though he were the last adult in the room. He said, "Just what are your intentions with William?"

It was fair to say everyone in the room was surprised by

the question, which seemed more of an accusation. Indeed, Tom was too surprised to know how to answer. Moll's blank look – answer enough to convey displeasure. All were habituated to seeing Nan in a state of inebriation. But it was only now that Billy noticed the fumes from his teacup, which appeared to be actually warping space and time around it.

"Nan is suggesting a house wedding to you, Tom," said Moll.

"Nan is suggesting no such thing," said Nan. "If Tom wishes the ceremony he may request one. I wish to know his intentions with that young man."

Tom could only shake his head at the spot he was being put in. And yet, drunk as Nan was, there was something strangely appropriate in the question. Had not Tom made clear he was not just another punter come to enjoy himself in a harem? Was not Moll's house intended to be a place of fantasy, tailored to the personality of each guest? Mr Baker, then, would be a youth asking Mama and Papa if he might keep company with their daughter. Billy might have laughed, only in the time it took Tom to answer he felt something like fear to know what he would say. How was it Tom already had the ability to hurt him with a wrong reply?

"Very well," he said at last, taking his partner's hand. "I wish to expose Will to experiences he has never known before."

No doubt this was the only good answer he could have made – pleasing Billy, silencing Nan, and producing a long, sing-songy "*ooooh*" from Moll at his chosen wording. She looked Tom up and down, straightening every wrinkle in his waistcoat, pulling taut every crease in his breeches before declaring they should all be so lucky as to have new, unknown, and no doubt delectable things *exposed* to them.

Believing Tom had now done his duty by his hosts, Billy was about to rise to lead them up, when a locomotive Henry Sparrow came into the room with a plate of biscuits. Upon setting them on the tea table, he bowed to the group, then made to depart.

Holding up a hand, Baker said, "Is the kettle boiling?"

Sparrow gaped at him, as though fearing to have somehow mis-stepped. "Set to boil a minute ago, sir. Perhaps two by now. Tea shall be brought presently."

"I will join you in the kitchen," said Tom, releasing Billy's hand and coming to his feet. Seeing the cook's frightened expression, he addressed his mistress. "If you'll agree?"

Reclining slightly upon the sofa, Moll looked up at the man towering over her and breathed: "Agree to what?"

"To tea as seafarers take it. Something punchier than you might have at this time of day."

"Seafarers?"

"Sailors, voyagers, sea-bound merchants."

As though experiencing a warm front blowing fresh into the room, Moll tugged at her silk wrap to expose the sharp line of her clavicle. "I see. You wish to perform a mutiny. To seize control of my kitchen and become Captain *Cook* yourself?"

"If you'll allow me."

"My darling man, I suspect you have skills I should never have dreamt of."

"One or two, perhaps."

"One or two, perhaps," echoed Moll, holding the words in her mouth like sugar lozenges. At last she waved her hand. "Go on then. Let us set out upon our expedition of discovery."

Tom followed Henry Sparrow out of the room. Nan was now in quite an irritated mood, unable to secure Moll's attention as the house mistress was some time looking at the place Tom Baker had just occupied. When Billy caught her eye she sighed and said, "Why did you ever leave me Billy?" before returning to Nan, who pretended not to have heard her.

A now wildly twittering Henry Sparrow began flitting

about the rooms, assuring them all he would produce the perfect vessels for the concoction, the *top-secret* concoction, Mr Baker was brewing, that he was not to say one word about as it was a great surprise. Then, much like the lid of the teapot piping in the kitchen he exploded:

"He's making Flip! Sailors' Flip!"

Shortly thereafter, Tom came into the front parlour with sugar dissolving into a pan of ale. He maintained the concoction in a perpetual stir as Sparrow fetched a bottle of brandy. Tom doused the pan with a measure and after the froth had settled, repeated the procedure three times to produce an evenly distributed, milky substance. Then he tipped a bit into the slender goblets Sparrow had unearthed from the back of a cabinet.

Upon sampling the brew Moll's eyes rolled back. "Lovely. It does transport one instantly to the deck of a sailing vessel. A group of hard-working men at the end of a day of sea adventures. A swig of Flip and a slap on the back; delightful."

This gesture of goodwill even pacified Nan, who was so pleased with the excursion he took the pan into his lap to cradle the warm remainder.

Without a doubt, Tom had now done his duty by the house and once his goblet had been consumed, Billy led him up.

THE ATTIC ROOM opened upon them, flickering with candlelight as Billy drew the blind on the dormer window. Tom noticed the newspaper set on the foot of the bed, but he took it up only to set it in a nearby bookcase. He became slightly formal, or rather professional, assessing the room with a critical eye, decrying the neglected bookcase, of good ash, which only needed a bit of linseed oil to bring up a lustre. And just look at the ceiling, that wet spot should be a concern. Had

Moll never mentioned it? Left unattended it might lead to significant damage.

Billy took these to be criticisms of Moll's house as an establishment. Tom seemed divided between appreciating of a place devoted to those of a like mind, where one could be carefree and open. And an abhorrence of the business side of things, that selling of human affections without which the rest would not be possible. When Billy stepped to the foot of the bed, Tom came forward and said:

"I desire us to be more than just bedfellows."

"As you like."

Tom blew out a breath, "*As you like*," shaking his head. "That we must come together in this, this *brothel*, a place which stands for everything I abhor. I am entirely conflicted. It's only been a week. One week. Yet I've come to feel something stronger for you than I have for anyone in a very long time. You seem to feel something like the same for me." Somewhat hastily, "Do you?"

Billy nodded, not trusting the words to sound like the drivel he had declared too many times before. "I don't know how you can like me looking as I do."

Tom stepped about the room, as though looking for the source of his discontent. At last coming to a group of flickering candles he said, "I hate that you have brought me up in the belief that you must oblige me. I hate that I cannot find a way to make this different for us both. It seems one cannot consciously do that. Why cannot you be a shepherd whose entire life has been spent on the lonely hills and who has never known a man?" Then he smiled, and said somewhat abashedly, "Why cannot I be one too?"

Billy stepped to a small wardrobe mouldering in a corner and withdrew a long silk sash. Centring it between his fists, he pulled it taut, then drawing it over his eyes looped it twice behind his head and returned to Tom.

"We can be shepherds."

"Will, games like this are exactly what I do not wish."

"No game. Tell me how you wish us to be without my eyes watching you. That's your only trouble."

He stood blindfolded in the middle of the room for some time. Tom's heavily booted feet paced about. Then after a lengthy pause, soft, meandering footfalls after the boots had been removed.

Another silence, broken at last by the buttons of a cotton shirt clattering with the hard back of a chair and with each other. Footfalls. Then a creek of floorboards as Tom knelt before him. The heat of a coiled body came into Billy's legs through his breeches. A coolness encircled his waist up to his chest as the buttons of his shirt opened bottom to top. The fabric was pushed aside, lips pressed briefly to his belly. When they withdrew, Tom said in little more than a whisper, "Take the sash away now."

Billy withdrew the sash. Tom was resting on his haunches, staring up. A tremendous heat radiated from him, from a body overdosed on the sun as though having taken it deep into the marrow where it must endure the winter.

"Let us be shepherds," he said. "Let us try, at least. At first sighting, let us tip our hats over the rolling downs. Each day let us circle closer, ever closer. Let us tend our increasingly rebellious flocks until at last we meet at the apex of a common hill, our herds now hopelessly intermingled. Then let us smile, for we cannot be troubled by it. For we have seen one other. Tipped hats, come together, and spoken at last."

Billy nodded, hoping he understood what was desired, hoping his eyes conveyed it. When Tom rose Billy pulled him into a tussle upon the bed wishing to break that studied dream. For even a dream might return to consideration, consideration to cerebral thoughts, thoughts to eat at themselves.

Lying beside each other, they revelled in lopsided equality tugging and tickling off every stitch of remaining vestments.

Then peering down each to each – at the absolute, the sloppy, the glorious honesty that was the male body – Tom encircled the waist of his young companion and brought them together. Pressing his nose to Billy's forehead he sought to draw out an essence, that thing which had gripped him as he had supported him into Souls Yard. The thing which had failed to relinquish him when he left him on Moll's doorstop, which could not be buried in manual labour, only polished it to a shine.

Then Tom declared dominance, pinning them together and closing over his eager companion – no trick, no bought exchange for here were Billy's own words, here was his body pulsing, begging now to be taken. Begging to know fully a man who had given without expectations, who wished to see though the crack in his exterior to something Billy hoped was there. And if it was there, he wished Tom to see it.

All then swiftly executed. Tom first into the cool depths before bringing Billy to the plunge, each in the belief it was boyish exuberance sending them tumbling over the edge when it was two men fearing to delay lest anything go wrong.

When they came apart, Billy was pulsing and awake, heart pounding, trembling at the glimpse of whatever he had seen.

Tom fell away, sinking to the seafloor. His kisses leading him to sleep. His tears indistinguishable from sweat.

As TOM SLEPT, Billy counted the candles flickering about the room. Seventeen in all. Some slender and nearly new. Some stubs. Some of spring-clean beeswax, some of stinking, smoking tallow. Far too many. But what mattered was the light to see Tom by. His back rising and falling, his body thinner than might be supposed when he was clothed. Billy ran a hand down the length of his back. Up. Then down, until Tom stirred, smiling at a touch so faint he had dreamt it was something else.

Telling Billy to touch where he pleased, he came gradually off the seafloor.

Then he roused them into a new embrace.

Gentle.

Silent except when a place thoroughly explored brought a shudder.

Drawn out to a honey-slow end.

At dawn, with Tom dressed to depart, they descended to the front parlour sofa, the house with the stillness of a lake whose surface they did not wish to disturb.

When Tom brought their mouths together Billy smiled and turned away.

"Can't you kiss me yet?" Billy nodded, though his eyes remained averted. It had been one thing, the only thing during a long and glorious night, which had not come naturally to him. "Look at me, Will; don't look away. I want you to kiss me."

Billy remained thinking. His mouth began to dry. Then he returned to Tom, coming forward to try again. As their lips touched he closed his eyes.

But the sun was rising.

…lighting Van Diemen's Land. And from there the coast looked to join with the land stretched before us. We could be certain of little out on a ship two leagues away. All came forward, green and woody. The shore stretched on – just a white sand and not a soul. A sea shower swept in, gentle as a breeze. Urging us forward, but with no place to make land, she resisted us just as powerfully. Gradually, then, up the coast, to view rocky points, crystalline shores. But always at a distance – suspended in a ship upon the azure blue – at 31 fathoms, sandy bottom.

Tom came forward, working Billy's jaw in his hand, kissing him until Billy kissed him back simply to place a stop to the endless question.

…come morning, we awoke to discover we had been driven three

leagues off course. By the tide, or the current, nobody could say what it was. As the day advanced observations were taken of the sun and the moon. Then come the PM, the surgeon's assistance began calling, pointing somewhere in the distance. We were just at an open bay. Smoke was rising. Not wild and uncontrolled, but as it will when a man maintains an eye upon the flame. Growing. Strengthening. But controlled. And so we knew: this place we had heard of and wondered about. Longed for, and slept beside all night, was indeed inhabited...

CHAPTER ELEVEN

Prigging

– riding

Billy was some time standing in the vestibule after Tom left, waiting to retrieve that part of himself which had left with him. But he never did.

"Oh God…" he said, staring at the closed door. "Oh God, not that."

The house would soon be stirring; he could not see people. Could not face the eyes. The snide questions about Tom as must be coming. As must send him over the edge, whatever edge it was. He took the stairs two by two then at Chandler's door had a change of heart. Chandler was an exception. Chandler might be just the person to understand. However a moment standing outside the door informed him he had company. Nothing was lost. He would speak to him later. He *should* be alone just now. Quiet and alone.

He went up, dousing the candles which continued to flicker, looking about the room which had so lately made him so exquisitely happy. And rather than sinking under the diagnosis he'd made for himself, the symptoms of which he had heard described too often to mistake, he was smiling at the folded newspaper they had never got round to reading.

Could Tom be the answer to everything? He might never need to see the Marquess again. Roger Calcroft was suddenly striding across the room of his memory, snatching his feathered hat from the corner, and saying: "That fat old man has set you free, Billy. Could you really pull on wet worsted stockings again?"

For so long he'd been considering how to win his wealthy benefactor back. But the Marquess *was* wet, heavy, itchy stockings which left you pale and pruned. And cold. Tom was – like wearing no stockings at all. Loving, attentive. And a remarkable man. After returning from his voyage, he'd built a home in Lambeth Marsh – with his own hands. Perhaps he was hesitant to move Billy in, having heard him mention the Marquess; perhaps he guessed the luxury he had been accustomed to. If that was the case, all he needed was encouragement. Because Billy had it in his power to tell Tom that he… liked him very much. So much that he would give up fine things. Fine things meant nothing at all compared with happiness. He would be overjoyed to be kept modestly. Because he would be kept happily.

Roger would be arriving at ten. After considering one last time, Billy decided he *would* go out with him, regardless of last night. He *should* go out, lest the endless remembrance of Tom drive him to distraction. An offer was coming, hopefully quite soon. But he had not made the offer yet, and Billy would not sit about this house missing him, all the time fearing Moll would fetch him down to meet a patron.

Roger would be arriving at ten. And he would be ready for him.

When Calcroft cantered into Souls Yard, Billy was enjoying a dignified breakfast at table – hot rolls, two rashers of bacon and a mug of small beer. Joining him was Caligula, now on his second breakfast, as well as O'Donnell, halfway through a glass of whey and indulging in an elaborate budget his late windfall had made possible. The largest item of this budget, with columns to contain six months of projected revenues, was labelled "Love Bundle". Here would accumulate the sums with which to woo the daughter of a wealthy merchant, as London was full of.

Glancing up, Caligula waved his fork as two horses passed the window: "Here's Money arrived."

Roger's showy display the day before had quickly circulated about the house, though few had seen the wealthy libertine. O'Donnell rose to peer out the window at the young man known in the house simply as Money. When he returned he nodded to Billy with the admiration of a developing sportsman.

Nothing had been vouchsafed as to what *keeping company* might entail. Billy emerged from the front door to find Roger modestly dressed, though his grin declared he hoped something would be noticed. He bid Billy remain on the stones of the front elevation so he could lead forward the second horse. Both animals stepped about silently as seahorses, as it was the custom in Little Barbary to shoe with leather.

"They lent you the horses."

"Lent *us* the horses," Roger corrected. "Entirely in compliment to you. And who is it attending you this fine day?" Somewhat grudgingly, Billy admitted to recognising Lancelot. "Your favourite of the two."

Having had little experience with horses or saddles, Billy hesitated. Leaping down Roger knelt, guiding Billy's shoe into the stirrup, then hurried around him, taking great pains with his bottom, cradling it with exceptional care, then urging it into the centre of the saddle with a light slap.

As Lancelot brought his rider forward, Roger stepped back to admire them. Then he announced they would be taking a leisurely ride in the country; the very thing sweethearts should do didn't Billy think? Bask in a bit of sun and in each other. And speak of the future.

The word *sweethearts* set Billy on edge. There never had been a chance of their being sweethearts, as he called it. Not before. Not in future. No doubt Roger got on in life with this kind of pushy charm, but he did not know about Tom. Knew nothing of that night of fantasy, of tenderness which needed no words, of lovemaking which had left Billy stumbling about like a fool afterwards.

Deeming Roger's announcement not worth a reply, Billy said only, "How'd you get the horses here?"

Taking no offence at the change of subject, Roger drew forth Galahad, leapt onto his back and, after circling twice, said, "My escort as far as Marshalsea was Miss Fanny Dempsey. You'll like to know your sister is now the widely regarded Flint-Hearted Fanny. Famed for destroying men of all ranks and religions – rich to poor, handsome to very ugly indeed. All driven to steal vast sums to win her – then to suicide for their unrequited love. Last night, over a lovely bonfire at Coxes Garden, I learned that she did long ago have a heart, only bestowed it upon a dashing pirate now languishing in Marshalsea. The very one she is visiting today as it happens; soon, alas, to swing at Execution Dock. Oh well-a-*day!* How I *adore* your family!"

They were soon cantering south on the High Street. Where The Borough became Black Man Street, it struck Billy he was actually sitting upon one of the two cherished steeds. They were communal horses, scheduled by the powers-that-be according to the importance of the errand. Roger, of course, was the important one, and whatever stardust he had been throwing in their eyes had somehow persuaded the community to lend them.

Yet, when he cantered slightly ahead and Billy had a moment to observe him, he knew it could not be mere stardust. Why did he so often fall to thinking of Roger as little more than the court jester? He'd already proved his knowledge while speaking of coaching inns, among other things. It seemed he went out of his way to be remembered as a clown. Yet when he was *with* you, when his pale blue eyes were sparkling, when the thousand eyes of his peacock's tail were turned in full display, he was no clown. Children though Billy's people were in some things, they were not gullible. Suspicion of others had been bred from birth. Roger was not only an outsider, but his also being the son of a City tradesman should have made him a laughingstock. Yet still he had won their trust.

As city gave way to country, Roger's silvery locks tossed about in the breeze as he continued ahead – utterly assured, utterly confident. At last recalling his manners, he pulled the reigns of his horse to let Billy bring up beside him. A sheepish grin seemed to say he'd lost his head for a moment, cantering ahead like that. Apologies if Billy had had nothing to look at but himself for a time.

Camberwell was a village of rambling timber cottages with thatched rooves, lately swelled by the summer boxes of well-to-do merchants, the ailing wealthy, and wealthy valetudinarians, wishing a breath of country air. This trend continued south to Sydenham, from modest, rusticated affairs to statelier abodes of brick or stone. Crisp carriage houses, gardens strew with shrubs, adolescent saplings all elbows and knuckles.

It was to see a selection of these homes that Roger brought them here. They cantered to one, then to another, never getting off their horses, simply continuing on a decidedly rambling tour. Roger made clear his ability to let them into any of these homes, but he would wait until Billy showed interest in one to do so. *Did Billy admire this house? Not particularly? Just down the lane was another – this was lovely was it not? – did he wish to know more of it?* Billy could only shrug, seeing little to distinguish the homes Roger selected for praise from those he passed by. No doubt the chosen were under consideration for robbery. Or perhaps had already been robbed and might be again, and at the slightest interest from himself he would describe the adventure, either planned or executed, in gleeful detail.

At last tiring, his bottom grown raw from the swaying motion of the horse, Billy picked a house simply to put an end to this endless ambling about. He selected a two-story cottage then, drawing up beside his escort, announced he wished to know more of the place. Roger brightened, commended him on his choice then directed them up the gravel drive. Upon securing the horses at the side of the carriage house, they advanced boldly to the front door. He produced a key and let them inside. He was a moment hallooing, announcing himself with a fake name and *apologies but the front door had been left ajar.*

After assuring himself nobody was home, he then presented Billy with a tastefully furnished newly built summer box. As they stepped across the wood flooring, of new, plump oak fitted tightly together, Roger began rummaging about, examining a drawer, then another, then on to a squat cupboard of bone china. The china he declared exceedingly lovely, before moving on to a tall white cupboard which appeared to be locked.

"Why did you bring me here?"

Feeling up and down the back of the cabinet, then stooping to peer underneath a nearby sideboard, Roger said, "On the contrary – why did *you* bring me here? We might have continued on."

"It was the only way to stop that endless wandering. I'd say this house is like all the others you showed me – it's the scene of a former invasion you wish to revisit. You were happy to come in because now you can try to discover what lies inside the white cabinet."

Apparently tickled that Billy still had not guessed, Roger simpered: "Alas, were it permissible for a gentleman to contradict the lad he so admires…"

"Then you have learned the owners have just returned to town and you intend to take something."

"Apologies, I must crave pardon here as well…"

Billy was too used to having his ignorance pushed in his face to suffer this for long. "You *should* crave pardon. You lead a cove about a village of valetudinarians and empty summer boxes and call it keeping company? I was courted sweeter by a retired cooper from Whitechapel, deep in his cups and crippled entirely up his left side. And after an hour on horseback in ever-increasing discomfort, I can tell you that saddle saw more fun than you shall see today."

The words came out harsher than intended and had an effect. After swallowing, his slightly bulbous blue eyes protruding just that bit more, Roger went red with anger. Striding forward, he said, "I've no intention of competing with your ungentlemanly saddle just yet – you've made your thoughts on that abundantly clear. As for keeping company, you seem not to understand the concept if you can compare the feeble poking of a cripple from Whitechapel to the excursion I have organised today."

Having silenced his tart companion, Roger stood to his full height of five foot six and came still closer. "You are standing in an inventory warehouse. I took possession of this place last year in quality of ratcatcher. In that time I have taken from it nothing but a spare key. Neither shall I take anything until I have a buyer for my goods. Until then, this is the ideal enclosure within which to house my inventory. Do you see? I have performed the perfect magic trick. The contents of this house are now my own, only nothing appears to have been altered. There is nothing even to charge me with. And will not be until what I have selected to sell has been carried off, and with the kind of meticulous choreography most hasty robbers could never even dream of."

Billy said nothing. This was quite beyond anything he'd ever heard of. What on earth could such a determined and creative young thief wish with himself, or indeed any of the riffraff of Little Barbary?

"A magic trick…" said Billy, trying to find the flaw in the scheme.

"That's what I love about you," said Roger, taking Billy's hands. "Your open, honest countenance. There *are* no flaws, as you are attempting to discover. One day the owners shall reach out to touch their belongings to find they are nothing but the reflection of light dancing in water. Who would ever suspect the neighbourhood ratcatcher, last here months ago and so long trusted in the neighbourhood? Patience, Billy, is all it takes."

"You have shown your face here today."

"I'm taking nothing today and likely won't 'til midwinter. If I am noticed and confronted by one of the neighbours I am simply come to maintain my traps." Roger mused, "Once, in my naughtier days, upon caging a troupe of five fat and lusty rodents in a home just down the street, I made shift to release them into the basement of the Dowager Viscountess Wainwright. When I appeared on her doorstep that evening she was so happy to see me she not only hired my services, she nearly ravished me right there upon the Turkish rug."

Reaching into a pocket, Roger produced a ring of keys of many shapes and sizes and held it forth. "No diamond, no purse of coin, nothing excites me as does the taking of a key. Define *key* however you like, but as we are speaking of physical keys I prefer a spare, which may be withdrawn for duplication and as soon replaced. But all this is not what makes one successful at The Stealth. Do you know what makes a success?" He tapped a temple with his long forefinger. "Your *aim*, as I said before. And that comes, ultimately, from one's motivation. One must be *motivated* by something bigger than oneself to succeed."

Then, rather like a canary, he chirped, "My motivation is hate!" and snapped his fingers. "All the planning in the world will not matter if you cannot *hate* the person you intend to get the better of. Break the houses of the rich, Billy, not because that is where the treasure is. Break them because you despise the rich man. When you rob him, you make a dent in all the injustices in the world! When you take his key, you turn his sense of security into a false sense. You expose the turtle's soft underbelly for he no longer has his house to hide under."

By this point in his speech, Roger had come quite close. Now he slipped an arm about Billy's waist and, bringing them against a wall, brushed his lips over the transparent hairs of his neck. "Clowning is my long habit, Billy. I wear the costumes of others for fear of showing myself, isn't that sad? Costumes are the shell I wear for fear of displaying my own white, sensitive underbelly. I fear being rejected." Taking him a bit closer he whispered, "May I show you my underbelly?"

"No."

"Why not? I have seen yours and do not despise you."

Pulling back Billy looked into his eyes. "Seen what?"

"Only the most solemn wish of your heart. The real reason I brought you here. Don't you like it?"

Stooping to kiss his neck, then pressing the front of his breeches against Billy's hip he murmured, "And now that you know that *I* know your deepest desire, there is an empty bed upstairs I wish to show you. Big… warm… *perfect* for two road-weary travellers…"

Billy pulled away, demanding to know what he was talking about, demanding to know just what he had seen. Roger slumped against the wall. Then, after a hasty adjustment to his breeches, he turned a large, knowing smile on his companion.

"A home. That is what you wish for and why we have

taken this little excursion. To see this *extra* home of people who have too much. I do not say I can give you this precise home; that would take some doing. The point is that *you* chose it. Choosing anything for yourself is a thing you have never done before. And if you have an aim firmly in mind, as you did when you asked to come inside, there is nothing you cannot achieve. Do you believe me?"

Billy stared at him. It took no genius to understand he wished for and indeed needed a home. And Roger did not actually believe this was his deepest wish. What he was offering, his actual lure, was control. For the first time in his life, Billy might *take* control – of the direction of his life, of where he chose to live, of how he chose to proceed. Whatever the reason, he had chosen to come into not just a house, but *this* house. The distinction was the point, and the application…

His view of his former apartment; The Marquess's apartment, not Billy's. Not for that year and a half. Not if the man allowed him to return. The Marquess had four homes. Homes in town, in the country, for different seasons and occasions, while Billy had been pampering and caressing him for a bed in just one.

Before that it had been Benjamin Sallow's apartment.

Before that Moll's house.

Nothing had ever been his own.

Then, his brow furrowing, Billy had another thought. What of the house in Lambeth Marsh? Thank God Roger knew nothing of Tom, but would it be any less true of that house? If Tom made him an offer, he would be accepting the home of yet another. A wonderful man to be sure, but *his* home, not Billy's.

But no, this did *not* apply if you actually liked the person. It couldn't apply, and he liked Tom very, very much. There'd been moments he'd almost thought he was in… Whatever the case, this did *not* apply to Tom, but the point about the Marquess was well taken. And were he still considering a return to that apartment, Roger's point was a good one and must give him pause.

Very well. He was strong enough to see the point without being overwhelmed by it. It *was* a new thought. A thought he had never had. With an atavistic power to allure – a home, and a direction, of his own choosing.

Billy lifted his eyes to look around the house once more. Seeing in a new way, both deeper and farther.

Roger had since returned to the white cabinet, as he had at last located the key and was now examining the contents. Without looking back, he said, "You see? We are a perfect match. The house for you, the inventory for me. A match made in heaven."

CHAPTER TWELVE

Dimber Damber

  – a topman among the canting crew; also the chief rogue of the gang, or the greatest cheat

---

They were to leave the horses at Pike's Yard, a notorious hovel in the Clink Liberty, a sort of Charing Cross of Southwark where much mischief was organised. Roger spoke of Pike's Yard with something like reverence, which Billy initially took to be a joke, as he had known the place as a child and recalled nothing to revere. The adage, *"First to St Thomas's Hospital, next to the Burying Grounds, then on to Pike's Yard"*, though accurate in its way, was not particularly helpful in locating the Yard. It stood not near the Burying Grounds but on the South Bank opposite the City, a series of rambling buildings some-what interconnected, with a view of the medieval prison and centred around a *lay stall*, that traditional centrepiece of court-yards: a dung heap.

In the mud encircling the lay stall a series of free-floating planks were placed to assist communication between the buildings. These consisted of Pike's Tavern, Pike's Gaming Parlour, an unnamed structure containing mattresses not daring to call itself an Inn, and for the very adventurous Pike's Eating House. Each building was strictly guarded, though at a remove by the many, and motley, millers-about in the Yard. This remove leant each building an appearance of openness – no heavies standing before entrances; the promenade always kept clear.

Dismounting before Pike's Tavern, Roger found this appearance of openness the most unnerving thing about the place. At a stranger's arrival, every eye turned to observe – the thickness in the air no longer just that from the lay stall, but of an expectation that one had best be able to justify a visit.

Upon arrival, Billy experienced a sensation quite different – a powerful sense of security he had forgotten existed here. Strangers and aimless vagabonds were of course anything but safe, but if they knew you, nobody maintained a better watch on your property and safety than did the criminal element of Pike's Yard. The Tavern was entirely without windows, yet there was no risk leaving the horses unattended as they would be known to belong to Little Barbary. Should anyone other than a community member attempt to take them, a swift and no doubt gruesome justice would be meted out – the name of the Yard had not, after all, come about by chance.

As they neared the tavern entrance a man, exceptionally large and dressed entirely in buckskins, took a step in their direction. By way of introduction he spat into the mud, at which point Roger looped an arm through Billy's, making clear his friend should speak. When asked their business, Billy said they were returning Galahad and Lancelot to Flint-Hearted Fanny, who was inside and expecting them.

"Come to see Fanny, have ye?" said the heavy, eying him. "Stripling like you?"

"I'm a brother," returned Billy, to which the man immediately became suspicious. "I ain't been around five, six years. Name's William Dempsey." The heavy continued to stare. Billy was on the point of telling him to simply fetch Fanny for the identification, when the man said something in the cant language of Little Barbary, slowly and concisely, and waited for a reply.

Generally speaking, London's cant language, sometimes called St Giles's Greek or Pedlar's French, and widely spoken in the underworld, consisted of a unique set of nouns and verbs stitched into ordinary English structures. This was often sufficient to baffle the general listener, however weaknesses existed particularly in its tendency to simply invent a noun from an existing English verb – a *wiper*, for instance, was not indistinguishable from a *handkerchief*. However the dialect of Wapping, one of London's chief centres of illicit trade, had evolved into something altogether itself. By blending the vocabulary of St Giles's Greek with a unique form of gibberish, that means of communication employed by gypsies, the dialect had become a fortress impenetrable to general ears. Indeed, even for those long associated with the underworld, using it could be a challenge had it not been learned at Mama's knee.

Billy understood the heavy with difficulty, not because he was out of practice, but because the man was clearly not from Little Barbary and had only a tentative grasp on the language. He had asked to know Fanny's age and physical description, but in selecting his *hard sound*, gibberish being formed by placing a consonant between each syllable, he had selected R. R, of course, was the first sound in robbery. When Billy responded, he asked why the man had not chosen T, which implied a meeting about the transfer of goods or property. He was obliged to repeat this. Only then, and only after receiving a nod from another in the Yard, did the heavy step aside, somewhat abashed, not even bothering to ask who Roger might be.

Fanny Dempsey had been scarcely more than a girl when Billy had last seen her. She was now voluptuous, brooding, and remote, a planet under a veil. Men fell naturally into orbit owing to her native gravity, though today only one or two admirers. She hadn't the heart for breaking hearts at present – this was a sad occasion. Today's visit with her incarcerated beau had likely been her last. Nevertheless, the reappearance of a brother after some years distracted her from her melancholy and the flint that was her heart softened. She embraced him, told him he looked just like Mama, and asked how he had been. They were soon joined by Tantivy, Freddy, and many others, all with the same seeming interest in him.

Their attentions, Billy knew, were like those of children; they loved novelty and were as quick to forget. Roger saw none of this, happy to believe these were the best of people, and that tonight was what everyone said it was: Billy's evening. But it was without question Roger's, his appearance tonight being the reason most had come.

Last night in Coxes Garden, like the salesman he was, he had promised to tell them something which would change their lives. A new scheme, possibly more than one, which meant new and hitherto undreamt-of riches. Word had spread throughout Barbary. Everyone wished to know what it was. The welcoming of Billy was only just got out of the way when the questions for Roger began. Groups began cornering him to ask what it was all about. Roger assured them all would be told presently. But now, here was Billy. Let us have a toast to Billy! The crowd compromised, pushed the two together then toasted them as *the lovebirds*, to the accompaniment of shrieks of laughter.

"Like David and Jonathan!" declared Tantivy holding up his mug. Roger was nearly overpowered, toasting in his turn, and with great emotion, the remarkable broadmindedness of

Little Barbary. This was followed by a second toast of even greater eloquence condemning to hellfire the rest of society.

All this left Billy baffled. As with business, where sex was concerned his kin elevated most what was not the norm – celebrated a thing, and themselves for celebrating it, simply because it was counter to culture. They were highly evolved. They saw though every societal norm. Their love touched the outer reaches of space.

Every evening of his boyhood around dying bonfires in boathouses, or under the stars in Moorfields, the children would giggle as the adults, just a few feet away, grunted and moaned and shrieked their pleasures with whomever had taken their fancy that night. All community children were *brothers* and *sisters*. A *father* was any man of the community at least ten years older than oneself. Even to a child the meaning was clear or should have been – ownership was a thing to be abhorred. Owning was just another societal norm – what greedy people did, with people and with things.

And yet this had not been clear to Billy. From birth, his strongest feeling had been for his mother because she was *his* mother. That was a role the community could not attempt to redefine. He'd wished, he'd longed, to be owned by her. When he had been left with Moll, he had missed the relationship with her the most – its specificity, its intimacy, something which did not exist in his other relationships, all of which seemed watered-down by comparison. Cherishing his mother was cherishing a person, not an idea of the role. And in his darker moments, he'd sometimes wondered if Mama had been encouraged to leave him at Moll's to break a bond which had simply grown too strong.

As Billy stood amidst his people in Pike's Tavern, he had one of the first true realisations of his life. Perhaps he had never flourished among them, perhaps he had never been good at The Stealth, because he did not truly believe in them. Whatever their professions of sharing and liberal-mindedness, they were themselves motivated by greed, as full of contradictions as anyone else. They were children utterly without direction.

Roger Calcroft *had* direction. His motivations were not called *love*, they were not thinly veiled excuses to take from others. Though it was well disguised, he had real anger driving him. Anger at structures which he believed marginalised him. Anger at expectations he had been raised to fulfil. This anger had honed his natural abilities into schemes for success Billy had never even considered. If he had a weakness it was in idolising such as Little Barbery, of misunderstanding their acceptance of his sexuality.

Presently Roger returned to him, charmed at having understood that David and Jonathan were in fact two of Billy's *uncles*, lovers throughout Billy's childhood, who had been oh-so-wittily named for the Biblical characters! Clapping and parading about, he appeared in the midst of a transcendent experience. He wished only, *only!*, to see the world as they saw it! To live as they lived! To be as they were!

Then he turned to the crowd and, as promised, gave them what they so wished to know, tossing into the air like a bride's bouquet a word they had never heard before:

Insurance!

Insurance?

Yes, Insurance! You might know it by the term Assurance. *The way of the future for forward thinkers!*

Freddy had never heard of it. Tantivy consulted his smallpox scars but to no avail. Fanny, however, silenced the crowd by asking if *insurance was not what businesses bought to protect against fire damage?*

"That is it exactly," said Roger, like an encouraging schoolmaster. "And it is nothing new. The Hand in Hand has existed for, oh, seventy-five years. Policies at Tom's Coffeehouse in St Martin's Lane if you are interested." As most of the revellers scarcely appeared even to understand, he continued, "But insurance is far more than a windfall should you *happen* to have a fire. *Happen*… remember that. International merchants might buy insurance to guard against losses at sea. Nowadays the applications are endless. Even – *even* – a person's life may be insured."

This was nothing less than shocking. The crowd grew hushed, drew in. Roger corralled them with one long, eloquent forefinger which stirred the ale fumes, then coming fully into his own, he boomed, "For too long, a *will* has been a thing for rich folks waiting to get richer by the death of an uncle! Based on my research thus far, I can tell you that *life insurance* is the will of a wealthy uncle for the rest of us! *One death!* and a fortune can be made. Now I shall not bore you with too many details at present – suffice it to say there are ledgers of risk and associated premiums, cross referenced by what are called *mortality tables*. Billy and I have more research to do. But this leads me to another idea still. Somewhat similar to what we've been speaking about, but to me, even more fascinating: *The Book of Lives.*"

The crowd oohed. *"The Book of Lives?"*

"Precisely that. You've heard the expression *every man has his price?* Well, some smart people in the City have taken this a step further. They can tell you just how much a man's life is worth, complete with odds. No more guess work. Think your friend will die of a heart attack tomorrow? Now you can make the wager. I believe a person has the right, perhaps even a duty, to put his money where his mouth is, don't you? This can happen, this *is* happening, right now thanks to *The Book of Lives.* Nothing so very formal as a life policy, but profit like nothing you have ever imagined. *If,*" he stressed, "*if* you can beat those City folks at their own game. That is where I come in. And what I hope to tell you about next time."

As he spoke, Roger shuffled across the sawdust floor, taking the hand of the tavern wench while lifting the very petticoats of his audience at large. He'd clearly taken a few lessons from street vendors selling the latest wash-balls and composition-cakes. Yet he embraced this without shame, and Billy could only shake his head as the people he'd grown up with and idolised for their abilities swooned under the power of his performance.

What in God's name to make of Roger? Was this all simply to spend the night with them in some miserable hovel in Wapping? He was offering calculus to their long division, so Billy had to believe much of this really was to impress him. Roger fancied him, he had said as much, but his motivation seemed deeper than just getting him into bed. This seemed a passion to change Billy's perspective of his own past. Of his history. And so of himself.

Once Roger had left the floor, he was mad to get Billy alone at a table. Entirely pleased with the excitement he had stirred in his audience, he asked breathlessly, "What *did* you say to that heavy outside? I've been dying to know! I understood… well, *some* of it, you know, but the gist I'm afraid was entirely lost on me. Do you know how notoriously difficult the Wapping dialect is to learn? That *was* the Wapping dialect, was it not?"

Somewhat taken aback, Billy flushed with that pride any native speaker of a language said to be difficult to learn will feel. When he explained he was in fact correcting the man's usage, Roger quite literally fell out of his chair laughing. He tossed handfuls of sawdust into the air. Still on the floor, he seized Billy's hand, kissed it, and begged to learn some. Would he teach him? Just a little? Billy agreed simply to get him off the floor, and when he rose, Roger leant in and kissed him full on the mouth – seizing him by the nape of his neck and pressing them together.

Billy drew in a breath.

Then he was kissing Roger. Fully. Heart palpitatingly. Completely. Knowing he should not, yet without the hesitation which had prevented that extraordinary night with Tom from being quite perfect. This kiss was without hesitation, and they kissed with abandon.

A cheer went up from the crowd.

Then Roger fell to his knees once more, laughing, setting his head gently upon Billy's lap. Then, resuming one of his most successful attitudes, that of beggar, he encircled Billy's legs with his arms.

WHEN THEY DEPARTED Pike's Yard, Billy wished to return to Moll's on his own. Roger, however, insisted on walking him as far as St Margaret's Hill. Then to St Saviour's Burying Grounds. Then, just a bit farther to Finch's Grotto Garden. He achieved this by forcing Billy into the role of Scheherazade, asking to hear the tale of his first exposure to Pike's Yard, then interrupting him with endless questions. Billy had been just eight when he'd proceeded to the Yard to arrange a job as a Petticoat Lane urchin, and it was a tale Roger believed deserved much close questioning.

But if the truth be told, Billy needed little prompting. He spoke at length as he was now glowing with pride. Roger might be a skilled performer, but he was not an actor when it came to this – he was truly interested. Interested in Billy's past. Interested in Billy. He had no actual need of him, or indeed anyone he had met tonight. His ideas were so far beyond anything heard of in Pike's Yard it could only be that he really did like and admire his new friend. And wish to be with him.

Once at the Grotto Garden, however, Billy refused to continue farther with him. Seeing his determination, Roger relinquished, then asked when they might see each other again. Billy found he was truly conflicted. Tom must not see, must not even hear about, Roger. There was no question that they must be kept apart, and though they were not sleeping together there was nothing for it but to treat the situation as though they were. So after informing Roger that his visits were arousing too much jealousy in the other boys, he asked that he stay away from Moll's house henceforward.

"Very well," said Roger, in a subdued tone. "Notes for me can be directed to Jonathan's Coffeehouse in the City. Or…" He hesitated, though for only a moment, "or rather come in person. To the counting-house of Calcroft & Son," and he gave the direction. "It's where I grew up. I still have my old room there, above the house. I shall spend every night there this week so I am easier to locate – midnight to nine I shall be there. Out most of the day but will stop in at two for my mutton – the good old City hour, you know."

Then, incredibly, after catching hold of Billy's eye, he swallowed as though from emotion.

"I shall be suffering every minute you oblige me to this. Forced to contend with my father and his endless harassing of me to participate in the business. But I will do it for you. Only promise you will come. This week. I have already set a plan in motion. A plan for us. You have your future prosperity to think of. And good as I am, this will be something new for me as well. I cannot do it without you."

CHAPTER THIRTEEN

The Cul Snylches

— the man eyes you

Billy returned to Souls Yard with a kind of heavy agitation in his heart. No sooner did he confirm Tom's wagon was not there, half expecting to see it though entirely without reason, than he regretted sending Roger away. He should have liked to see Tom, and by embracing him try to quell that bit of guilt for his behaviour in Pike's Yard. Yet with no Tom, he should have very much liked to speak more of his past. Recall another story with which to entertain Roger. Recall and keep his restless thoughts occupied. Because after the events of the last two days, his thoughts left unattended were tending to a strange, unsettled place. And it didn't help that a light rain had begun to fall.

Walking into a noisy game of loo in the dining parlour, he immediately sensed uneasiness. A brash, obese man dominated the scene, Chandler clinging to his side rather like a barnacle. The boy met Billy's eye though with none of his usual spriteliness. He looked somehow pathetic, like he wished to be anywhere else. Joining the card game were the Tower Princes, each with a client, and Moll standing to one side, questioning a dripping Henry Sparrow who appeared only to have come inside himself.

An agitated Moll quickly came forward wishing to speak. Billy extended a wrist, this being her preferred mode of trans-porting him, but not before he had nodded to Chandler that he should find him the moment he was free. Chandler nodded in return, attempting to smile. Then his loud companion pushed a hand of cards into his face and directed him back to the game.

Moll spared no word as she hauled Billy up the stairs, directing him up the steep box staircase into the attic room. Once they arrived the scene explained itself. A section from the roof beams lay on the floor leaving a head-sized hole of drizzling sky. A tarpaulin lay cast aside, as though a useful item were doubly resented when one could find no useful way of employing it. A posset bowl placed under the leak was serving only to launch the falling droplets against the wall and nightstand.

"Is Tom coming?"

"He wasn't in. Henry ran all the way to his house to fetch him, then was obliged to leave a note on his door. Oh Billy, you cannot imagine my anxieties. Business has been good this last year. Exceptionally good. And I have been complaining about those dreadful shutters for a decade at least. Tom is very good at what he does, but he is not cheap and… and perhaps I have been rash. Perhaps I should have saved—"

Billy said something about all working out, to which Moll cried, "Will it?" then draped an arm across her forehead. "Oh my dear, my saviour. How *very* kind – I was so right to follow my heart and let you back. I shall bring up a bottle of cognac when Tom arrives. A few visits should set us right, don't you think? Four visits, say… and half a month's rent shall be waived…"

Without a head for figures, Billy could only suppose he would be coming out behind by such an arrangement. On the other hand, Moll would be employing all her resources and charms to attract Tom to the house, which could only be a good thing. At their last parting, he had been unable to say just when he could return, so perhaps this was for the best.

When Moll departed, Billy had a full wash at the basin, adjusted the tarpaulin and the posset bowl to help minimise the areas affected by the endless, sputtering assault, then brushed out his hair. After he had donned a nightcap, he crawled under the counterpane and stretched out on his back, his eyes going to the grey sky above.

NIGHT DREW on without a knock at the door. No Tom, no Chandler. Only the continual arrival of thoughts. There was happiness, of a sort. Yet such uncertainty – a tangle of vines returning to Moll's had somehow tricked him into planting. The vines had become a beanstalk, and he had climbed to look down upon his former lives: in this house, in Southwark, with a glimpse of Wapping in the distance. Only here was the point the vines divided. Different directions, into unclear skies.

He thought of Mama, who was used to call him her saviour just as Moll had done tonight. As Mama grew older, she had wished away from the community, and was always after some man to place her in keeping. When she complained of growing old, Billy would praise her for being as dark, as alluring as ever. When she despaired of securing an offer, he would reword some old scheme she had for trapping men and recommend it anew. Then she would take him in her arms and praise him as her saviour. So very wise. So insightful. So pretty himself. And it had felt wonderful. He'd felt useful. And loved.

One night she had fallen into hysterics, certain she was losing her navy officer. Billy had taken her head into his lap, stroked her hair, telling her what to do. Only this night she had failed to listen. No, she had heard all that before – this time it was serious. Her officer was to be sent off somewhere, she hadn't time for any of that. She *must* think what to do. And Billy understood she had not really been asking his advice before. That she knew every idea repeated back had been her own. And that now he must think of something of his own to tell her.

At last he had said, "Don't worry. It's always darkest before the dawn." A bit of tripe he'd heard a balladeer singing in Covent Garden. And the words had no sooner left his lips than he knew he'd let her down. Without a word, she had risen to her feet and begun pacing. And whatever she had decided, whatever scheme to get her offer, it had been invented without him and with steely resolve.

And dawn had come. She'd secured an offer and an apartment in just a few days. Before she'd gone off, she'd brought Billy here to Moll's. Saying little of why. Only that she could not take him where she was going, and Billy hadn't the courage to ask to stay with the community, because they both knew that in thirteen years he'd never pulled his own weight.

Determination had done it for Mama; she'd sought the dawn.

And this is what Billy would do. It was time to push Tom to make an offer. He could not continue at Moll's. Tom knew what staying here would require of him, and if he truly felt the things he claimed to feel, now was the time to prove it. Or else risk losing him.

Because Billy had another option now; he had Roger Calcroft.

And that made all the difference.

By MORNING, a clearing but cool sky produced a rolling fog which lasted until well after noon. When Chandler arrived carrying his trusty tub of *medicament* it was on towards tea time. It seemed an age since they had last spoken, and he was clearly in a bad way. Uncharacteristically timid, eyes like a fish searching for a way back into the pool. Upon coming forward and observing a marked improvement in Billy's nose, he looked as though he might cry.

"Suppose you don't need my care any longer." Then in a moment he had rushed into his arms, bringing them tumbling onto the bed, simultaneously apologising for his neediness, and drawing the counterpane about himself. "Never mind my nonsense!" he sobbed before burying himself.

Billy could do nothing *but* mind it. He crawled beside him, pulled his head from the counterpane, then attempted to tame the lad's errant fringe. "What's happened? Just say what it is. There's nothin' you can say that I ain't heard before."

Whatever he had expected, it was not an odd, meandering tale of searching for rooms nearer the theatre district, encounters in Fleet Market with such as Sally F. and terrible anxieties about approaching the great madam of King's Place. "An advertisement within the pages of *Harris's List* is crucial to my entire plan," said Chandler, "only I have hesitated and procrastinated for fear I shall be laughed out the door. Promise, *promise*, on your heart and soul, that you will tell Moll nothing of this or of what I am about to say."

Billy braced himself.

"It has long been my wish to leave this house. Moll is a good mistress, but she is demanding. Very demanding indeed of those she prefers, you know how she is. I was seventeen last month and I begin to feel the years slip away. Then *you* arrived. And when I saw Moll would take you back, it seemed my chance. My first, my only, chance. Now here you are, reformed and attracting plenty of custom even with your injury. Deep down she's always adored you and so my exit will hardly be noticed. Yet here I am, with a brilliant idea which, if I can execute it, will have me living north of the river with my freedom well before the Season begins. Only… only rather than executing my plan, it seems to be executing me."

"Executing?"

"Arrangements for my new lodgings have gone rather too far; I am committed. I have turned over the money, I have very little left. I *must* move. Only I fear my plan was no plan at all, only a delusion. Listing myself in that book, even in the very back, even if Madam Hayes does agree, must be done with utmost discretion. But discretion might hazard a lack of clarity. And should some man read the advert, misunderstand, and arrive on my doorstep to find what was not expected – it could be disastrous…"

"Listen," said Billy. "Why haven't you secured a keeper? You must have had twenty offers."

"Hundreds!" wept Chandler, burying his face in Billy's neck. "But a keeper is just that! He would keep me under lock and key, even tighter than Moll does. Yours made you wretched – he never let you breathe – and I wish to… to *breathe*. I must be free to pursue my own interests!"

The boy's befuddled eyes swept wildly about the room. He leapt up and paced about, first to reposition the posset bowl, then to look out the window. From the window he looked back to the leak in the ceiling, his brow furrowing. He repositioned the bowl, then returned to the window. His eyes were once more drawn to the ceiling, and he clapped a hand to his mouth then shrieked, "Who's that? Billy, there's somebody on the roof! *MOLL*, come quick! *Robber! Thief! Ravisher!*"

Billy turned to look skyward and observed an eye peering down from the aperture in the roof – no more the eye of an intruder than the eye of God – only that of Tom Baker.

"Mr Baker?"

"None other, Mr Chandler. The rain has cleared so I came up directly."

Chandler looked to Billy, horrified at having shouted at one of his admirers. "*Vastly sweet of you Mr Baker!*" he cried, quite literally crying. "*Is it bad wrecked?*"

"Nothing that cannot be mended. Will, you down there?"

"Present and accounted for. It's Christly of you to come so promptly." Turning to his friend, he added loudly, "Upon my honour there's a great man, Sukey."

Chandler nodded, then his eyes filled with tears, for he had nobody Christly to descend from the sky and save him. Seeing he was too fragile to continue the conversation where they could be heard, Billy motioned to him to proceed down to his room, they would talk there.

"Even if the weather holds, Will, it's another hour up here at least," called Tom. "Unless I can roust up some help."

Not quite hearing him, Billy said, "If it rains the repair will have to wait. You'll catch your death. I'll see Henry Sparrow puts on a pot of tea. You shall have every possible comfort once you are done."

Having bestowed these stimulating promises, he departed the room, slamming the door and clattering down the stairs into Chandler's room.

Tom was nearly two hours completing the repair, during which time three potential advertisements for the *Harris's List* were hashed out. Each described Chandler with a distinctive flavour – amusingly, seductively, mysteriously – as it seemed wisest to present Hayes with an array of options when seeking an audience. However as they honed and embellished, Billy grew increasingly uncertain about his friend's prospects, though for his sake spoke with most confidence when Chandler's own began to flag.

Boy punks, especially those with a fondness for women's clothing, were particularly loathed by female sex workers. Nobody was more outraged should a young male be caught loitering about for trade, and should he be placed in the stocks, no one equalled the vitriol and abuse heaped upon him by his sister entertainers. It was just possible that a Madam might think more of profit and so consider a discreet listing, but the ire roused in the women of the *List* must weaken the prospect considerably.

If Billy did him any service, it was convincing him to delay the move. He should attempt an interview with Hayes as soon as possible, but he must not think of moving yet. The foolish boy had already bought new furnishings for the place, but in the end this was what convinced him not to move hastily. His money being nearly gone, he must build up his reserves before a transition, and he could earn the most right here in the Mint. One month more would allow them the time to break his departure to Moll, perhaps even bring in someone new from the Registry Office to ease the news.

When Tom's voice was heard in the vestibule, he patted his friend's shoulder and assured him things were looking up. They would speak again soon only now he must go down. Chandler took his hand and kissed it, sending down another apology to Mr Baker. Billy achieved no more than the first-floor landing when Moll arrived with Tom, motioning them all into the attic to inspect the repair.

Inspect was a strong word where Moll was concerned. They arrived to have a look, but Tom never could get her to see just where the problem had been. She wished only to be assured all was well again and left it to Billy to examine the new boards fit snugly into place. She busied herself tipping out cups of hot tea topped with a good measure of cognac. "There you are my dearest, strongest man," she said, sitting Tom down and sliding a teacup into his hand. "There. You. *Are.*"

"Much obliged."

"I shall leave the teapot and the cognac here. Everything in this house is yours tonight, darling, *everything*. You have prevented the very walls from crumbling down. Now – what do I owe you for the repair?"

"Nothing at all," said Tom somewhat stiffly, as he wished the topic dropped and Moll away. He seemed not entirely in the best of moods; wet through, the repair having taken longer than expected. "Scrap materials from the shutters were all that was needed. A warm drink and a quiet chat to Will is all I require." Upon which he took down half his cup in one piping hot mouthful and nodded appreciatively.

"Payment in kind then, very well," said Moll. "Billy, if you would be so kind?" then tossing her head with a girlish simper, she departed the room.

Actually wincing when the latch on the door clicked, Billy attempted to introduce a new topic. The damage, however, was done. Tom's mending mood soured; he turned to look out the window, his mouth gone rigid. They might have proceeded to bed directly but Moll, tactless, one-note Moll rather than lubricating the way had hurled a chastity belt into the room and closed the door.

Billy took some pains to undo the damage. At last, with soft words, with praise, with tea and cognac and that blessed relief of stepping from dank, sweaty clothes into dry bedlinens, all began to come right. Once in bed, Billy took on his chill. Tom settled over him, taking his warmth, working it into a common, deeper heat. With his face buried in Billy's neck, he said, "I've a mind to leave without sleeping with you. Hand Moll my bill for services rendered then watch the colour drain from her face."

They laughed. It felt good to laugh. To hold again a body so powerfully recalled, though not yet familiar. This thought was so identical between them they needed not a word, just sweet, knowing laughter and exploring caresses. Soon they let off laughing. Tom was stirring; Billy exhaling, glazing over as one does when feeling adored. Grinning as Tom demonstrated that newly acquired knowledge of what pleased his companion. Very nearly smirking as Tom took his time, a pupil intent to prove just how closely he'd been paying attention…

Billy allowed his mind to slip.

Time passed; he could not have said how much.

Roger Calcroft strode across the room. He retrieved his feathered hat from the corner, donned it, then vanished. For a moment – for one long, thick moment, like a child's finger pulled through a glob of oil paint – it had been Roger.

When he vanished, Billy followed. He found Roger running down Cannon Street Road. He had snatched the white *wiper* from him, holding it aloft, waving it in the wind as he ran ahead…

Tom was by now quite far along, but he paused to bring his companion round, as Billy was staring into the corner appearing flushed and bewildered. Tom turned to look into the corner for himself, unsure of what, or whom, he would find there. Billy dismissed it as a spell of faintness, quickly passed, and Tom was somewhat disinclined to question him further just then.

They were soon asleep. Or, rather, sleep was the role assigned after lovemaking. It was a hard, hollow interlude. By his breathing, Billy understood Tom, too, was often awake. Stealing a stealthy glimpse, he observed Tom staring at him as though at a silhouette inside a paper lantern. Billy had understood the episode no better. He supposed he *was* thinking of Roger rather a lot now. Almost as often as he thought of Tom. Even so, as he found himself repeating to himself quite often, the roles they played in his life did not overlap. Not really.

Not at all, in fact. Back in Pike's Yard, Roger had wrapped arms around his knees and, with head on his lap, begged to learn the language of his youth. He longed to know everything about him – his first experience in the Yard, every mishap, every adventure.

Tom wished a dreamland divorced of the unclean past. Where was his curiosity to know what had happened to bring Billy to where he was in life? What kind of man stared at the swollen eye and bloody nose of his lover and hadn't the interest, or the courage, to ask what had happened? He would not even speak about himself. True, Billy had encouraged them to be shepherds and were he only a punter none of this would matter. But by taking hands as shepherds, they had crossed a stream into someplace quite different. And silences could not remain here long, or the land they stood upon would crumble away until it ceased to be.

Seeing his bedfellow was rather intensely awake, Tom asked if anything were the matter. Billy almost failed to hear him. He shrugged and turned away. Then he smiled to himself, as he heard in Tom's tone that he was looking at himself as the culprit in whatever rift had arisen between them.

When Tom said, "I have forbidden us to speak then wonder why we cannot," Billy understood not just why Roger had come into his mind at a very indelicate moment, but how he might use the knowledge.

To his credit, Tom discerned quite a lot of this inner dialogue. "I do wish to know about you, Will. Everything about you, how can I not? I only wished us to dream a while. To be – it may sound absurd, but the word I favour is *pure*. Give a man the opportunity to pretend and he will take it, no questions asked. But not if it will drive a wedge between us. If it means speaking more of myself, let it be so. Let us speak."

But Billy was now too fixed upon obtaining an offer to hear these words as a genuine and heartfelt wish. *Let it be so?* he thought, like a ruling from a magistrate. *Let us speak?* It was all he could do not to laugh. Tom might have said, *Let us change*

our very natures when we are together. Let us snap our fingers and alter
everything we have been.

This was one of the most bizarre speeches Billy had ever
heard. It left him not merely amused, but cold. Tom might be
lyrical lost in a dreamland. But living in reality? A laughingstock! But no – Billy could *not* laugh; he must not laugh.
Laughing at Tom would be like laughing at a child trying to
walk – a toddler who crossed one fat leg over, rather than
ahead, and fell over.

He knew Tom's time at sea was, for whatever reason,
something he did not wish to speak about. So to test this
supposed commitment to forthrightness, he said: "What was it
like being two years aboard the *HMS Dolphin*?"

As though he had foreseen the question, Tom said,
"Demanding. Very demanding." There was an unmistakable
tone of irritation in the words. As though by now Billy should
know this was not a favourite topic, that there were a million
other things he might ask.

But he checked himself, and continued, "Demanding:
What does that mean? Imagine you have been three months
at sea. You are anchored somewhere off the coast of Brazil
and most of the crew, yourself included, believe your journey
home is to begin shortly. You were told your voyage was for
commercial and diplomatic purposes in Rio de Janeiro and
that Rio de Janeiro is the midpoint. Then you are gathered
before the Commodore and informed you are not in fact
returning. Your frigate, the *HMS Dolphin* and her companion,
a sloop called the *HMS Tamar*, are to continue into the
Southern Seas. The mission is to make such discoveries and
observations as will promote the interests and understanding
of Great Britain. For the additional year and a half of your
life, you will receive double pay and so live very well when,
and if, you return to England, there being much danger and
uncertainty in such undertakings. What would you think of
such a proposition?"

Somewhat taken aback, Billy required a moment to respond. "Reckon it would be a surprise. But if life at sea is not entirely miserable as I've heard it can be, I should like to go exploring."

Tom's nod said such thoughts were entirely as they should be, what was a man without a thirst for the sea? Yet as clear was his wish to change the subject. And that now he had the right to ask some things he had been curious about, and Billy guessed this would be about more than what had happened to his nose.

"I wish to know how you came to be in this house. Not now, I'm speaking of before. You are intelligent and able. If it is not too distasteful to speak about."

Tom may have been surprised to know just how many had asked him this. Depending on the humour of the man, Billy would sometimes preface his arrival with a story or two about the antics of his kinfolk. With Tom, he deemed it prudent to prune all that and commence with the purse tied with a cord of hemp.

Inside, coins in an amount Moll had never disclosed to him. Mama had taken the purse, and after a thorough perusal of the contents, kissed Billy on the head, told him to be good, then exited the house. That had been his last sight of her, standing in the front parlour as she closed the door. With the reek of lavender oil stinging his eyes as it crackled in a crucible in the fireplace.

He had turned to Moll, who was studiously assessing this thirteen-year-old carrot just pulled from the garden. Turning her grubby purchase about with a bony finger, pinching between thumb and forefinger, end finger, naturally, extended. "My boys are *tableaux*, young William," she was saying, Billy now in his second revolution. "*Tableaux vivants*, as the French say."

By this she meant that each boy was to encapsulate one single, powerful image. A living representation which, once understood, might then be employed to stun a patron into enchantment. After which she could send a taproot into the earth of his desire, growing a passion which would keep him obedient, generous, and addicted.

In Moll's view, men with a taste for youths sought an idealised image or experience from some pivotal point in their lives. It was her job to discover what this was. It might be the swaggering youth one had once been – or the swaggering youth one had never been but wished dearly to be. It might be a fellow pupil at school loved passionately when the Head Boy was away. It might be an unfulfilled fantasy about the Head Boy himself, punishing the young scholar for his misbehaviour and then letting things go a bit too far. Moll drew, expertly and often without their knowledge, this information from her clients. She then sought to match him with a young man who was never told just what she deemed to be his greatest attractions, for it was her belief that few could support the knowledge without ogling and primping and bloating it into parody.

Billy had come to see the truth in this. He also understood that maintaining the secret leant a level of uncertainty, and therefore dependency, because Moll's caress always ended in a nail. The nail being the threat that a boy kicked from her house would be doomed to the basest bulk-mongery. Marathon Moll, only, knew his *tableau vivant*. Marathon Moll, only, could fetch his best price. Marathon Moll, only, could see he was treated well.

Tom had that look of horrified fascination Billy fully expected. He said, "Left here by your mother? I had supposed you ran away from home."

"More like being put on the doorstep of some church. My people never had nothing, no doctors' visits or such like. Always hand to mouth livin'. So Moll took me in. Cleaned me up and fed me and had a surgeon in to examine me before sellin' my maidenhead."

This last had been calculated to shock, for Moll had

taught him that a man who is betrayed into tears, into anger, or into shock will show you more of his true nature than he will ever tell. Billy quickly proposed to stop the narrative, wording it to imply he himself, not his history, might simply be too distasteful. Tom, of course, said a man could surely bear hearing what a boy had had to endure, so Billy continued.

"Every night before the auction Moll rubbed a bit of saffron oil on my chest – right about here. Over my lips, which was rough as sandstone. Over the backs of my hands, and up my Fundament. Night of the auction, Caligula brought me out on a large, black tray. I was dressed in naught but a silk robe. The bidders sat at the dining table, puffing pipes. Cali knelt to set the rim of the tray on the table, and the guests rose and circled round. Moll tugged the wrap from my shoulders, then swept my hair around to the front so that the candlelight lit my skin. Then she had me taken out of the room, saying as how whichever of her guests liked me must walk through *the dark curtain* before placing their bids.

"In the corridor between the front and back parlours there's a bar up near the ceiling. We called it the trapeze. Moll had me hang there upside-down, so my hair hanged down. Each bidder had a silk sash tied about his eyes, then stumbled forward until he felt the tickle of my hair on his face. Then he would just stir around awhile, as long as he liked, smelling that lavender oil I had been marinating in for a week. While he did that, I said:

'Pray, Papa, let me down
You'll find me the best boy in town
I'll never while I live offend
I promise you, you will find me mend.'"

"Christ Almighty," said Tom. "Weren't you scared?"
"Nah, I thought it were a lark. Cali was holding my legs so I wouldn't slip, hissing at me to be still and it was all I could do

to keep from laughing. Each guest had just one bid upon exiting *the dark curtain.* The bid was made without talking to the other guests or knowing the other bids. Moll is a bitch, reckon you know that, but she's a right smart businessman. After the bidding, the patrons returned to the dining table to await the announcement of the winner. I was dressed again in the robe and set back on the tray. Cali brought me back into the dining parlour, took me around the room ten times, before setting me before the winner."

Tom could only shake his head.

"The winning bid was £52. A man of trade."

"And?"

"I stood up on the tray, said 'Sir, you are the winner', and took off the robe. Moll escorted most of the others out, telling them they must come back another time if they wished to see me again. She let the second highest bidder remain, though. To watch."

"That's enough now," Tom nearly hissed, wrapping an arm around his companion and placing a kiss on his forehead. "More than enough. You poor boy."

Billy smiled as he set his head upon the warm chest, happy to confirm what he had already known – that Tom was a decent sort and would find nothing titillating in the story. Tom Baker was not like that. Only now he must have a fire in his belly to take poor Billy away from the horrible, dreadful place which had debauched him. Far, far away…

CHAPTER FOURTEEN

Pike on the Leen

– run as fast as you can

As the sun broke over the room, Billy rolled backwards into a sudden, terrible hollow. He was alone in bed. Quite alone. Rubbing at his eyes, he sat up and looked about the room. Tom was sitting at the table, staring out the window with a cup of cold tea. Though relieved, Billy's heart began pounding harder than ever – he had a surging fear that he had misjudged in what he'd said last night. Misjudged and driven him away.

He felt a sudden stab of pity for Tom. They'd spent just two nights together, two actual nights. The first, extraordinary – for himself and for Tom. The second, far from smooth. Indeed Billy may have ruined it. And why? Tom had shown him more true affection, more tenderness, more... love than any man he'd known. Billy had only laughed at him – silently, yes, but had it been so silent? Something was clearly altered in his manner now and he wondered if it had been silent at all.

The scene which was to follow began with kindness and kisses. Seeing Billy was awake, Tom came over and knelt by the bed, kissed his forehead, asking how he had slept. The distracted look in his eyes caused some alarm. When he refused to say what was the matter Billy became even more alarmed. Perhaps he'd been talking in his sleep again. Perhaps he'd said something he should not. Soon enough, however, he understood the damage had been done while he was still awake.

"I shouldn't have said so much of my first week in this house."

Tom's continued silence made it clear this was indeed the problem. He had asked only to know how he had first come here. He had not asked to hear anything like what he had been told. Billy had known full well it would dismay him, and it had.

"I don't regret what you said of yourself," he said, "but it has upset me more than I can tell you. My feelings have not changed. If anything they are grown stronger, as you now have my compassion. Perhaps rather too much of my compassion."

Billy sat up and took his hand. Kissing it then holding it to his heart, he asked how it could be too much.

"Because I cannot return to this house after today. I've abhorred such places all my life though I'm ashamed to say that for a few months I've pushed my reservations aside. I've been lonely. I've had nobody to speak to these many years. Nobody to love. I've found myself returning here under the pretence of these odd jobs. Not for companionship... well, yes, for a kind of companionship, even it was only to be near those who understand the kind of companionship I desire. But they do not understand that here. They understand nothing of the kind. In my opinion, this place should be burned to the ground, because it knows what loneliness is, but seeks only to exploit, and in the filthiest…"

If this was an offer it certainly did not sound like it. If anything it felt like an attack on Billy's entire life. "And I am too dirty to——"

"Don't you dare twist my words." This silenced Billy, and after a look of warning not to do it again Tom continued, "My meaning is quite the reverse. I cannot stomach the notion of your remaining in the house which left you——"

"Left me what?"

Fixing his eye: "With those same fears of intimacy as I have. Though our histories are different, we are very much alike. I feel a responsibility to you now. All I can do is think of you. All I want from life now *is* you. You've a laugh which gives me hope. A resilience. A tender way almost despite yourself, despite what must have been a very difficult life. And I feel important to somebody again. And yet…" His words trailed off, before coming to what all this was leading to.

"Yet I must be honest – I feel as though my hand is being forced. You knew what you were doing telling me all that. Paraded about on a tray, your innocence auctioned off like a side of beef. You wished my reaction, now you've got it: I despise myself. Last night, Moll sold you again – for the price of a roof repair. And I did nothing but try to laugh before taking you straight to bed. I wish you to come with me out of this house. Only I do not wish to keep you. I *shall* not be your keeper. I wish a relationship of equals."

"Equals?" said Billy, hearing a euphemism for what must be the very thing he did not want. "And I am not an equal livin' as I have done?"

Though suspecting he was being pushed into words he would later be hated for, Tom said, "You are a perfectly able, perfectly intelligent man. You are curious about the world. A great reader of novels and newspapers – you've read all about

Captain Cook. Yet can wish nothing more from life than to be kept? Will, haven't you any pride?"

"I got heaps of pride!"

"Not pride as I mean it. A man with pride would not be layin' with every Tom, Dick, and Harry wants to stick it in him."

"Just the Toms?"

Tom turned bright red, angry almost beyond words at being deliberately misunderstood and toyed with. "I am offering you a home. My home in Lambeth Marsh. Not as your keeper. As a partner and helpmate. A partner to somebody who will *come up* when next I am on the roof and ask for assistance. Not remain inside like a prince to be waited upon."

Remain... inside like a prince? He had been helping his friend! But here was Tom, never bothering to ask, God forbid he open his mouth and ask! All was best left a dreamland in which Billy ambled aimlessly about a warm house, a worthless layabout.

Until now there *had* been indecision. But not anymore. He knew what he would do, and further talk would not help the matter. "How about you speak direct for once? How about be *honest*? You don't like what I am or ever have been, so there's the end of it. Two nights have been enough to take the measure of me. Measure twice, cut once, right?"

Billy felt the satisfaction of a blow well-landed. Sounding as though the wind had been knocked from him Tom said, "I am *not* cutting you! Let us talk this through!"

But these words are as clear a sign that a conversation is at an end as any in the English language. As Tom refused to leave the attic, Billy dressed, grabbed his shoes, and, pounding down the stairs, was out the front door.

HE WAS RUNNING. At first neither from Tom Baker, nor towards Roger Calcroft. The mere act of running was enough. As he ran, he let fall like so many weights every care, every expectation, everything that had come to burden him down.

He sought to outrun a view of himself so demeaning Tom had believed he might disguise what he was actually offering. An equal? A helpmate? *Carpenter's apprentice* was what he had meant! And a house in Lambeth Marsh indeed – thank you very much, but William Dempsey could do a *bit* better for himself than a house in Lambeth Marsh. He needed a home, but not at that price!

A home *was* important. But there was a distinction. A distinction even the Great Clown of the Borough High Street could understand. A home should be of one's choosing. In some manner of one's making. Tom had built his house; he'd forgotten what it was like and now assumed Billy must grab for it, regardless of the requirements. But Roger had not forgotten. He refused to succumb to his father's wishes for him. Rather than submit, he had opted for the streets. He was seeking a place, and a future, of his own.

Even with his costumes and tomfoolery, perhaps with a fear of showing himself he'd tried to play off as a joke, Roger had never wavered in his interest in Billy. Billy as he was, not as he imagined him to be. Now he needed to know more of Roger. To understand not just his techniques, but his way of seeing the world. Anger there was, though never getting the best of him, scarcely ever apparent, but ever-present and the fuel for all he did and accomplished. Bloody hell, Billy had more right than most to feel a bit of anger at the world! Why was he always so uncertain, so frightened to take just a bit of that happiness and security so long denied him?

When he neared the couple loitering near St Saviours church, each trimmed in velvet, with that air of visiting Germans or French, and far finer than was usually seen in

Southwark, he knew what he would do. No time to consider, time only to recognise the enemy. Upon passing by, he doubled back, snatching the richly embroidered reticule the Mrs had just closed. Then, partly intentionally, partly from his native clumsiness, he collided with her husband, sending both tumbling to the ground. The husband, being his only real threat of pursuit, was in an old-fashioned three-quarter-length frockcoat, which twisted about him like a constricting viper. But Billy resumed his footing quickly, darting towards the Triangle before anything more could be done than the shrieking of the bewildered lady in a foreign tongue.

He had done it. Not cleanly, not elegantly, but he had done it. Once alone to examine the take, he discovered a vial of smelling-salts, a gilt-framed mirror small enough to fit into a palm, and nine gleaming *Yellow Georges*. Nine whole guineas! The reticule itself was a fine thing – once he'd stowed the contents into the pockets of his breeches, he tucked the glittering reticule into his waistcoat under an arm, knowing it would be worth retaining for the clothes vendors of Monmouth Street—

The clothes vendors! God in his Heaven, he would fit himself out top to bottom! Toss these old duds, sell the reticule and in a beautiful new suit promptly at two o'clock, he would arrive to meet Roger. Oh, for a new frockcoat and slippers. He would take a chair to that counting-house in Botolph Lane. Then he would learn everything about insurance. Everything about the *Book of Lives*. Everything about Calcroft.

As Billy continued toward Monmouth Street, he reflected on just what had happened to him, what had changed in himself. Roger's words returned to explain it to him. Because in the moments before he'd snatched the reticule, he had felt hatred. *Break the houses of the rich, Billy, not because that is where the treasure is. Break them because you despise the rich man.* He *had* despised the lady holding the reticule. Despised that she had something when he had not. How dare that couple wander into Southwark to see the sights? They deserved a bit of street justice!

This would be a day devoted to fashion. By one that afternoon, Billy was transformed into a careless libertine about town, splendidly arrayed. He'd decided upon a short frockcoat of periwinkle velvet, dressed, with a wink to the military, in ropes of frogging, trimmed along every delicious edge in white silk. Knee breeches of velvet trimmed in the same silk, and slippers of blue calfskin completed the ensemble. At one-thirty, he was between the river and East India House, springing along Botolph Lane in a chair powered by the enormous calves of four lusty Irishmen. As he reclined under the sun visor, it seemed the very city glimmered behind a layer of silk. All was safe, secure. All was beautiful again. And with four strong men ready to defend him at all points of the compass, he felt a privilege so vividly recalled that his eyes stung to know it again.

The chair was only just setting down and Billy alighting before the counting-house, when he observed Roger talking to a man down the street. They had been enjoying a lazy afternoon observing the dress of gentlemen and tradesmen, wagering upon the colour of the stockings and frockcoats of the next round the corner into Botolph Lane. Roger was soon settling with his companion, then he sprinted over with a cry of, "*Ecod!* but you are dressed to set the city alight! Be still my heart!"

Billy grinned, trying not to show just how pleased he was to see Roger. His growing attraction to this sprightly fellow was not the physical ache he'd come to feel for Tom – rather, it was a sort of admiration so keen he wished to take him by the lapels and shake him. To toss him to the ground like children in a schoolyard, force him to be still, and tell him everything he knew. It seemed an attraction to his mind, rather than to his body, though as Roger knew his history intimately, he felt the attraction in his heart.

Somewhat amused, though hardly surprised, to learn what Roger did with his free time, he asked to know the odds on costume betting. After an attempt to wave off the question, Roger admitted that odds on frockcoats were fair, colours abounded. Long odds, however, on any but white stockings – the days of colours and clocks, those lovely designs at the ankles, tragically passed. Only the meanest countryman would dare anything but white today, yet it was just possible some free-thinking rake would strut by, and it could make one's fortune. "Enough of that. Come upstairs while I change, we shall dine out."

With somewhat more liveliness than his heeled slippers were intended to endure, Billy rattled up the stairs between the counting-house and the neighbouring business. "No mutton chop at two o'clock?"

"Bugger the mutton," said Roger, coming into a well-furnished sitting room with landscapes in radiant oils of destinations the world over. "We must have something grander. Shin of veal at Chapman's Eating House, perhaps. Later though, I am not hungry yet, are you?" and, already half undressed, he came forward and seized Billy for a kiss. It was a jolt returning him to Pike's Yard. That surrendering to what he might become. That pride in himself and his history. Not a particularly lustful embrace, a mere holding of their lips together as Roger hummed. Yet when Roger withdrew Billy savoured the taste of him, that first step towards knowing him more intimately.

Roger said, "Let us go wherever we list, as the saying is. Shall I don the emerald velvet? The same as I wore when I visited you at Moll's the first time? Just now it is the only thing I have to match the splendour which has just graced my apartment. Yes, let us have the emerald velvet in honour of that meeting."

Billy nodded, grinning somewhat stupidly as he strode about the apartment, still dizzy at his transformation. Looking around, he was somewhat surprised to see such wealth on display. Roger was quick to inform him it was all his father's. The man had furnished the place in his youth and had since moved to a house in Cornhill. These days it was most often used to host visiting international merchants, dignitaries, and blah blah blah. He would be coming into his majority next year, at which time *Papa* expected him to leave off sleeping in down-at-the-heel pleasure gardens and behave like the son he was raised to be.

"Only you and I have other ideas, don't we?" he said, grinning as he pulled on a bag wig which had been specially tailored to accommodate his full head of silvery hair. Billy fetched a container from the vanity and powdered him, then slipped him into the emerald frockcoat. Roger strode to a floor-length mirror and, slim as he was, inhaled as he buttoned the coat. Then he undid the buttons, posing to take in all sides. Appearing pleased, he then descended for another kiss. However Billy was far less inclined for a second embrace. They had already done that and too much of this must raise the expectation of bed. Kisses were beginning to recall Tom to him. Tom with his cup of cold tea brooding at the window, and how he had wished to kiss him and retract everything he had said the night before.

Roger seemed not to notice and enjoyed the kiss fully. When he withdrew, he took care to take Billy's lower lip between his teeth. Then with a devilish grin, he said, "Let us fly, my charmer," and led them outside.

They soon hired a Hackney, the streets, though decent in this part of town, forbidden to gentlemen in fine dress. In Billy's opinion they were a dazzling pair: his nose was now almost healed, Roger looking as well as one could look in a wig. Wigs, for most indispensable in finishing off a fine costume, were scorned by Billy. His long, thick hair made them impossible, so he'd taken to simply tying his hair into a tail which leant him the aspect of a Continental. Yet despite their differences in this and, indeed, many other things, Billy felt an odd, almost primal unity with his companion.

He was actually going about with someone his own age – a thought so extraordinary he was obliged to confide it. Roger found this very amusing, affirming it was high time to relinquish the role of Ganymede. No more lecherous older men, so doddering, so fat, so smelly! Together they would be two of the freshest bucks of the new generation. They would be leaders. As leaders, they would lead in all that was new, which Billy would learn of presently. But so too was it the prerogative of youth to revive the old – did Billy know that?

Letting his head fall into the soft lining of the Hackney as it rocked along, Roger considered. Then he straightened up, set his feet on the floor, and after considering his knees with great seriousness, crossed one leg over the other. Taking a golden pin from the cuff of his frockcoat, he tugged his stocking top from beneath the breeches line, folding it and pulling it taut over one knee, to produce one perfect, snowy Alp. He held it aloft for Billy's inspection. He then informed him it was a fashion early in the century to pull one's stockings rakishly over the knee rather than concealing them beneath the breeches line. Fastening the pin to secure the stocking in its new position, he appeared quite pleased.

"Let us revive the fashion, hm? Once we are rich enough to be reported upon in the papers, all the young men of London will wish to copy this." Roger made an identical adjustment to his other knee, fastened it with a twin from the opposing cuff, then placed his knees together. Not quite right. He was soon entirely distracted attempting to discover that precise manner of folding and pinning to allow for movement in all positions. "But how *did* they keep them in place? Upon my honour, it is no easy thing. They never quite lay as you wish them to. Was it only for portraits, do you think?"

Ambition, be it grand larceny or the not so grand, Roger did have. And as stupid as some of these ambitions were, and from Billy's perspective stocking tops should always and without exception remain tucked beneath the breeches line, he could not but admire the charms of Calcroft. Roger was the golden pin fastening, then refastening, Billy's attention, though by the time they reached their destination, with adjustments continuing to be made, Billy wondered whether a dirty sole rubbed rakishly across his rakish knee tops might not do the boy some good.

CHAPTER FIFTEEN

Tickler of Rome-vile

– the knowing fellow of London

Lloyd's Coffeehouse was London's premier meeting place for the business-minded. A champagne flute overflowing with brokers, stock jobbers and general gamers who crawled about the rooms, stuffed themselves into doorways and lined the surrounding alleyways. Everywhere the air was hot with new schemes for profit, new ventures, and new splits divvying up the risk of these ventures. Sweating men waiting to get inside leafed through papers, haggled over quotes, scratched calculations with chalk upon stone exteriors. One tradesman, unwilling to fight the crowd to get inside, was signing a contract on the back of another, a third man serving both as witness and inkstand, complete with inkwell, wiping paper, and sand shaker.

Billy reckoned the chances of a table inside were nil, but

as they were to seek out an underwriter long employed by Calcroft & Son, Roger promised a box at some point. Once pressed through the doorway like so much wet laundry through a mangle, the scene inside Lloyd's unfurled.

Underwriters in their highbacked boxes carried on a brisk business. Tri-cornered hats hanging from wall hooks jostled about as be-frocked and be-wigged gentlemen, many large and ungainly, settled down amongst their compatriots, then rose again. This was a world Roger had long known and his expression was one of tolerance. In heeled slippers, he clipped about like a colt newly shod, and in a wig, he was not unlike George III in appearance, his blue eyes pronounced and a bit austere like their youthful king.

These chameleon-like changes in Roger were almost hypnotically captivating to Billy – as beautifully as Tom when he worked a plank into shape, Roger altered his posture, the motions of his wrists, his facial expression to bend his surroundings to him. Equally able, it seemed, to descend as to climb ladders, as he had spent his life observing human behaviour. If his lively demonstrations could seduce a motley crew inside Pike's Tavern, his genteel manners could as quickly gain him access to the best drawing rooms.

The man he sought was an insurance underwriter by the name of Moffit, currently occupied in his box. While they waited, Roger moved to the bar where alcohol and food could be had and commanded two steaming mugs of coffee. Pipes, for hire or purchase, were also available, and on a whim Billy bought a slender clay pipe similar to one he had owned while living with Moll. Either because of poverty while tricking outside the Hook and Crook, or from the dislike of tobacco of his subsequent keepers, it had been three years since Billy had enjoyed a good pipe. He took up his newly acquired purchase, stuffed it with cherry tobacco, and lit up.

At last there was movement from the box of Mr Moffit, quite an odd-looking man who, as an aid to his poor vision, was employing what appeared to be a large set of opera glasses. These were in fact two Galilean telescopes fused together by a celebrated Venetian optician. He was perusing a contract under the light of a smoking candle as a pair of men rose and departed.

A second man inside the box, a Mr Welch, was waving the boys over. As they picked through the millers-about, Mr Welch withdrew a golden flask leashed by a chain into his coat pocket. In an agile motion he drew out the sparkling tether as though his pet might wish to roam about the rooms. With an extended hand, Moffit offered the newcomers a place beside Welch.

The two businessmen were joined as links on chain, Welch being the broker sent by merchants to search out quotes for insurance on various ventures. Moffit, in his turn, one of the underwriters who calculated the risk and provided a price on that portion he was willing to represent. Welch received his quotes, then would go on his way to secure representation on the remainder and shop for better rates.

As the boys settled in Welch brought the flask to his lips to douse himself with that accelerant which kept him at full flame. To which Moffit stared down the double-barrel of the glasses and said, "You are under a physician's order to abstain from drink. He says it has stripped away the coating of the stomach entirely."

"Then my stomach must make do in its waistcoat," said Welch, wiping his mouth then holding up his flask to the boys. "Anyone recommend a good tailor?"

Moffit asked after Roger's father, then proposed the man come see him before the end of the week as he had a deal on space aboard a merchant vessel bound for Virginia. Or had Roger taken up the reigns of this end of Calcroft & Son? "Not just yet," was the response, leading Billy to believe the elder Mr Calcroft had been recruiting his business associates in the task of chastising his son for lack of participation.

While introducing the men to his friend Mr Dempsey, Roger made clear his lack of participation in the family business was not for lack of knowledge. He spoke in some detail about the international grocery trade – sweetening the air with raisins and figs from Greece. Adding tang with lemons from Cyprus, then garnishing with almonds from the Balearics.

Mr Welch lifted his flask and cried, "Could your father hear you now, Roger my boy!"

"Could he hear me now," said Roger, "I would be locked sixteen hours a day in his counting-house pouring over ledgers and contracts. That said, I *am* here on behalf of Calcroft & Son. My father has been fourteen months battling to collect a debt from a fish merchant, a Mr Longfellow of Billingsgate, whose business he helped establish with a loan but who has yet to make a single payment to him."

The businessmen regarded each other, a thing to be done carefully given the sweep of the Galilean telescopes, which never left Moffit's eyes. "A Mr Longfellow of Billingsgate," repeated Moffit. "Never heard of him. Have you?" Welch shook his head.

"Hardly a surprise," said Roger. "A man who cannot be bothered to pay his debts will not bother to insure his wares. But I wish to inquire about a different sort of insurance, what they call *life assurance*. I don't wish to purchase, I am merely gathering information, but I should like to know how a policy on the life of Mr Longfellow might be obtained to help secure my father's interests."

"*Life* assurance," groaned Welch, "these young dogs will insure anything nowadays, upon my honour. Never heard of such a thing in my day. Sir, report your debtors to the magistrate and let bill collectors and bailiffs do their jobs."

Slightly flustered, Roger said, "Yes sir, of course. That is what we have done, which under normal circumstances would suffice. But I have it on good authority Mr Longfellow is ill, quite ill indeed, and will likely not see another summer. In the event Calcroft & Son will never recover the money and suffer a loss I wish us to avoid."

Though he had again returned to his contract, Mr Moffit said, "Move with the times Welch, you don't need to like it. Equitable Life Assurance Company, Roger, Nicolas Lane on Lombard Street. First, and best, in the business, been there about ten years. They require their members to have a *life interest* in the insured, which as a holder of a debt you have. Can you document your interest?"

"Yes, of course," Roger replied, a gleam coming into his eyes. Then in a tone of offhanded banter, "You know, it's too bad our delinquent fellow, Mr Longfellow, is not a well-known fellow, ha-ha. How's that for a rhyme?"

The telescopes came up and around. "What was that?"

"It is said – perhaps you know – that the debts of the vastly wealthy, members of the Nobility etc, are so well-publicised that creditors often insure the lives of their debtors quite freely. No questions asked, just take out a policy."

"I doubt it," said Moffit, "the life insurance industry might not be... quite up to snuff just yet, but I don't believe——"

"*Believe*, sir!" cried Welch, slamming his flask on the table for emphasis. "The boy is quite right. Insurance men have become so lazy anymore, yet so greedy, that common gossip, or a piece of printed gossip in a rag like the *Morning Star*, is quite enough to sell a policy. I know for a fact that very thing has been going on over on Lombard Street, and the potential for fraud is really quite appalling."

Roger leapt from the table, nearly colliding with a pot boy's tray of coffee. "Thank you Gentlemen! I've just recalled a prior engagement. William and I must depart. Say, Tuesdays and Fridays are still the days for the *Book of Lives*, yes? At noon?"

Welch nodded. "That's right."

"My friend's mad to see it, he's never been. We'll be back tomorrow then. Promptly at noon."

Now aiming his lenses across the room, Moffit began waving over another pair of men. As they made to depart he said, "Go with God, as the Spanish say."

At the word *God*, Roger's eyes lit. Then he licked his lips as he had done after taking Billy's lip between his teeth.

DEPARTING LLOYD'S COFFEEHOUSE was rather a relief to Billy. Keen as he was to understand Roger's ideas, it seemed so much astrology his head was throbbing. Until now, he had believed the skilful lifting a timepiece from a coat pocket to be the height of stealth.

They piled into a Hackney carriage, which at Roger's direction headed toward a street in the West End advertising townhouses for sale. Of their visit to Lloyd's, he gleefully confided that all that muck about life insurance, useful for future schemes though it was, had not been his primary aim. He had wished to have confirmed the name of a newspaper – the *Morning Star* to be precise. And the *Morning Star*, Good God in his Heaven, had been confirmed. That was crucial, absolutely crucial, to know before proceeding with their own scheme in the *Book of Lives*. Mr Welch might disdain the idea of life insurance, but the *Book of Lives*, that celebrated invention of Lloyd's, was scarcely any different. It operated in just the same way, but without the need for written policies, it was open to anyone willing to place a bet. He promised to tell Billy more that evening, only now he must organise his thoughts. Why not look at town homes for a while?

Initially, Billy did not wish to go into the West End; all those homes seemed too much the stuff of dreams. But Roger insisted. They advanced much as they had done while looking at summer boxes. First to one, then another, then just one

185

more choice home in a choice location until Billy's eyes dilated, pulsing at the thought of himself once more amidst splendour. Unlike in Sydenham, there was no need to go into any of these, as Billy knew what they contained. For two years he had lived, dined, and masqueraded in this very area. He knew the neighbourhoods, the byways. Oh, the comforts! He had even had his own footman for a time.

He told himself not to be hasty in his expectations. Hastiness might lead to disappointment – only hours ago he had been holed up in a leaking attic in the Mint. Yet as they rolled down street after street of gleaming façades, of finely liveried servants helping even finer men and women into personal carriages he found himself believing. He wanted to believe. And when one was with Roger Calcroft, it was hard *not* to believe.

To think he had actually been considering what could scarcely be more than a life of poverty with Tom. Tom was nice enough, but you accomplished nothing if you could not be business-minded about your future. Take away Tom's caring, his skill, his reliability, his tender lovemaking, the eyes which said he had never loved like this before. Take all that away and he was – well, just a labourer, really.

They dined at Chapman's Eating House then returned to Botolph Lane. Out came a bottle of Old Hock and a copy of the *Morning Star*. The paper had been laying, folded and untouched, in the kitchen when he first arrived. Presently Roger brought it into the drawing room, Billy, with his new pipe, following and settling beside him on the sofa.

"Now, what is the latest on my darlings the Crawford sisters?"

It seemed Roger was quite interested in two young starlets of Society, daughters of a wealthy Lord in Norfolk, who had spent their entire lives at a school in France. Six months ago, it was learned they would be coming to London to seek husbands, so for five months they had been reported upon, in particular their beauty which was said to be extraordinary. They had arrived three weeks ago in the metropolis and now their every outing, every diversion, every cough, was reported upon. What did Billy make of this?

Billy sighed and lit his pipe. It took some doing to acclimate yourself to always feeling six months behind another person. You could not say of Calcroft that he actually looked down on those who failed to match him in schemes – he was too often caught in joys verging on mania to feel superior. But really it would be nice to occasionally meet him in ideas. Or at least guess what he was thinking.

"Two of us plus two of them equals a marriage scheme?"

"Bandbox!" groaned Roger, taking Billy's pipe for a puff before returning it to its owner. "How perfectly seventeenth century! Oh no, we are neither of us so low as to stoop to marriage – not yet."

"What's to *make* of it then?"

"The power of the printed word. Let me explain." But before he began, he pulled the pipe from Billy's mouth and kissed him. "My God, you are a delicious boy. How I should like to… but I digress. Wait. Where was I?"

"The power of the printed word."

"Ah yes. My two darlings. They have been, as I said, in town about three weeks and are indeed the toast of it, though rather at their own expense. Their invitations now come to confirm the reports, which began the day of their arrival, that they are *not* two visions of Venus as had been first reported. A cruel bit of popularity, nobody knows if they quite understand it. But Londoners do hate being lied to, even if it was not the sisters doing the lying only the ever-reliable rumour mill. So now there have been many little articles complaining how very ordinary the sisters are, how all of London has been taken in. That the only thing remarkable is that there are two of passable prettiness, who, unless we receive some touring Saudi

Prince who might take both, will be nothing at all once separated."

Billy could not help chuckling. This was the very thing the Marquess would have appreciated. Indeed he had read out a report about the sisters during one of their last mornings together. Still, any particular interest in them was quite a mystery.

"My interest in them is this," said Roger, as though replying to his inner thought. "In the Tuesday edition of the *Morning Star*, Miss Eleanor Crawford was reported to be ill. No details, so it was believed to be nothing serious, but enough for a brief mention. That very day at noon, she was listed in the *Book* at Lloyd's with even odds on survival for the next twelve months. I ran about buying up every newspaper I could find, but the *Morning Star* was the only paper to have reported this. Others did that evening, which means the report was sound and substantiated. Don't you see? It is supposed to be some great secret just which reports are used for getting names into the *Book*. Lloyd's declares they personally know well-informed people, and perhaps they know some, but the *Book* has grown far too large for personal communications about everyone listed. These days they must rely on newspapers for information. The *Morning Star*, I am convinced, is one. It has a fairly good reputation and all the gossip. Surely one need only speak to the right people, some columnist who trolls about in the Bedford or some coffeehouse like it, to get into circulation news which can then affect the odds on someone listed in the *Book*."

Roger was by now done perusing the *Star*. He tossed it aside and grinned at his companion. Billy could certainly see the potential of such an idea, though controlling so many moving parts seemed to him a rather daunting prospect. He asked one or two general questions, the second coming out as more of a yawn.

"You've had a long day," said Roger. "Listen, I've just had

an extraordinary idea and must go out. But you *will* stay here tonight? You cannot wish to leave."

Though not having fully considered spending an entire night with Roger, Billy had no intention of returning to that room in the Mint – a room now full of uncomfortable memories. It was about this time last night he'd been working to get Tom into bed. And only this morning the sight of him sitting alone with that cup of cold tea. Roger might not be enough to keep every melancholy thought at bay, but his apartment would provide a needed distance from Tom. So too that further intimacy with Roger himself, whatever that might entail. Billy agreed to stay.

"Stellar," said his host, rising from the sofa to change clothes. From the bedroom, he called, "And I am not yet allowed to make love to you, is that right?" Billy was too tired and out of sorts to field any such impertinent question. At his silence, Roger returned to the room with a fresh shirt over his shoulders. "Well, am I? If I am to the Devil with my idea, I shall remain—"

"I'm dog tired."

"Of course. Perfectly alright. As expected. You will take my bed and when I return I shall have the sofa." Billy objected, but Roger overrode the objection, returning to the bedchamber for new breeches, saying something Billy could only just hear about not wishing to have any accidents.

WHEN BILLY AWOKE NEXT MORNING, it was with a kind of surging clarity. He was in Roger's bed, quite alone, with the knowledge that his friend had kept to his word and stayed away. He had a vague recollection of hearing him return in the middle of the night, though so enveloped in the intense comfort of his bed he could no more have moved or spoken to him had he been made of stone.

A particularly bright, undiluted sun pouring through the bedchamber window said it was about eight. The light of the exterior world seemed strangely like that surging clarity inside him – coursing with bright energy, illuminating, yet threatening to surmount the illumination by its own glare.

It was a moment before he could credit what he was seeing.

Just a few feet from the bed, Roger was standing in a robe before the full-length mirror. He was, incredibly, fiddling with those damned stockings again. Did he never sleep? There he was: in nothing but a robe and stockings, pinning, then re-pinning with his fingertips the tops of the stockings over his knees, standing at different angles and in different attitudes to judge the effect. *Durable but not pleasing to the eye*, he seemed to say. Then after another adjustment, *Pleasing to the eye, but must come undone before noon.*

Feeling somehow tightly wound, Billy came from bed, naked and stealthy, and at an opportune moment, unable to resist, applied one foot to Roger's bottom, sending him crashing to the floor. Agile as Roger was, he struggled for a moment to gain his bearings. At last coming to his knees on the Turkish rug, he grabbed his opponent by the ankle and pulled him down. However Billy was more than ready for the move, half jumping as he was pulled, bringing Roger into a scrimmage in which he never truly gained the upper hand. Billy soon prevailed, pinning him on his back, panting as his hair fell forward, where it mingled in a kind of otherworldly beauty with his opponent's platinum halo of hair.

Calcroft, for once, remained motionless. No clowning, no jesting. No dazzling schemes. When his arms were pinned over his head, he complied. Directing his eyes to the ceiling, he shifted his hips, then drew his legs gently but firmly around his combatant in a way to make Billy's eyes expand. Billy bucked to re-exert supremacy. No effort was needed – Roger merely winced, then, smiling, closed his eyes like a child told not to peek.

It appeared, like everything else with Roger, Billy was rather late to understand what was going on. First informed was his body: coiled now like an iron spring trembling to expand. Roger was not asking for dominance. Perhaps he never had been.

"You win, Billy," he said, a vein pulsing in his neck while the sun streamed through the windowpane. "You win."

CHAPTER SIXTEEN

Bingowaste!

 – get you hence!

At noon they were once more inside Lloyd's coffeehouse, the blinds drawing, a candle lighting to announce the bringing forth of the *Book of Lives*. This was all meant tongue-in-cheek, as soon enough the *Book* would open, additions, deletions, and any significant alteration in the odds would be read out, and the betting commence. Still, the drama of the moment sufficed to bring Billy from his hedonistic stupor, if only briefly.

They had made love three times that morning, and as the light went down inside Lloyd's, the sight of those snowy kneecaps crossed primly beside him in Moffit's box were nearly enough to drive him to fresh desire. What was worse, Calcroft appeared not one iota altered from their boisterous morning.

As a lover Roger was eager and tireless, nothing pleasing him as much as submitting to absolute, boyish selfishness in his partner. He seemed always at a slight, almost amused, remove, both spectator and participant.

That first time he had covered his eyes, looked again, asked to be restrained. Then, grinning, he bit his lip as his companion, having never had a thought of fulfilling this role, found himself at a conclusion before he rightly understood he had begun.

Upon which Roger had pulled away, stretched, then collapsed into bed. "Lord, the things a fellow must do to be allowed back in his own bed. I've a crick in my neck from sleeping on that sofa, you brute."

Still stupid with surprise at himself, Billy was attempting to rise from the rug, having attained no more than his hands and knees. At last, rubbing the glare from his eyes, he joined his partner in bed. Roger brought him in, kissed him, gave him some praise. Then with a sigh *supposed Billy intended something more – he had heard about boys from Little Barbary.*

Billy did not know what Billy intended. Even as they descended to tussling and he went rigid from the wish to dominate he didn't know, only that this was the only way to feel anything like the upper hand with Roger Calcroft.

The *Book of Lives*, however, roused him from his puppydom and carnal thoughts. The light inside Lloyd's was restored, and with it his curiosity about the *Book*. Roger gave him a thorough explanation, and though the underlying mechanics of what he intended were still obscure, the idea of the *Book* was simple enough. The *Book* contained the names of people whose chance at a long life could be wagered upon. The names of noted public figures, members of the Nobility, and the very wealthy, entered its pages after news in some form called into question their continuing to exist. A name was entered, then odds were given based on mortality tables which converted age, gender, known illnesses, and lifestyle into a number. This number was then passed through a calculation in a column called either *Risk due to Detestability* or *the John Wilkes Factor* – the certainly that the hated MP John Wilkes must lose his life to violence having first opened the *Book* at Lloyd's.

Roger's idea consisted of getting a name of his own choosing listed, then influence the odds. While Billy had been asleep the previous evening, he had rounded up his costume-betting companion for an excursion to the Bedford Coffee-house in Covent Garden. They had manoeuvred for a seat near a man known to write for the *Morning Star*, then had a noisy exchange in which was disclosed the shocking news that it was not Miss Eleanor who was ill, but her sister Miss Elizabeth, who might have consumption.

The outing proved unsuccessful. The name of Elizabeth Crawford had failed to appear today in the *Book*. This was because, he was certain, it had failed to make the *Morning Star*. Roger put that omission down to the dismal acting abilities of his betting companion. And, really, they had been no more than two idle fellows chatting in a coffeehouse. What was required was an informant who had more credibility, and for the next venture – his and Billy's venture – he would make sure credibility had been established before seeking to proceed.

Then, almost in passing as they exited Lloyd's, he said, "All shall be quite different when we drop our information about the Marquess of Argyll."

Billy said nothing, partly to avoid looking a fool for not having understood the Marquess was to be their aim. Partly because he *had* known, in some dark part of himself. But mostly because he didn't quite recognise himself anymore or know what he should think.

Just who had reversed the role he had always taken in bed? Who had made the reversal like a revelation, so overpowering it was now nearly insatiable? Who had put Roger so fully in control that he was now quite comfortable displaying it? They were small things, a little grin to himself, a new term of endearment. Yet small was all that was required. A change had happened – it was obvious and quite acceptable when you suspected you had a puppy at your side.

Over an early dinner in Dolly's Steakhouse, Roger expressed optimism in the plan for the Marquess, which *would* work now he had tested the waters. All had not gone to plan with the Crawford girl, but he had learned some things from the experiment. Now they simply needed to get the Marquess listed. After a perusal of the *Book* today, he had verified the man was not yet listed, so he would begin inventing some juicy gossip about him, this time making certain it was convincing and reported upon. This would both prove he could influence what was reported about the man and ensure the man was being talked of before a sudden change in health.

"Change in health?" said Billy, a glass of claret halfway to his lips. This was the first mention of that. And he had not changed so much as to wish anyone physical harm.

Roger met his eye. Then, smiling, he opted for a mouthful of steak before answering.

As he studiously chewed, Billy watched him not only seize control of the relationship incontrovertibly but flaunt it. Just *look* at him! He wasn't even bothering to be subtle about it. Billy could not match him in scheming, and information on the schemes themselves was doled out in such a way as he could never quite see the entire picture. Other than his connection to the Marquess, admittedly of prime importance, he really had nothing to match him in the relationship. Yet he had only pursued Roger to try to take control of his life for once. He was sick of merely taking what was given. He *needed* control and as yet had discovered only one way of feeling it. And if he chose, Roger might withhold that too. But that was intolerable! Sexual politics was *Billy's* game!

"Whatever my past with him, I don't wish the Marquess

harmed," said Billy. "If you intend to hurt him, I shall find him and tell him, and all your plans will be ruined."

Roger swallowed, then took a sip of wine. "You are a sweetheart. That's why I like you so much, Billy. He will only have a temporary bout of ill health. An accident, a bout of flu. I favour flu actually. Something from which he can recover in about a week. That's all."

Billy should have liked a more dramatic or unreasonable ambition, something he could more strenuously deny him. "That really all?"

"Yes. Only it must *seem* serious for a time. Never fear, there are plenty of little powders to do the trick. You will simply ask for an interview, slip it into his drink, and that will be that. Lloyd's will hear of a serious illness and put him into the *Book of Lives* with slim chances of recovery. We will bet heavily the other way and make a mint."

"But what if what I give him accidentally kills him?"

Roger sighed. "It will not. And really, can you care after the way he treated you? He put you out without a penny to your name, not caring what became of you. You devoted yourself a year and a half to that man. You must have *some* anger about that. Tossing you out meant nothing to him – he continues in his comforts and parties, four houses, a coach and six. No doubt he replaced you within the week. But that episode destroyed your *life*. Everything you had built to that point – gone."

But Billy was not hearing him; he was avoiding his question and it was beginning to scare him.

"Alright," said Calcroft, smiling. "I see you are concerned but you have not the slightest reason to be. I can guarantee what I give you to give to him won't kill him."

"How?"

"Because if I am not careful in what I choose, all of my plans *will* be ruined. The plan only works if he gets ill and survives. A dead man will not be listed in the *Book of Lives*, only the *Obituaries*."

DAYS PASSED.

Roger was now almost every night at the Bedford, establishing his credibility with someone writing for the *Star*. How he was doing this and exactly what kind of gossip he was spreading about the Marquess Billy didn't know. Or particularly care. He had agreed to do his part when the time came, but a growing guilt over the plan discouraged too much discussion about that man. The discussions which did arise were often peppered with kisses. Then with touches. Then tumbles.

Billy was now living nearly as well as he had in the West End. Exotic fruits set by the front door each morning. Runners from the counting-house to fetch whatever they wished from market. A musical evening in Covent Garden. Yet he understood he was not terribly happy. Roger insisted the feeling was trepidation before a big win, that nothing worth doing in life came without risk and a level of uncertainty. Uncertainty, not unhappiness, was what he was feeling.

"And do you know how to rid yourself of that pesty uncertainty?" asked Roger. "Hate!" he said and snapped his fingers. "You wished to learn from me Billy and I want you to hear this now. This world is a corrupt and horrible place; the odds are stacked against all but the wealthy and connected. Think of your Marquess not as a person, but as a representative of all that is wrong with this world. Hate him enough to be *willing* to kill him," Roger held up a silencing hand, "even though you won't. But you *could*, given what he represents. You see? Then giving him a little stomach ache will cause no apprehension, for it will seem mere child's play by comparison."

There seemed to be something in this. He was considering

the idea when Roger added, "And when you think about it, can he really be as – well, as human as you and me?"

Frowning, Billy said, "He's human."

"He inherited all he has, so he's never known what most humans know, which is work. Much less scratching and conniving to make ends meet or selling his body to get by."

This was true. All of it. Everything Roger said sounded right and well-reasoned. Yet to say the Marquess, the man he had known, if not particularly liked, for a year and half was not human, seemed a bridge to far.

His eyes flickering as he studied him, Roger came in to nip at Billy's ear. He said, "Listen to me now. The Marquess of Argyll is said to be a very robust and sportive man. And you've said he is also a very arrogant man. Perhaps getting sick for a time, a week when he cannot jump his horses and hasn't the breath to shout at servants, will help him appreciate what he has a bit more, hm? Why not think of it that way?"

Billy turned to him, speechless. This was a revelation. He *would* think of it that way. This was quite brilliant, it set everything to rights. Painful as it was to lose his apartment in the West End, he had been forced to appreciate what he'd had in a new way. And some good *had* come out of it. He had made amends with Moll. Chandler had helped him through those newspaper articles and in the process answered many of his questions. And he had met Tom.

Yet after a few days, the comfort of this thought began to fade. He could not have said why, but it did. And now, rather than seeking rationales for comfort, he sought comfort from his memories of Tom. Meeting him *had* been a good thing. And it was not just Tom that he missed. He missed how *he* had been when he was with Tom. There were times these days he felt almost a stranger to himself. Times he thought he should leave Roger and try to make amends.

Yet what would he say? And what would be the consequence? Wouldn't seeking him out be giving Tom the upper hand? And wouldn't giving him the upper hand change what had been so special about their relationship? Because there had been something special. And whatever he had meant by a *relationship of equals*, he had not meant using him as a carpenter's apprentice. He might have stayed and asked just what he had meant. But really, did he need to? Tom had been asking him to ask more of himself, that was all.

Ten days on was a hell of a time to admit that he had understood this.

Ten days on, what did it matter?

One night he awoke to feel Tom's hand withdrawing from his, as it had done the day in Souls Yard when he'd first approached him. Only now he was withdrawing for good. Billy had taken up that hand without caution. A hand numb from use, and disuse. And so he must be rejected if he tried to take it up again. It was too late to return to what they had had. Billy had ruined it.

At last he fixed upon writing to Chandler to see if he was alright. This, at the very least, he could arrange, and it would ease his mind about him if about nothing else. Not surprisingly, Roger told him to forget that silly house in the Mint — they had their note to compose to the Marquess and so many other little things to organise. As Roger spoke, it became apparent that he knew Billy could not write the note himself. When or how he had discovered it was unimportant; it would have been more surprising if Roger Calcroft had not discovered it.

Knowing that Roger knew produced a moment of panic. He could easily refuse to write the note, and Billy would be at some pains finding someone to assist. But seeing an agitation which seemed likely to continue, which might itself disrupt the focus they needed to execute their plan, Roger scratched something to the effect of:

Bad cold. Very catching. If need be, send a note to Roger Calcroft at Jonathan's Coffeehouse. Will return to see you when able.

W. Dempsey

BILLY SEIZED the note and read it over as well as he could. After bringing the note himself to the penny post, he breathed a sigh of relief. All was likely perfectly well in the Mint; Chandler still had plenty of time to sort out his worries before telling Moll of his coming move.

After two weeks living above the counting-house in Botolph Lane a note arrived from the Mint. Three days before Roger had written to the Marquess *on behalf of William Dempsey* to request an interview. He was now expecting every day to hear back. As such, they woke early every morning and proceeded to Jonathan's Coffeehouse to collect post being held for him under an assumed name. Nothing yet from the Marquess. Then the attendant handed over a letter directed to Roger Calcroft. In rather a sour mood, Roger took the letter and looked it over. Then he stuffed it into his pocket, dismissing it as nothing. By now Billy could read him well enough to see that it was, in fact, something, and so grabbed it from his pocket and flattened it out on a nearby table.

Its brevity was its only saving grace; he could make most of the words. He saw it was signed by Chandler, having worked with himself to learn the names of everyone in Moll's house.

Seeing Billy's alarm Roger made a face. "We *cannot* have any distractions now. Please. We *must* see our plan through to fruition, and going to help that boy now will only—"

"*Help* him?" Billy had got the sense of Chandler's wishing him to come, but nothing of his needing help. "What did he write?"

"What does it matter? We have other things—"

"We *ain't* got other things. The Marquess didn't write back yet. You tell me what that note says. I know it's from Chandler and I know it's something important."

After a long exhale, Roger took up the note. After making Billy promise on his soul he would be back in Botolph Lane by evening, he read out:

Billy,

Something dreadful has happened. If you are at all able do come quickly.

Sukey Chandler

CHAPTER SEVENTEEN

Tumbler

— *a cart or wagon*

Whatever Billy expected to see when he arrived, it was not Henry Sparrow cowering by a tree at the edge of Souls Yard. With his hands in his hair, he appeared on the very brink of sanity, the crossroads of his life, unable to go further in his flight from Moll's yet unwilling to return. A bed of leaves to crouch upon, and no less than eight sets of eyes staring at him from cracks and holes in the Yard's neighbouring structures declared he had been by the tree some time. The young man leapt into his arms, professing he hadn't meant any harm, really and truly he had not. Though quite taken aback, Billy soothed the ailing creature, however his requests to know just what had happened produced nothing but wailing.

"No questions! No questions alright?" he said, a promise

which at last doused the flames. The task of coaxing him back inside Moll's had only just begun when Caligula appeared in the doorway, arms akimbo. This daunting sight was too much for Sparrow, whose cries began again.

"Stop that confounded pipe!" shouted Caligula. "And you, Billy, I knew your returning to this house boded nothin' but ill."

"What'd I do?"

"Upset the balance of this cuckoo's nest, that's what. Lord have mercy, you know it don't take much," he said, stepping aside as Sparrow was guided into the front parlour.

The room contained every member of the house except Moll. Chandler was facing off against the Tower Princes, O'Donnell in the attitude of a mediator, the house fiddler lounging on the settee, puffing a pipe, and observing the show. As Billy had feared, news of the forthcoming departure had escaped. Chandler informed him he intended to be out of the house today, and when Billy asked where exactly he was headed, he cried:

"I had supposed all of London knew by now – 13 Craven Street, Strand!" Clapping his hands over his ears, Sparrow let out a howl as Chandler continued, "I do not regret what I have done. The room was available immediately and the location suits my interests exactly. I shall be settled two months before the season begins with plenty of custom to pay my expenses." As he said this, he turned from Harper to face Billy, his voice filled with triumph. His eyes, however, as filled with apprehension as any Billy had seen.

"Take custom from this house and I shall personally have your hide!" shouted Harper, in the tone the highly religious adopt when defending their Lord, each word crafted for heavenly scribes. "I shall haunt 13 Craven Street, Strand and if I see one familiar face coming to your door Moll will destroy you and your reputation!"

Now blinking back tears, Chandler continued in his

perfectly modulated stage voice, "I have no need to take custom from this house. My name is to appear in the *Harris's List*. The '72 edition arrives at your nearest booksellers in December. Circulation – eight thousand."

"You are a bald-faced liar!"

"Purchase a copy and see if I am."

"That list is for men seeking women. Real women, not nymphs of your sort."

"I can assure you all that is needed is a bit of fancy verse and a reference to *the Italian gusto*. Voilà."

"Voilà and you are dead, Chandler," said Harper. "Punters do not cotton on to such tricks. And you," he continued, rounding on O'Donnell, "you can wipe that smirk from your face. With Chandler's departure, *I* shall be top boy. Well, the Tower Princes will be tops."

O'Donnell's smirk said otherwise. "A lad doesn't become tops simply because has been lounging around this house longer than anyone else. My stellar dance card *guarantees* me top spot—"

Having heard enough, Caligula somewhat unceremoniously corralled Chandler, Billy and Sparrow into the dining parlour and shut the door.

"It was to be a great secret, Billy," said Sparrow, whose gift for declaring the obvious nearly equalled that for spilling secrets. "Only I could not quite believe it. Even after we went up the Strand and Joe showed him the room, and took the money, I still couldn't believe it! Then one day I *did* believe it. And the moment I believed it, the very moment, well… Mr Harper and Mr Applegate sort of… heard. Oh Sukey, you will still come to my wedding! I am to be married to Miss Susan, of Spitalfields, someday. Did I mention her to you? Her family feeds a stray cat…"

After Chandler gave his assurances, Caligula took charge of the cook, directed his eyes to his own and, holding them, asked if making them all a nice pot of tea might not help matters. After some consideration, Sparrow judged great sense in this plan, and once he had departed, Caligula said, "Moll's run off in a flood of tears, Billy. I expect to Nan's which can do no heart any good. She shall be slow to recover her senses, but when she does it'll be hell for Chandler if he is within strangling distance. You hear what I'm sayin'?"

Billy turned to his friend. "Pack your things. We must get you out of here before she returns."

Appearing dazed, Chandler allowed himself to be hauled up to this bedchamber, which was in complete disarray. Billy deposited him into a pile of silk breeches, sprigged muslin day dresses and errant parasols. He was just collecting his thoughts when the shattering of a bottle of cologne announced the appearance of Eva Marie atop the vanity, frozen with a hind foot dangling over the edge, aghast at what she had done.

With increasing dismay he had every fear of the direness of Chandler's situation confirmed. As the fog of cheap *eau de cologne* rolled over the room threatening to suffocate every living thing, Chandler admitted he had exaggerated his prospects while speaking to Humphrey Harper. He was not, in fact, scheduled to appear in the '72 edition of the *Harris's List*. Or, indeed, in any edition.

"We still have our ideas of how to approach the Madam. We shall get you moved and then——"

"I have been to see her. Last Tuesday evening. And was laughed out of the establishment."

Billy's heart swelled to see his friend wilt like an old flower petal. Still, he felt obliged to say, "It was a stupid plan. It wouldn't even work on the stage."

At this Chandler began silently to cry but Billy was sparing him the worst of it. 13 Craven Street, Strand might be closer to the theatre district, but it was far from the best of London. And Harper was right. Popular as Chandler was, taking patrons from Moll's house would be breaking one of the cardinal rules of the business. As the industry saw it, Moll would be within her rights to harass not only Chandler, but ex-patrons daring to visit an ex-employee, even with threats of exposure to the outside world. And without the clientele of the house or the protection of a bawd, Chandler would likely be left trawling for trade in parks and alleyways. He would be every minute of every day open to violence and brutality of every kind.

An idea came. Not quite a new idea, as it had been, somewhere in the back of Billy's own muddled thoughts, simmering ever since his friend told him of his ridiculous plan. A frightening, horrible idea, all the more horrible because he suspected it was their only real option. He could not ask Roger for assistance. Roger had no feeling at all for the boys and no reason to do him the favour.

Billy paused in the midst of his frantic thoughts. He needed a moment to process just how true this was. Roger had *no* reason ever to help him, much less one of his friends. Billy was entirely dependent, and they both knew it. Roger had taken over his life. He was the smart one. The knowledge, the schemes were all his. Could he even be sure Roger liked him, other than as a means of getting at the Marquess? He did still wish to be around him, to learn from him. All the same, the dependence upon him was almost exactly what it had been with the Marquess. He'd even had to beg to be let out on his own today. Just as before.

Billy pushed this from his mind and began pacing the room – a thing to be done carefully, as there were rolling parasols and shards of the bottle Chandler was placing into a rubbish bin. He thought over his idea, trying to find a fault, even hoping to find one. Potential pitfalls there were, those were out of his control. There *was* no other option, not that he could see. This was what they must do. To be completed in two phases, and there was nothing for it to begin on the first.

"Where are you going?" said Chandler, leaping to his feet as Billy made to exit the room.

"With luck I won't be more than an hour. Get your things together and yourself too if you can. Deep breaths. If this works you will be having a very bumpy ride across the river in the back of a carpenter's wagon. I am going to fetch Tom Baker."

BILLY WAS RUNNING. Running towards Lambeth Marsh as two weeks before he had run from it. With only a general idea of where the house was located, and no idea at all what, if any, kind of reception he would have. He ran across Gravel Lane where it crossed into Melancholy Walk. From there through a large fruit orchard to Lambeth Marsh Road, turning where it became the New Road. Continuing south would lead him to Westminster Bridge. North, he hoped, to Tom.

He ran through an apple orchard bright with autumnal colour. Through an acre dancing with the drying textiles of a tenter ground. He ran to outrun the fear never far from his heels. The fear that this would not work. The fear that Tom would not be home. The fear that Tom *would* be home…

When the cottage came into view, he could not have said just how he knew it was Tom's. It sat amidst a garden on half an acre, with a thatched roof upon a stout framework of seamlessly blended stone and timber. A barn somewhat larger than the cottage stood to one side, and as he approached, he observed coming into view Tom's wagon within the open doors. No sign of its owner. And somehow the sight of the old, worn wagon with its rusted hinges, the wagon which was meant to do so much, and with no Tom to command it, halted him in his tracks.

"I'm an idiot," he panted, his breath coming short. "He ain't here and even if he was we parted terrible. It *was* my fault. I wished to manipulate him and could not forgive him for seeing through it." Then, almost cheerfully, he continued,

"Anyhow he is not home. I don't see him, and this trip's been for naught." Some small voice in his head said that an open barn door might even the odds that he *was* home. Another said the presence of the wagon left unsecured might make it a certainty. Another part still said a far better method of figuring this out would be to knock on the front door. Yet even as the front door opened and Tom stepped onto the front porch, Billy did not see him. Because it was only then that he heard, that he truly heard, the offer Tom had made him.

I am offering you a home. My *home in Lambeth Marsh.*

Tom came down the front steps and down the path, a path of flagstones winding about beds of primroses and new box hedges still too young to be cropped. He came closer, and if Billy saw him, it was only as a painted landscape in his mind – an image merely to be gazed at, idealised, longed for. Something upon canvas which only a Henry Sparrow believed one might step into.

"Will?" said Tom, taking him by the shoulders. Then, his voice rising, "What has happened?"

"I don't know." Billy looked from the cottage to Tom, to the features now so familiar. Features he had sensed merely from the smell of him, which he had dreamt of before he had quite seen them. And which now confused him beyond description. "That's a lie. I *do* know, I just... ain't sure it's the lie I thought it was..."

Still at arm's length, Tom looked his visitor up and down as though he might see tracks from a Hackney carriage run up his back. Then he said, "I've missed you. No, not missed – these last two weeks have been absolute hell for me. I haven't returned to Moll's because—"

"I haven't been there. I never went back. You were right to stay away."

Looking quite alarmed Tom said, "Who have you been with?"

For a moment he saw himself as Tom must see him. The

question would never be *Where have you been?* He could never be anywhere without a *someone* to assist him. William Dempsey was utterly helpless. And how could such a wretch even think of helping anyone else…?

"Chandler," said Billy, coming to, determined to save that bit of self-flagellation for another time. Then in as few words as could be managed, he laid out the problem at hand. He had hardly begun when Tom was leading them back to the barn, lifting the hitch and bringing the wagon forward before fetching the old grey steed. When he returned, he told him where he wished to bring Chandler. Tom paused, frowning. Yet after a short explanation, he saw the sense of the proposition. He agreed it was likely the boy's best option. Then he stepped up to the driver's bench. He reached down, took Billy by the hand, and pulled him up beside him.

In the time it took to fetch Tom, Moll had returned to the house – according to Harper staggering from the death blow she had received. According to O'Donnell from rather too much of Nan's cheap liquor. She was now sealed inside her bedchamber being comforted by Caligula still unable to face her betrayer. But soon she would mend, the wound clot, and she would storm forth in righteous indignation to have her revenge. Billy judged they had about half an hour to get clear of the house before all went to hell.

Given Chandler's profound love of scents, cosmetics, and frippery of all varieties there was decidedly less to take from his room than one might have supposed. This was owing to Eva Marie's having damaged nearly every one of his belongings. By the time they had loaded all her master's worldly goods into the wagon, the cat was at the top of his bedpost, hanging quite literally by a thread near the ceiling, having shredded an entire bedcurtain in her mania to flee the whirl-wind of boys, silks, and parasols.

They were all soon out in the Yard and making to depart. Tom had resumed the driver's bench, Chandler settling beside him in a somewhat catatonic state. Inside his coat he held Eva Marie, who had gone rigid in one long, petrified hiss. Billy climbed into the bed of the wagon with the last of his friend's belongings. He was some time placing them amidst the mountain of every bit of old wood Tom had ever collected.

Billy called out that all was secured then looked back to the house. The door they had closed behind them now stood ajar. Moll was in the doorway, Caligula just behind. Moll met Billy's gaze but said not a word. When Caligula set a hand on her shoulder, she crossed an arm to place a hand on his, then remained as though caught in a one-armed embrace. Her eyes remained on Billy's. Her expression was benign. As though asking, perhaps daring him to make of her house what he would.

The old grey steed pulled forward with a start. Billy stumbled, then caught his footing.

Then Tom's wagon pulled away from the souls of Souls Yard and was soon rattling toward White Cross Street.

CHAPTER EIGHTEEN

Bingo Swag
  – a brandy shop

S oho was an area of London lately come into fashion. During the previous decade, as Covent Garden had begun to stagnate, Soho's gaming parlours, taverns, and coffeehouses had become quite the thing. It followed that a molly house, though obliged to maintain a much lower profile, must benefit from the new activity. All the better if that house stood above a brandy shop, situated on a bustling corner, and the resident bawd had a proven history as a good provider, active in the health and safety of his boys.

Such was Moll Dowager's establishment, the destination of the wagon and Billy's gamble as the best possible home for Chandler. It boded well that Dowager was said to have lost many of his boys over the last few months. What might not bode well was that the introduction was to be made by

William Dempsey, who had parted with Dowager on particularly ugly terms nearly two years before. This parting had discouraged him from approaching the man after he'd been kicked out by the Marquess. Yet he had won back Marathon Moll. And Chandler, being an unknown in Soho, should have an introduction. If Dowager could get beyond their parting, he would see that Billy had nothing to gain but a wish to make all parties happy. And if Billy were ever to make amends with the bawd, it must be by introducing him to a very able and experienced boy.

After directing Tom into the alleyway behind the brandy shop, Billy asked him to wait while he and Chandler went round the front. They arrived to discover the shop entirely dark. No sign of life inside or in the living space above the shop. Trying not to envision the worst, Billy rapped smartly on the door. The door creaked somewhat ominously inward, displaying the dark interior of what had always been a very lively drinking house. Now, not a customer, not an employee, to be seen.

He cleared his throat.

"Let us in, Moll. It's Billy…"

"Let us in, Moll. It's Billy, come with a peace offering…"

"Let us in, Moll. It's Billy. I've brought a fresh face for you…"

This continued for five minutes, to no avail. The boys circled the establishment, peering up at windows frosted with old lace. The place seemed utterly removed from the bustle of Soho, which avoided it like a pit in the road. No one approached to go inside, though they were often clipped by passing chairmen, whose *"By your leave!"* was not always sufficient to announce a passing hazard – Billy nearly lost a shoe to the stampede carrying a young woman in a full hoop.

Tom remained striding about in the alleyway, glancing up at the building, not much caring what was inside. As five minutes of pacing became fifteen, Billy noted an increasing restlessness to speak to him. Two weeks of reflection and regret were making this added delay intolerable, yet Billy felt little inclined to listen just then. What could a conversation do but muddy the already muddied state of his mind? He was committed to his plan with Roger, and his own regrets and reflections might well be alleviated once they'd collected the money from Lloyd's. He hadn't an idea of what Tom should say to make things right. But there were countless things he should not say. Things which might make the rift irrevocable, which might make returning to him impossible. And wasn't an illusion of choice better than no choice at all?

When Tom came forward, Billy cut him short, telling him the front door of the shop was ajar and he was about to go inside. They had done too much to get Chandler here; he would go in uninvited, up the stairs, and into every room of the house before giving it up as lost.

"Do what you must," said Tom, "only I *will* speak to you once this is sorted out. I've waited too long… I'd very nearly lost hope."

Avoiding his gaze, Billy nodded as he departed the alleyway. As he came round the front, he thought he observed the faintest shift in a lace curtain on the uppermost floor, like the remembrance of moonlight from a night which had yet to move on. Chandler confirmed the movement, upon which Billy pushed open the front door and stepped inside.

All stood in a dusty blue haze. The brandy shop was a narrow lane of the darkest wood imaginable, age like tar in every crevice, giving nothing back from the light swallowed from dirty windows. Chairs around a long table ran most of the length of the room, which ended at a locked liquor cabinet. In addition to a lock, the cabinet was secured by a plank of wood set in an iron brace finishing the room in fittingly Medieval fashion.

Billy started as a floorboard creaked overhead, compelled to remind himself this was indeed the same place he had known at various times over the years. Never had he seen it so completely dead. Scarcely had he even noticed the room itself, such had been the crowds, the noise, the merry-make.

At last, an inner door leading to the back parlour moved not by a hand but by a change in air pressure, as though from the opening of a window. A creak was heard on the stairs descending into that room, known as the entertaining parlour. Then through the open inner door a blue shadow emerged.

"Wilmot?"

Wrapped in a woollen blanket which flowed behind him like a train, a living wraith emerged. His eyes went first to Chandler, who had brought up beside Billy and whose own had gone wide. Chandler shot a questioning look at Billy, who had neglected to mention that Moll Dowager, despite his name and this ghostly and frail attitude, was in fact quite an attractive man still shy of thirty. His name was Edmund Wilmot, and though with a pallor played up by the sick-bed hue of his blanket, it was obvious he had not become a consumptive and was only indulging in a bit of theatrics. Nevertheless, this strange, dark mood was quite unnerving, for even after a three-day bender, Billy had never seen him reek of so strange, so foul a temper. It struck him that 13 Craven Street, Strand was perhaps not such a bad destination for his friend.

"Death, then," said Wilmot, addressing both, "in the form of nubile youths I would once have loved to entertain. Young boys used to be the lifeblood of my party house, filling it with laughter and song."

Furrowing his brow, as though trying to decide whether this was in fact Billy or the Reaper taking the form which would most torment him, he said, "William Dempsey," deciding in favour of his former employee. "'*Let us in Moll, it's Billy*', you say. '*I bring a new face*', you say, but I see the old."

"I've come to make amends. We ended in a bad way but there was a lot of good before that. What's more, I've brought a dear friend – top boy at Marathon Moll's what's now seeking other representation. A dazzler as I never saw – popular and kind and generous. Draws men like flies…" Billy frowned, supposing he might have done without that last.

"Does Moll know she is losing him?"

If this lacklustre swipe at his trustworthiness was to be the extent of Wilmot's anger, Billy would be grateful indeed. All might not be lost. Perhaps the greater challenge would be to convince Chandler this place was not the dungeon it appeared – that whatever its current problems, Wilmot was more than capable of hosting a lively house overflowing with devoted patrons.

Billy continued, "Chandler, Sukey if you like, had it all out already with Moll. His wish is to live closer to the theatres as he is a great and rising stage actor when he ain't entertaining patrons. You know living in the Mint never did nothin' for nobody and it's the same for actors. I can add he's nothing like me – and so long as he's free to pursue his acting commitments he'll be true as the day is long. Your absolute best boy."

A snort from Wilmot was somewhat discouraging. Nevertheless he was examining Chandler who was blinking rapidly with almost no expression at all.

At last Wilmot said, "He would be a *good* boy, William, no more." Billy at first took this for a putdown, and the man continued, "Let me explain, sweetheart, you never were good with words in any form. *Best* is a superlative. *Good* modifies a noun in the singular. *Better* compares two. *Best* three or more. Your lovely friend could be no more than *good* because there is no longer anyone here to compare him with." Wilmot was enjoying this bit of correction when his face altered and, raising his voice, he said, "May I help you?"

Tom had taken a couple of steps into the brandy shop. Wilmot was quick to see Billy's sudden uneasiness and smiled. "You must be with these two." Tom's silence contained no more than a nod, but Wilmot continued, "or... with Billy? You've that certain look about you."

With a steel edge in his voice, Tom said, "And what look is that, in your professional opinion?"

"My *professional* opinion..." said Wilmot, letting his eyes fall to the front of Tom's breeches – a vulgar, but not ineffective, way he had of unsettling a man he'd taken a dislike to. Billy was now bright red, understanding that bringing Tom here was quite possibly the worst decision he'd ever made. He knew how nasty Wilmot could get. When he had the upper hand, he was less likely to explode from unbridled emotion and more inclined to tease out his torture. Even when they were on good terms, it was a quality Billy had hated about him. A quality that had made it easier to betray him when he'd had the opportunity. Yet still he had brought Tom here, believing his distaste for such houses would simply keep him in the alleyway.

Wilmot said, "My *professional* opinion... what was the name again?"

"Tom."

"My opinion, Tom, is that you seem a decent sort who will do anything for him. He has a quality which makes one wish to go the extra mile. I did." He turned to Billy. "That introduction to the Marquess of Argyll was my contribution, remember? Establishing a correspondence with that illustrious man because my pretty little boy could not read or write. That letter of introduction and subsequent correspondence saw you into the highest circles, though your betrayals of me continued long after that."

Billy turned toward Tom, his nostrils flared as though recoiling from a hot iron. Tom, however, maintained eyes on his host, who held his gaze a long moment before raising his brows in a kind of *c'est la vie*.

Then Wilmot turned to Chandler. "My dear, I have nothing to offer now but a bit of plucky humour to see me on in life. My reputation is trash, my house empty of boys and furniture; very well, I am at least free from worry now. No ambitions to betray, nothing to steal. I have, simply, my existence." He retreated a few paces before smiling expansively. "But a prettier pair of Grim Reapers I could not have wished for. So since you have come all this way, let me take you on a tour of ruins which were once a great house. Laugh at me, tease me, ravish me – do what you will. Then leave me to die in the afterglow."

Chandler said something to the effect that continuing the visit was perhaps not such a good idea when, as sometimes happens in life, the *deus ex machina* awakened and clanked, changing the course of the interview and of Chandler's life.

From the street came a hideous screech. This was followed by a grimy grey cat through the open front door of the brandy shop. It darted passed the loiterers, around Wilmot's train into the entertaining parlour, where it skidded across the dust of the empty room before continuing up into the bowels of the house.

"Do follow the footman," was Wilmot's quip, as he was the only one still believing the interview was not at an end.

Suddenly bursting from Chandler's lapel, Eva Marie tumbled to the floor and tore after the grey cat, sliding through the dust and into the back door before continuing up the stairs.

"*Eva Marie!*" shrieked Chandler and, not waiting to be invited up, ran after her. A moment later, he was calling for Billy to grab the grey as they were fit to tear each other to pieces. Having no intention of remaining downstairs with his host, Tom pounded up the stairs after them. Wilmot, then, lest he be left an utter fool standing alone in his woollen wrap, cast the blanket aside then proceeded upstairs.

Shocking as it was to see most every room of the Dowager's house empty, it was a miracle of good fortune where collecting cats was concerned. With scarcely anything to hide behind, destroy, or dive under the animals were caught without too much collateral damage. In the end, Eva Marie had torn just one hole in Chandler's sleeve. Tom contained the grey without more than a few scratches, though the cat let out a stream of urine directly across Wilmot's shirt before he could wrangle it downstairs and out the front door.

"*What in hell did you bring into my house?*" Wilmot screamed at Billy.

"Sir," said Chandler, stepping forward, "that was a stray. This one is my own cat. Really very sweet, only a bit testy when other males are about. If you wish to yell at anyone, yell at me. I am quite sorry—"

"Other males?" spat Wilmot. "Eva Marie?"

"Yes, that's the name. And she's normally very docile. Just look – she likes nothing more than to be a visitor in your home." Eva Marie went down into a cloud of dust. With an instant hiss, she lifted one foot and froze like Lot's wife turned into a pillar of salt.

A look of such bewilderment came over Wilmot he seemed about to unravel. He gazed around his nearly empty bedchamber. He looked at Billy, then at the hole in Chandler's sleeve. Then down at his own clothes, drenched in piss. Then he began to laugh. It was an odd, hacking sort of cackle, but to Billy's ears most heartening. He laughed until tears came. Laughed as Tom returned to the room with a look of caution. After a time, it became apparent Wilmot wished to say something if he could only collect himself. At last, he turned to Chandler and said, "And now, what do you think of Moll Dowager's party house? Was William Dempsey a dear for bringing you here? Does it fulfil every wish of your heart?"

Chandler set a hand on Wilmot's arm and smiled. Without a hint of irony, he said, "You've a very spacious abode. Spacious abodes are nothing but blank canvases if you are an artist, as I fancy you are." To which Wilmot's laughter subsided, at last punctuating his long, trilling hysteria with a small smile.

"Remind me of your name again, fresh face."

"Chandler. Sukey if you like."

"I do like." Then, displaying a hint of that allure for which he had once been known, Wilmot smiled and brought his visitor's hand to his mouth. "My only regret is that I must meet this lovely and promising flower at this stage in my career when I have so very little to offer him."

"You've living space," said Chandler. "And I've got a wagonful of clothes and perfumes, and a couple of pieces of furniture in the alleyway out back which need a home."

Chandler also had an almost pathological desire to help people, and Wilmot had seen enough to sense this in him. He repeated what Billy had said of the demands the theatre would likely make of him. But if he could be allowed this one freedom, he would give everything he had, every effort, every invention, every spare bit of love to this house and to Wilmot. Together they would fill the house with patrons, employees, and song. Chandler *would* be a good boy. A very good boy. Until, at last, he was the best.

From this point, nothing more needed to be considered. The two spoke, planning out a room just down the corridor, occasionally falling into whispers as though not wishing to shatter something neither could quite believe. After changing his shirt, Wilmot led them downstairs, then all Chandler's worldly goods were brought inside. After all had been stowed upstairs, the group paused in the entertaining parlour for glasses of water, after which Billy was quite ready to depart.

Tom, however, turned to Wilmot and asked, "What really happened to this house? To your custom and belongings?"

This was said in an accusing way, as though daring him to answer. Wilmot, who was now so taken with Chandler he could scarcely look away from him, dismissed the question with the appearance of generosity. Merely nodding in Billy's direction he seemed to say, *His fault, as you suppose, but I am a tough old boy.*

"Will has received nothing but abuse from you since arriving," said Tom. "Perhaps he deserves some, I do not know what caused the rift between you, but whatever it was it cannot have caused you to lose every patron, every employee, every item of furniture in your house."

This was challenge enough to rouse the ire of Wilmot, who, with a raised eyebrow said, "Cannot it have? Then you don't know much about our business."

Billy didn't believe him either, hadn't the energy for any of this, and motioned to Tom that it was time to go. Wilmot caught his eye and said, "In your friend this sort of ignorance is excusable Billy. But you appear to doubt it as well. I find that quite provoking. Do you think it was merely that musical instrument that I lost?"

"*What* did he do?" said Tom.

Stepping about the room, Wilmot considered. "First you must picture how this house once was. An intimate sofa here. A lovely billiard table of richly polished oak over there. Everything was sold to avoid a stay in a sponging house. The Bailiff, to my great good fortune, was used to dandle one of my former employees on his... *knee*, so allowed me a week to sell before he threw me into his house and sold my items for me."

"That was kind of him."

"Very kind. Had he locked me in his house as is customary in such situations he would have charged me rent for the stay. Kindnesses like these... well, I cannot say they restore one's faith in humanity. They leave it merely maimed."

"You are avoiding my question, Wilmot," said Tom, appearing heartened. "So could it be that Will is not, in fact, responsible for the state of your house?"

"I *am* avoiding your question. The genius of what he did, Tom, is that it sounds almost too silly in the telling. Others have laughed. And I don't like being laughed at."

"I'm sorry," said Billy. "I was a stupid, selfish punk and I got my comeuppance. The Marquess of Argyll kicked me from my apartment, and I lost everything I thought I had gained."

"You seem to have recovered," with a glance at his companion. Then Wilmot continued, "Alright Mr Tom, here it is. It started with the virginal. A virginal in the middle of a bawdyhouse, how very droll. My house, you see, was known for its musical entertainment as much as its brandy and boys. The virginal was a little keyboard my sister used to play as a child, and which stood next to the sofa in this room. Just behind you was the jewel of the room: a breathtaking Italian harpsichord. Many of my boys were trained musicians, so my house attracted a great musical crowd. In a fit of generosity, I quite foolheartedly lent the virginal to one of my best patrons, himself a musician, for one week. When he failed to return it as promised, I found myself at some trouble to know how to ask for its return.

"About that time I saw William Dempsey strolling in St James's Park. I had not seen him since I'd ejected him from my house for stealing, but he was in keeping somewhere in Mayfair and seemed to have changed. I told him I had just had a visit from the Marquess of Argyll, a wretched prig who had the gall to tell me none of my boys suited him. Billy, I suspected, would suit him exactly. It seemed a stroke of good fortune for all. Billy told me he was ready to move on from his keeper and would be eternally grateful for the introduction. So while we were working on the Marquess, he was often back in this house. Then the weekend before he was to move in with His Lordship, while I had a friend visiting me and we were the entire time drinking and raking, Billy offered to arrange for the return of the virginal, I need not spare another thought for it. And as I happened to be in a jolly, expansive mood that weekend..."

"The virginal was returned," said Billy.

"Yes it was. And I had a new place to put it as, when I came out of the stupor of that admittedly debauched weekend I discovered my exquisite Italian harpsichord no longer graced the entertaining parlour. It was made of the finest wood, Tom, and along its long, sensuous body, the underside of its top, and over the cypress soundboard, I had commissioned cherubs painted by an understudy of Gainsborough, no less. It seems that, while requesting the return of the other, smaller instrument, an offer was made to ease the loss, which was the sale, at the great bargain price of just £200, of my harpsichord. All of which vanished the day the Marquess took possession of your friend here. The instrument, the money from the sale, and dear Billy – all gone. Billy had been installed in a secret apartment somewhere – the Marquess being always impeccably discreet in his private affairs.

"I went promptly to His Lordship's home to inquire after my instrument. It was no surprise to hear he knew nothing of the affair. However it *was* a surprise to be informed that I had been telling all of London that the fee he paid me for discovering this gem called William Dempsey really should have been five times what I had accepted, and so I just might invent a story of losses to help make up the difference. And now, just as his newly purchased treasure had told him might happen, here I was requesting £200 for the loss of some supposedly priceless instrument."

Seeing Billy about to speak, Wilmot interrupted, "Why? That's all. Why?"

Chandler was now looking at him too. Not accusingly, but eyes of any sort were unbearable.

Billy muttered, "We told the Marquess I was in the keeping of some Lord in Bath. I should have been humiliated to bring only two silk suits into his house. I needed new clothes." The words hung somewhat lamely in the air. At last Wilmot blew them away with a sigh. "Anyhow," said Billy, "I'm here to make amen—"

"How does one make amends for the loss of a reputation?" said Wilmot. "A Marquess with tastes which are, shall
we say, somewhat *niche*, has vast influence within his set of intimates. He was so enraged at my accusation he made it his
mission to destroy me. This was easy enough of course – with
his connections and my tendency to tipple overmuch. I could
not be trusted. I could not be associated with. Moll Dowager's
was no longer the place to be. Soon I was unable to maintain
my staff of domestics. I was then obliged to sell my possessions to pay my bills. My boys, with no instruments to play
and nowhere to sleep, soon went too. And in the end, Billy,
that virginal you so kindly retrieved for me was sold as well."

It was full dark when they returned to the wagon. Both were
relieved to be out of Dowager's house, however Billy was not
relieved to be alone with Tom. Tom, he knew, wished to
speak, and to speak kindly. To show he understood, to agree
that what Billy had done was terrible but that the consequences could not have been predicted. What mattered was
that he wished to make amends now, and that he had given
two people a new lease of life.

Inexplicably he said, "I'm sorry," and though Billy did not
wish to hear him, either to condemn or absolve him, he was
compelled to ask what he could be sorry for. "Sorry that the
work you did today to help your friend has left you so
distraught."

"Tom—"

"I'm sorry that the life you were born to has led you to
grasp so desperately for happiness where no true happiness
can ever be found."

"They was my own choices—"

"And I'm sorry that I have done the same. That in
grasping for happiness with you I stunted any hope of growth.

Blank canvases are well for painters and for the rooms of a bawdyhouse one wishes to reimagine. But people cannot be blank canvases, or else they are not people. In trying to allow us freedom from the baggage of our previous lives, I relegated us to a kind of infancy too malnourished to grow. I saw where we were going wrong, but when you told me something of yourself, something deep and personal, as I have not done, I reacted very poorly."

"I said that to get a reaction. To make you have to take care of me. To force your hand."

"My hand *cannot* be forced. I should never have used those words. Neither will I be forced to condemn you for what you did to Wilmot. Living in these houses in which affections are bought and sold like newspapers, in which the men who were in effect your guardians did nothing but debauch you in every way imaginable—"

Billy dismissed this. Perhaps Wilmot's tale had made no difference to Tom, but it had made a difference to himself. Had he ever bothered to consider Edmund Wilmot afterwards, he might have guessed what that accusation had done to him. But he had not considered it, because he had nothing in his heart to tell him right from wrong. Nothing to prevent this continual need to make amends with everyone he'd ever known. Perhaps it was how he had been raised, it hardly mattered. It mattered only that his first, most basic, instinct was to speak the cant language. Not the language of decent people. No matter his guilt, he could never speak it as he spoke his own. He would always say *best* when he should say *good*.

And Tom Baker was too good for William Dempsey.

So he told Tom he would not be returning with him in the wagon to Southwark. He would proceed on his own to another place on foot. Alone.

Looking suddenly desperate Tom said, "Is it true you are illiterate?" Smiling, Billy shook his head, as though this was the only thing missing to make him feel truly low. But Tom continued, "This explains so much. I never would have asked why you had no ambition other than to be kept had you admitted—" His words trailed off. After a moment he said, "But we were to be shepherds wandering in a dream world, weren't we?"

Billy said, again, that he would be going.

"I am offering not only myself, but peace," said Tom, taking him by the shoulders. "That space to be still and to find your way. And to see yourself more clearly. As I have seen that I might be stronger, more resilient. And yet not lose my spirit, or the laugh I laughed when I was a child. I am ready to be an adult and *speak* as adults. Because I wish you to know me as I wish to know you."

This was enough to break Billy from his determination, if only momentarily. As he looked at Tom, he understood that this was what they should do. This was what had stood in their way. That failing to be quite open was nothing done from malice or intentional selfishness. Only an experiment which had everything, and nothing, going for it.

But what he could not, what he would not, say was that he no longer wished to know about Tom or his past. He liked the image he had of him. He wished to keep it. It was enough to know there had been this good and caring man. Hardly perfect, but more perfect than Billy had believed existed. He did not wish to hear Tom Baker was not everything he imagined him to be.

Appearing to see this in his eyes, Tom said, "Please, Will! We must give ourselves this chance! The chance I would not allow us to have. The chance to be truthful one to the other. To be open. And to speak honestly."

After a moment considering, Billy could say nothing beyond, "I don't know that I speak that language. I don't know that I want to."

CHAPTER NINETEEN

Whisker

– a great lie

Upon returning to Botolph Lane, Roger appeared somewhat peevish, though he could not quite be angry. As promised Billy had returned within the day, if only just. An exhausted look silenced any tart comments. Billy passed him without a word as he made for the kitchen. He was utterly knocked up, utterly famished, and could think of nothing but that damned loaf of bread on the kitchen table he should have taken before departing that morning. He avenged himself presently, tearing it apart and stuffing it down.

Now somewhat checked, Roger confessed to being on edge – the afternoon post had confirmed the Marquess had yet to write back. Then he fetched a glass of water and once Billy had drunk it and collapsed into bed was right beside him. Roger smoothed his hair, kissing his ear, his nose, saying how much he had missed him, how he had ached for him. However when he touched their mouths together Billy pushed him away and turned his back to him.

Losing not a beat, Roger came up behind. "If that manoeuvre is meant to cool a growing fire you don't know as much of men as I supposed you did." He dropped his head into Billy's neck and let his hand slip to his hip. "I'll do all the work then, shall I?"

Casting his hand away, Billy flipped onto his back. "Lie still and be quiet or I shall go to the sofa. I am dog tired."

Roger sighed. But then, showing a bit of the old whimsy, he slipped his hands behind his head like a child sitting on his hands. They exchanged a look. Nothing but a little grin on either side, but it was enough to reassure Billy he was not wrong in returning. Somehow, the lack of that feeling he had for Tom was rather a comfort just now. Roger expected nothing so very elevated from him. There was no need for long rationalisations for why he had acted as he so often did. Roger knew most of it, and what he did not know would hardly be a surprise. He accepted him as he was.

As Billy was born to be.

Next morning a note arrived from the Marquess, agreeing to meet at one that afternoon outside the old apartment. The plan was simple: they needed just one interview during which Billy would slip a vial of something tasteless into his drink. That something would make the man ill for a week or so, an illness long and serious enough to get him into the *Book* with slim chances for recovery. Roger had been feeding the reporter from the *Star* all sorts of gossip about the Marquess – gossip which, according to Roger, the reporter believed and was printing. The details were unimportant, only that he was now a credible source of information on the man. And should the

Marquess's illness prove not quite sufficient to produce slim odds for recovery, a word from himself about a dire outlook would be taken as gospel and promptly printed.

His Lordship's note produced joy in Roger. In Billy, a mixture of excitement and impatience to have it done. And uneasiness. Though now blaming himself, rather than Roger, for a return to uncertainty, he could not be quite comfortable with the plan. He could not say what, but something seemed off. Roger reminded him that approaching the Marquess was what he had intended from the moment he'd been kicked from his keeping. Well, wasn't it? *Yes.* And, as intended, Billy would be asking to be kept by him once more. *Yes.* Only now, he would be going in without a care, because it would not matter in the slightest what the Marquess answered. Was this not so? And was it not so much better this way? *Yes.* Then why the concern? Why the worry?

Yet when Billy arrived at his former apartment, well before the agreed time, he could scarcely breathe. Roger was just down the street with his gaming friend, every few minutes casting Billy looks and making reassuring gestures. Yet he could not but feel alone in what he was about to do. He did not quite trust Roger. And yet he knew with certainty Roger would never risk all he had done by failing to get an appropriate potion. Roger was brilliant, he had taken care of all that. Now it was Billy's turn – tipping potion into that drink was something Roger could not do himself. The man's former lover was unquestionably most qualified to do this. And it was a mere nothing.

Yet when the *"By your leave!"* sounded from down the street and the chair arrived on the wings of four trotting Mercuries, Billy felt a wave of unworthiness bordering on nausea. After their ugly parting, why had His Lordship even agreed to this interview? And if, by some miracle, he had cooled and actually wished him back, then what?

As the chair was lowered, Billy turned away, wishing to

look anywhere else, and so began a minute study of his shoes. The blue calfskin slippers he had purchased on Monmouth Street, the shoes which had made him fine for his reunion with Roger. But at last, fearing his intentions might literally be written across the back of his frockcoat, there for the Marquess or anyone else to read, Billy turned around to face his former benefactor.

The Marquess of Argyll was a sour-faced gentleman in his late forties. Bald but for the wig, which he wore at all times except in bed when he swapped it for a woollen nightcap. He was long-legged and large-boned, which aided in concealing an extra five stone so that many took him to be robust. Before he had even stepped from the chair his eyes met Billy's – looking as he always did, his face entirely unreadable. As expected.

What was unexpected was the man's accepting the hand of one of the chairmen to rise to his feet. He came out carefully, then employed a cane to support his right leg as he stood to full height. *Oh Christ*, thought Billy, *he's had a mishap and I am to send an already injured man to his sickbed for a week.*

The Marquess told the chairmen to wait, then advanced. Keeping a distance of a few paces, he told his former companion he was looking well. Billy said nothing, thinking only that a meeting after four weeks was really quite surreal. Four weeks, when you came to think of it, was an absolute age.

His Lordship directed them to the apartment and produced a key.

"Ain't you got a new cove in there?"

The man merely directed Billy inside. It was too much to say the place had been kept as a shrine – this was Billy's first thought. His Lordship was not sentimental in the slightest, yet things did appear almost exactly as they had done the fateful morning he had departed to meet Mr Evans. In his bedchamber, slung over the back of a chair, were the breeches he'd decided against before the rendezvous. On either side of the bed stood two vases, moved at his desire from the parlour so he might awaken to the scent of flowers each morning.

But no. Those were not his breeches; they were too long and of that rosy hue he abhorred. A small bottle of cologne beside the washstand, a hand mirror – neither was his.

The Marquess had replaced him. *Replaced* him. That caused a pang. It shouldn't, but it did. It had only been four weeks. Four weeks was nothing. Nothing at all! It was an insult to be replaced so quickly, like a set of soiled bedlinens.

"Your clothing and trinkets are stowed in the sideboard in the parlour," said Argyll. 'I've had no time to dispose of anything. Depending on how this meeting proceeds, you may have them back. Any hint of blackmail and you will quickly discover that contacting me was the worst decision of your life. Well, one of the worst."

After a moment he gestured at the dining table, then took out the brandy decanter as was his habit when hosting a guest. When he set out the glasses, Billy looked away, and for once the inability to disguise his feelings was rather to his benefit. Seeing his discomfort, verging on fear, the Marquess said, "Forget what I said of blackmail. I don't suspect you. I should never have met with you if I did." He glanced at Billy's healed nose, for the first time observing some alteration though unable to say quite what it was. Still, it was enough to soften his tone, and he added, "I do... regret how we parted. I am not displeased to see you again."

"That's a comfort," said Billy taking the glass though his eyes fixed upon the one in the Marquess's hand. He crossed his leg, slipping a hand into the pocket of his breeches to assure himself of the location of the glass vial.

The Marquess's eyes flicked over Billy's face, still unable to place what exactly was altered. "What's happened to you?"

"Nothing's happened."

"Where have you been?"

"Here and there. I ain't grown so soft I can't make shift when the need arises, though with only the clothes on my back and just one pound ten in my pocket."

"Why did you wish to meet today?"

Billy took a stinging sip from his glass, then, rubbing his eyes said, "See if you'd take me back. That was to come after the apology for deceiving you, and saying you had every right to cut me. But I see you got a new cove now and it's a mute point. So let's say this visit is to ease a guilty conscience."

"Moot," said the Marquess, then with another look at Billy's nose he said, "it is a *moot* point."

Corrections to his English were nothing new, indeed Billy scarcely heard it. He nodded. After taking another sip of brandy, he noted the extended pause in the conversation. The man was studying him. He could not have said just how he understood it was owing to that passive acceptance of the correction that His Lordship was studying him, but he did understand it.

After a moment, the Marquess set the cane on the floor and rose from his seat, saying he would retrieve his things from the parlour. Billy remained motionless as he saw his opportunity. Another would likely not arise, no time to consider anymore. He slipped the vial from his pocket, pulled the bit of cork, tipped the contents into the Marquess's glass, then stirred the concoction with his finger. When the man returned the powder had dissolved, his glass precisely where he had left it.

He set a canvas bag on the floor, one glance into which revealed a number of belongings Billy immediately recognised. In his hand the Marquess held a piece of paper with a crease down the centre. It was a moment before Billy recognised it as his own. When he did he looked up into the man's face. Then, his own flushing scarlet, Billy said, "Where the bloody hell did you get that?"

The Marquess tossed the paper at him. "Raise your voice

to me again and you will be removed from this apartment. *Comprenez?*" Billy remained silent. "Everything here is *my* property. I did not *get* the paper. One does not *get* something one already owns. The paper was mine to discover. Agreed?"

Billy nodded.

"A week after you left, while I was preparing the place to move in Joseph, I recalled finding it in that copy of *Gulliver's Travels* I have on the bookshelf."

Though refraining to touch it, Billy maintained his eyes on the thing laying on the table between them. "You recalled?"

"I recalled. I do not know how long it was there, but I discovered it about three months before we parted. After that, every week or two, I would have another look when you were out of the room, and there would be added another line, words crossed out and done over. I saw they were questions you were compiling as you wiled away the boring hours in this place." Then, with a disdain Billy failed to comprehend, he said, "I waited for you to ask my assistance and you never would."

Matching the man's tone, Billy said, "You mighta *asked* if I needed help."

"I might have," said the Marquess. "I might have made a brilliant scholar of you. And it might have been a thing to bond us, Billy, because we never were close, not in eighteen months. A man can become close with his concubine; it is not unheard of. We had our amusements at masquerades and in the homes of my friends. Certainly no complaints in bed—"

"I should hope not."

"—but we were never intimate. When I understood you meant to keep those notes to yourself I chose to believe they were kept from mere idleness. A pastime, not a wish to improve yourself…" Billy cast him a derisive look, to which the Marquess said, "Because another thing which is not unheard of is a scholar becoming so scholarly he is able to turn tables upon his teacher. No good deed goes unpunished, I firmly believe that, and with a little reflection you should believe it too." For one bizarre moment, Billy was certain the man knew about his bringing Chandler to Soho and the consequences it had had on his feelings for Tom. "The tools you give a man to improve himself are often the same tools with which he will destroy you."

"Blackmail? I never even—"

"I know that," said His Lordship. "I know that now. It is neither here nor there. A *mute* point, as you say; let us remain so about it. Still, when I came across this paper after you had left, it seemed to mean something. I thought keeping it would be a reminder, as I move forward with Joseph, to remain… more balanced. To not be too cynical. But now that you have contacted me, I should be remiss if I make the same mistake again."

"Remiss? About what – the questions?"

"Yes. If you still desire the assistance, I can answer them."

Billy touched a corner of the paper and turned it towards himself. Rather to his surprise, he observed a couple of errors. The substitution of letters for words of the same sound, among other things. He folded the paper and pushed it aside. "I got help with all that now."

The Marquess merely nodded, but for a moment, Billy saw a stranger sitting across the table. Their relationship was over. What had been could no longer be altered. Yet had they not met again he would have kept a far different memory of it. A limited, two-dimensional relationship it had been, but not without reasons or regrets. In his way, the Marquess had come to care for him though they would never know the outcome had either of them surmounted their fears, offered assistance, or asked for it. Where might the discussion have led? Might Billy have been less inclined to seek a second patron if his absolute dependence upon the Marquess not driven him to it?

By habit, His Lordship, rather than taking his drink and settling back in his chair, had a way of settling back first, then bringing the drink to him, like one does before bringing a small dog into one's lap. The moment he settled back in his chair, Billy shot one hand out, sending the man's drink crashing to the floor.

"Sorry!"

"Oh for God's sake, Billy…" he said. "Stay back now! I shall fetch a rag to clean it."

"No pray, I'll do it," said Billy jumping to his feet to retrieve the rags from a cupboard in the kitchen. "You cannot with your leg like it is. I merely wished to take that piece of paper and rather overshot the mark, as the saying is. I'm ever so clumsy – you know how I am." He felt an overwhelming need to leave this place, to find Roger, tell him they must think of something else. The Marquess was far too paranoid ever to let his glass from his sight.

The mess was soon cleaned from the floor, the shards of glass collected without injury, a miracle in itself considering Billy's shaking hands.

"I shall go now," he said, rising up and almost running for the front door. "Much obliged for the brandy. I never deserved half your generosity."

His Lordship struggled to his feet, wincing as he came down on his leg before making to follow his guest out. Upon reaching him his brow furrowed. "Whatever is the matter? You've gone quite pale."

Billy had frozen in place, his breath coming short. After a dry swallow, he said, "Your leg. I meant to ask you. Is it bad hurt?"

Letting out a sigh of disgust, the Marquess said, "My horse threw me one morning a couple of weeks ago."

"What, Shakespeare?"

"It wasn't his fault. Some hooligan lit a smoker, one of those Serpents, and threw it in the byway I take to return home. Then a second lit a Cracker and hurled it into Shakespeare's mane, causing him to rear up and cast me onto the cobblestones. No doubt the intention was to rob me, but they took nothing. Never even came at me, at least from what I can recall. I suppose with Shakespeare's stamping about they were scared off. By some miracle my leg, which took my entire weight, did not actually break, though it suffered some manner of splintering fractures which have been the most painful thing I've ever experienced."

His eyes growing wide, Billy threw himself against the front door in his mania to escape.

"Improving under a surgeon's care if it eases your concern…" was the Marquess's somewhat bewildered call after him. For Billy had already run past the waiting chair-men, cut up an alleyway and was gone.

The powder. The powder he had been given to put into the man's drink.

The powder had been meant to kill him.

Of course it had.

When Billy found Roger in the street, an exchange of looks sufficed to communicate failure. Roger pushed off the wall he had been leaning against, holding a hand up to his gambling companion, a raggedy young man Billy supposed must be one of the two hooligans who had attacked His Lordship.

Coming forward, Roger said, "Do you still have the vial at least?"

Billy handed it over. Upon seeing it was empty, Roger looked confused. "Last minute change of heart?" Then with a smile, "He's taking you back."

"He's filled that vacancy."

Somewhat surprised, Roger brightened. "Very well. We have other options. I didn't wish to, but I should be able to talk my way into his house. If I can somehow get to—"

"I was sent in there to kill him."

Roger went silent. His jaw worked a moment, then with an edge he said, "Christ, I explained all that—"

"I was sent in there to kill him."

"Toxins taken moderately only sicken, they don't kill. How many times do I have to explain? You don't trust me as far as you can throw me, *that* is your problem."

Billy simply stared, wishing only to repeat himself. Because with each repetition, he was confirming the details of what he knew, pounding them into place to assure himself they were sound, forcing himself to believe what he had almost been tricked into doing. "I was sent in there to kill him."

Something in his tone at last caused Roger to falter. Blinking rapidly, he frowned. Then he whispered, "You have a heart, Billy, that's why I like you so much. I haven't much of one, as you probably know, but what I have is for you. But a person doesn't always know what is in their best interests. Once it was done, you'd have had nothing to reproach yourself with. You see? You must believe I am sincere. You *must* believe that."

But it made no difference if Billy believed him or not. Only once had he experienced a greater betrayal. And nothing he could ever say, or ever do, would sufficiently express what that had done to him. But Roger *was* here. Here to be confronted. Here to be spoken to.

So at last, which was indeed the last thing he would ever say to Roger Calcroft, he said:

"You sent me in there to kill."

CHAPTER TWENTY

Tom's Tale

Billy performed the journey to Lambeth Marsh on foot. This was not his intention setting out from the West End. Neither was it a grand gesture, for William Dempsey was far too disorganised for that. He simply hadn't any other means. As he was long used to do, he had left all his worldly possessions in places he could no longer return to. His money he had left at Roger's. His clothing, now for a second time, in his former apartment, in possession of one Joseph, new concubine to the Marquess of Argyll. When you came to think of it, it was quite annoying, really. A hassle to be continually starting over. But that was his life, such as it was.

He returned to the second-hand clothes merchant in Monmouth Street, the same as had sold him his silk suit and calfskin slippers more than two weeks before. When he departed, it was in a smock, waistcoat, and knee breeches of cotton, his shoes once more those of a messenger boy. In his pocket a bit of coin – his purchases being modest, as it should be as he wished as much as possible for Tom. Tom, who seemed doomed to perform acts of unpaid charity as long as he kept company with the likes of Blue Billy. There was an obscure thrill at the thought of showing up on his doorstep and forcing him to take his money for once. Like throwing a bit of sand in the eye of Fate.

As Billy proceeded, he considered buying a copy of the *Morning Star* or perhaps trying to locate a copy of the list printed by Lloyd's from two weeks back. He didn't doubt his reading abilities would be soon up to snuff, but in the end he found he did not need more proof of Roger's actual scheme. Being thrown from his horse two weeks before had seen the Marquess entered into the *Book of Lives*. His steady recovery would have bestowed a healthy pay-out after his death today. But Roger was too smart to let slip a second opportunity. Because the man's death must have also meant an insurance pay-out from Lombard Street, had Roger let slip to the gossip columnist that the Marquess of Argyll had sizeable and unpaid debts to Calcroft & Son.

He decided to forgo the endeavour, though, thanks to Roger Calcroft, he had more reason than ever to hunker down and study his grammar. When the Marquess got wind of the libel printed about him in the *Morning Star*, his retribution against the paper and against the business which no doubt started the rumour, would be worth reading about.

And thanks to Roger for one more thing. Because whatever had risen inside him when he'd understood the potion had been intended to kill – indeed, whatever had risen when he'd simply begun seeing His Lordship as a person, and not the representative of a class which must have no problems or cares – he knew it came from that same place as his continued love for his mother. Something at the core of himself. Something which had not been taught, and which reason could not talk him out of.

Time must tell if what he was to hear of Tom's past would

leave him in the same elevated place he now was. Try to avoid the thought though he might, he was now terrified that whatever Tom had to tell him, whatever he had been so disinclined to say about his voyage, would change the image he had of him. Because Tom had tempted him to those same fantasies as he was himself so tempted by. But if there was to be a future with him, a future with something more than a house of cards as a foundation, he must listen to what he had to say. Then let the cards fall as they may.

When he stepped across the flagstones leading to Tom's door, he stopped to peer in the window. Tom sat looking into a blazing fire, a newspaper draped over his knee. Billy had not intended to stand there long, just long enough to consider where in his life he was about to go. In truth he believed he was no more than a minute. But a face glowing in the glass of an outside window cannot long go unobserved. Tom saw him with a start. Then, just as fast, he started up from his chair, crossed the small room, and opened the door.

THE GRAND TOUR of the cottage experienced something of a delay once they reached the bedchamber. This was only the second room Tom led him into, but as the cottage only had three, and with the tour more than half complete, they decided the East Wing could wait. They were some hours making up for lost time, and when each had slaked what at times seemed a near unquenchable thirst for the other, Tom said, rather like he was coming up for air, "How's that for your welcome, then?" entirely pleased with his performance, which, in fairness, he had every reason to be.

"Better than being called the Grim Reaper."

"I expect so," said Tom, grinning with a glow which lit him from within, appearing happier than Billy had ever seen him. He leant in for a kiss, a kiss Billy returned with grateful and increasing ease. Still, it was a kiss kept brief as it was meant more as a full stop than as the start to a new paragraph.

"Can I ask you something?" said Billy before his companion was quite done punctuating.

Tom withdrew, touching Billy's dark hair from his eyes, and nodded.

"What have you been doing these last weeks?"

"These last weeks? Is that all the further we are to go back?"

Billy nodded, pleased to have him eager to speak as they should have done from the beginning, though his heart was now fluttering with uneasiness. "For a start."

"Nothing special. Endless hours sitting on the docks of the river watching the ships come and go. Believing my life was over. Or, rather, wishing it to be over if there was no chance of your returning to me. The docks are a place I've gone for years. It's soothing somehow, watching the comings and goings. Lately it seems even the docks have lost some of their charms – had I gone tonight then discovered who had been waiting for me at home they would have lost all of them."

"You waited weeks for me to get my head on straight. I should have waited 'til you returned."

Tom took his hands. He held them until Billy looked in his eyes. Then he said, "Thank you."

Billy knew what he must ask then. Tom needed to finish the story he had begun about his time on the *HMS Dolphin*. Perhaps even more he needed Billy to ask to hear it. So he said, "Finish the story."

Tom brought Billy's hands to his chest. Then after a moment he began, returning him to the deck of the *Dolphin*. Three months into the voyage, believing the voyage to be at a halfway point and that the ship was about to return home.

"It's funny," he said. "I can almost recall being angry at the deception, indignant that we were not told until so late of the change in plan. But I don't recall it because I wasn't angry. I said just what you said. That I should like to go exploring. That I was up for the adventure. And I was. It was the natural progression in a career which had seen me serve many years at sea. So I was, as much as anyone can judge of these things, ready. The entire crew was ready. Everyone but Nicolas."

Billy caught his eye. "Nicolas?"

"Nicolas Cramer," said Tom, his mouth going momentarily askew at having said the name aloud. "We'd scarcely spoken in all that time. Three months, and we had been only shipmates who'd done scarcely more than nod to each other. And I know that, had we returned to England as planned, we never would have spoken. I know that as I know that we must have come together with the change.

"It was the end of October; we were anchored off the coast of Rio. Commodore Byron had just concluded a commercial and diplomatic mission in the city. The evening he returned to the frigate he told us of the change in plan. We were to continue down and around the coast of the continent, through the Straights of Magellan, and chart the South Seas for reasons not entirely explained, at least not to me. The expectation was that every red-blooded member of the crew would be overjoyed at the prospect of adventure and double pay.

"I had no reason to return to England. So when a double ration of brandy was produced at the announcement, I was soon singing with the rest of the crew. I made a point to touch mugs with every crew member. That's when I approached Nicolas. He was a marine, no more than twenty. I'd seen him standing sentry once or twice, spoken to him for some reason I can't recall. He was tall and slim, with a chin which gave him a look of stubbornness, a bull set in his ways. He was singing and toasting with everyone else. Saying he was ready to go. But I saw in his eyes he was terrified."

Billy's relief that it was to be this kind of story felt out of all proportion with the revelation. This was all it was – an affair which had not lasted, from which Tom had yet to recover. Could this be what he had come to fear so much he had nearly turned his back on the man rather than hear it? He said, "Reckon he needed a friend to confide his fears to."

Tom nodded. "That was it. I saw his need, and so remained near him that evening. I asked what was troubling him, supposing they were tales of treacherous crossings through the Straights. Or French pirates. Or regret for some sweetheart back home. It was none of these – he feared the weather might be cold where we were going. The crew, he said, were absolute fools to expect all to continue as it had been. Hot and muggy. Meat which stank within three hours of butchering. Water requiring turns at a ventilation machine before we could consume it. He expected it would not be so where we were going. He had sold all his warm clothes and bedding for goats and fowls in various ports along the way, as had much of the crew.

"I laughed and lent him a spare blanket. And yet after Rio, his fears proved all too valid. We experienced some very cold nights. After a few had passed, Nick returned the blanket – we had made port and he was embarrassed by the entire exchange. We continued to be friendly. One night I told him some dreadful tales I had heard about crossing the Straights, and when he was good and terrified smiled and said my blanket would be at his disposal again if he needed it. And the blanket's owner, too, if he liked.

"Nick blushed and said little to me for a couple days. But we understood each other. He had awakened desires in me that, until then, I'd scarcely acknowledged to myself. Much less expressed. Even if things went no further with him, it was enough that someone else knew. That was really all I wished – that somebody else would know.

"The evening of November twelfth, land was sighted. Distant hills had been seen in the dusk, appearing blue as they will in rainy weather. The boy on the mast announced waves breaking upon a long, winding beach – an island, he said, lay dead ahead. Then the beach, the blue hills, the island itself dissolved. It was only a fogbank, and the trick it had played greatly unsettled the crew. Next day we saw a flock of what they call at sea Mother Carrie's chickens – a sure sign of a coming storm. A short time later, a squall blew in like none on board had ever experienced. Before we could raise the main tack, it laid us upon our beam-ends: the tack was cut, but the main sheet struck down the First Lieutenant, beating out three of his teeth. That's when we reefed our main sail. It had begun to blow very hard again, and so we lay to beneath it all night.

"Such was the violence I could not simply take Nick into my arms. I grabbed him and dragged him to the lower deck. He was weeping, terrified that he should never see his family again. Terrified that he should never do so many things. So I kissed him. Kissed him as I had so long wished to do. And he accepted me. Again, and again. At first with confusion. At last, with a confession; that he had loved me long before I'd given him that blanket. For months, since he'd first seen me. And if we survived, he wished to give me his body – only I must promise to see him through the gale.

"I did see him through it. The gale slackened about dawn. When it was light, the sea in all directions was a deep, loosely coagulating red of blood – the surface was blanketed with thousands of small, hard-shelled fish, like crayfish. All slaughtered in the storm. The men commenced casting their nets and baskets into the sea, hauling up great quantities of what seemed manna from Heaven after a plague. But to Nick and to me, it was the remanence of our defences. A sign that God had not only saved us but wished us to be together. And so we would be.

"From that day forward, I no longer worked for Commodore Byron. No longer was I in service to Great

Britain. All the repairs, the maintenance, all the care heaped upon the *Dolphin* and the *Tamar* was done for Nick. My purpose was to see him to safety. To love and to guide him. Most of our days were spent working our separate duties – yet we were working in tandem. Each day we cast our nets off opposing sides of the ship, then in the evening placed them together into one memory. One imagination." His voice growing thick, Tom said, "It is something, Will, to be young and unafraid. Never once did I fear losing my grip upon him…"

Then he ceased speaking. After a silence, when it seemed right, Billy asked him to continue.

"Just before the Straights, at Port Desire, men wishing to do so might return to England. Places existed aboard our supply vessel which would go no farther. There was no question that I would continue; my job made me indispensable. A marine, however, might return if he chose. We were no longer at Rio when we had no choice but to continue. Nick had a choice. And he made it. He chose to stay with me."

Billy stopped him here. The tears had come. Nick had clearly not completed the voyage – a question was enough to learn that the crew had collapsed under an outbreak of scurvy six months later. Nicolas Cramer had not survived. But he knew Tom must complete this tale. Nothing would be right until he did, and so as soon as he seemed able Billy asked that he would.

The end came soon enough. Tom spoke of growing ill himself and expecting each day to join Nick. He spoke bitterly of a body which protested and instead grew well. He spoke of frantic mixtures of brandy and lemon water, always consumed too late, always in short supply. He spoke of deckhands dousing every surface of the frigate with vinegar, the smell of which he could not encounter even today without retching.

As he spoke, Billy brought Tom's head to his chest. He understood it was not hearing about a Nick or of some skeleton in his closet which had caused him such fear. He had feared having Mama in his arms again. And having only the tripe sung by balladeer singers with which to comfort.

But Billy was no longer a child. He had lived. And loved. He could summon his own words now. And he could simply hold when words were not needed.

Tom said, "Nicolas's corpse was delivered into the ocean; mine at Deal. Still, I found a manner of living after returning. Until you, my great joy has been my work. And I have succeeded in it." Then with a small laugh, he added, "When you have a bit of talent, and nothing else to do, it is quite easy to become an artisan."

Billy smiled and stroked his hair. When he leant down to kiss his forehead, Tom took him by the nape of the neck, holding Billy's lips in place to feel the words he was not yet saying.

Tom said, "I've spent years watching cargo loading onto ships, the crew gathering, setting sail. I've watched vessels set sail round the world and been present for their return. But observing from the docks does not make one a traveller. That is easy to understand when you are sailing. Easy to confuse when you are not. And I wish to be a traveller again."

Then Billy whispered that he loved him too and held him as he had once been held.

As a shepherd with a kindred shepherd.

As a speaker of a common tongue.

BIBLIOGRAPHY

Canting Vocabulary taken from:

**The Surprising Adventures of Bampfylde Moore Carew, King of
the Beggars /
Containing his Life, a Dictionary of the Cant Language, and
many Entertaining Particulars of that Extraordinary Man**
by Robert Goadby (1749)

and

**The English Rogue: Described in the Life of Meriton Latroon, A
Witty Extravagant**
by Richard Head (1665)

ABOUT THE AUTHOR

A native of the American Southwest, David Lawrence has spent much of his life in Great Britain, France, and Finland. He now lives in the American Northwest – Helena, Montana – with his Finnish partner.

By day he loves hiking under the Big Sky of his beautiful adopted state.

By night, however, he prefers editing lost manuscripts and wandering the byways of 18th century London…

You can learn more about David Lawrence and his penned works by visiting his website, https://www.david lawrenceauthor.com/ and subscribing to his newsletter!

ALSO BY DAVID LAWRENCE

Hugh – A Hero without a Novel

Blue Billy's Rogue Lexicon

Printed in Great Britain
by Amazon

21733466R00150